FAIRY TALES BY
HANS ANDERSEN

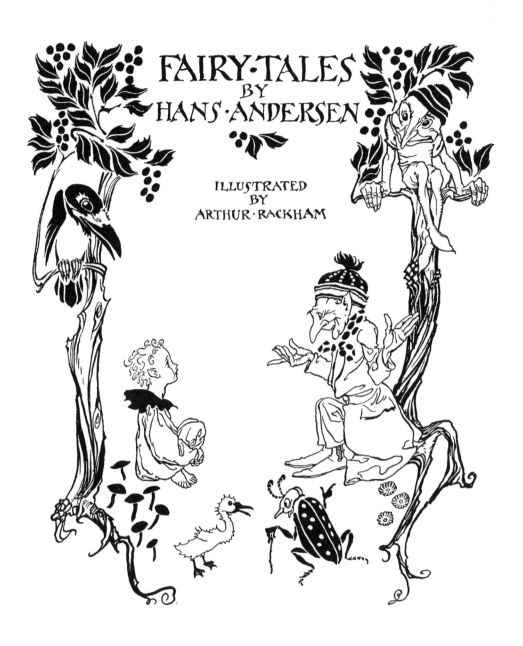

FAIRY·TALES
BY
HANS·ANDERSEN

ILLUSTRATED
BY
ARTHUR·RACKHAM

WEATHERVANE BOOKS · NEW YORK

Library of Congress Catalog Card Number: 77-72114
All rights reserved.
This edition is published by Weathervane Books
a division of Imprint Society, Inc.,
distributed by Crown Publishers, Inc.
c d e f g h

NOTE

By the Illustrator

IN making this selection of Andersen's fairy tales I have used the convenient edition published by Messrs George Allen and Unwin, to whom my thanks are due for their permission. At the same time I should like to thank my Danish friends for their assistance, particularly those who gave me opportunities of seeing the indoor life as well as an outside view of the people to whom Andersen belonged. While in Copenhagen on a recent visit I had the good fortune to meet a lady who in her childhood—her very early childhood it must have been—had listened, unsuspected by the author, to Andersen himself reading for the first time some of his own newly written stories. While he read she sat on the floor under the table, silent as a mouse, hidden from Andersen's view by the tablecloth—a little scene illustrating his well-known reluctance to be treated chiefly as a writer for children, but also providing a subject in which, had he known it, he would have found just such another incident as he had so often turned to account for one more of his immortal children's stories. On this point one cannot read his autobiography without realizing that he was by no means insensible to the recognition gained by these *smaating*—trifles—as he called them. Indeed, how could he be? A recognition so immediate, so widespread, and so affectionate that few have had the happiness to win anything like it.

I should like to add that I have made no attempt in my illustrations to look through Danish eyes. But I think that my visit to Denmark, which, with all its modern progress, happily preserves in town and country a genial atmosphere of old dignity in comely everyday use, did give me just that nearer view of the author's country that I needed—a view that helped me to realize again the sensation I felt as a child when I first read Andersen. This sensation experienced in childhood in foreign fairy tales is a foretaste of that encountering of familiar things in unfamiliar guise which later is one of the joys of foreign travel.

A. R.

1932

CONTENTS

PAGE

LITTLE IDA'S FLOWERS — 15

THE GOBLIN AND THE PROVISION-DEALER — 24

THE UGLY DUCKLING — 28

THE SHEPHERDESS AND THE CHIMNEY-SWEEP — 40

THE SNOW QUEEN — 46
  Which treats of the Mirror and the Broken Pieces — 46
  A Little Boy and a Little Girl — 47
  The Flower Garden of the Woman who knew Magic — 53
  The Prince and Princess — 60
  The Little Robber Girl — 68
  The Lapp Woman and the Finn Woman — 72
  Of the Snow Queen's Castle and what happened there at last — 77

THE SWINEHERD — 82

THE BEETLE — 87

SOUP FROM A SAUSAGE-PEG — 96
  What the First Little Mouse had seen and learnt on her Travels — 98
  What the Second Little Mouse had to tell — 102
  What the Fourth Mouse had to tell, before the Third One had spoken — 107
  How it was prepared — 109

FAIRY TALES BY HANS ANDERSEN

	PAGE
THE ELFIN HILL	112
THE STEADFAST TIN SOLDIER	122
OLE LUKÖJE	128
Monday	129
Tuesday	131
Wednesday	133
Thursday	135
Friday	137
Saturday	139
Sunday	141
LITTLE CLAUS AND BIG CLAUS	143
THE TINDER-BOX	155
THUMBELISA	163
ELDER-TREE MOTHER	176
THE PRINCESS AND THE PEA	185
WHAT THE OLD MAN DOES IS ALWAYS RIGHT	187
THE LITTLE MATCH GIRL	193
EVERYTHING IN THE RIGHT PLACE	196
THE LITTLE MERMAID	205
THE TRAVELLING COMPANION	230
THE EMPEROR'S NEW CLOTHES	251
THE SNOW MAN	256
THE GOLOSHES OF FORTUNE	262
A Beginning	262
What happened to the Councillor	263
The Watchman's Adventures	269
A Critical Moment: A Most Extraordinary Journey	273
The Clerk's Transformation	278
The Best Thing the Goloshes did	284

ILLUSTRATIONS

ILLUSTRATIONS IN COLOUR

FOLLOWING PAGE

"Why do my flowers look so faded to-day?"   32

When night was come and the shop shut up   32

Kay and Gerda in their garden high up on the roof   64

Gerda and the little robber girl in the robbers' castle   64

Just as the swineherd was taking the eighty-sixth kiss   96

The banquet where the really grand company were assembled   96

"He says you may go and open the chest in the corner and you will see the devil crouching inside it"   128

In the midst of the tree sat a kindly looking old woman   128

There she was sitting under the beautiful Christmas-tree   192

She came across a whole flock of little children   192

She put her arms round the marble figure which was so like the prince   224

"But he has nothing on at all," said a little child   224

11

ILLUSTRATIONS IN THE TEXT

	PAGE
Headpiece to Illustrator's Note	7
Headpiece to Contents	9
Headpiece to List of Illustrations	11
Headpiece to *Little Ida's Flowers*	15
" The Professor can't stand things of that sort "	18
Tailpiece to *Little Ida's Flowers*	23
The poor duckling was hunted about by them all	31
He was himself a swan	36
Into the garden came some little children	37
The Shepherdess	40
The Chimney-sweep	40
Overandundergeneralwarcommandersergeant Billygoatslegs	41
Headpiece to *The Snow Queen*	46
The old woman went right into the water	55
" They are only dreams," said the crow	67
No one was in the house but an old Lapp woman	73
The Lapp woman wrote a few words on a dried stockfish	74
Then she was met by a whole regiment of snowflakes	76
Kay sat all alone and gazed at his pieces of ice	79
" They are the sweetest children, and very playful "	90
Tailpiece to *The Beetle*	95
" That was an excellent dinner yesterday "	96
" Then began a wonderful music "	100
She had been running day and night	106
" Will the King now be pleased to dip his tail into the boiling water? "	110
" You are invited to the Elfin Hill this evening," said she	113
The Elfin Girls were already dancing on the Elfin Hill	115
She took him by the wrist, and he laughed till he clucked	119
Suddenly the lid of the snuff-box flew open	123
The rat followed, gnashing its teeth	125
He comes up the stairs so quietly	128

ILLUSTRATIONS

PAGE

" Listen now! " said Ole Luköje   130

The furniture immediately began to chatter   131

The water came up to the window-sill   133

" Will you be good enough to sit in your mother's thimble? "   135

" We wish you would come and drive them away "   137

" One must not even give one's opinion any more," said the old
    portrait   140

" Good evening! " said Ole Luköje   141

In the night the door opened   149

" I'll draw my sword and cut your head off! "   157

" Don't speak so loud, or she will wake up "   164

The mole hired four spiders to weave for her   171

The man who can tell fairy tales   174

" We went hand in hand up the Round Tower "   179

In the morning she was asked how she had slept   185

" Well! now I must really kiss you for that "   192

The little Goose-girl   196

All day long they used to play   205

Where the ocean is deepest stands the sea-king's palace   207

The polyps shrank back from her in terror   221

The little mermaid was slowly rising up out of the foam   227

Then he led him out into the princess's pleasure garden   240

All the little goblins in the room   246

He took the princess by both hands, and they danced about   247

Tailpiece to *The Travelling Companion*   250

He held himself stiffer than ever   255

" And I have lost my voice too—do you not hear how hoarse I am? "   259

He tried to pull his head back again, but he couldn't   275

Tailpiece to *The Goloshes of Fortune*   288

13

LITTLE · IDA'S · FLOWERS

M Y poor flowers are quite dead," said little Ida. "They were so pretty yesterday, and now all the leaves hang withered! Why do they do that?" she asked the student who was sitting on the sofa, for she liked him very much. He knew how to tell the most beautiful stories, and could cut the most amusing pictures out of paper: hearts, with little ladies in them who danced, flowers, and big castles in which one could open the doors. He was a merry student. "Why do my flowers look so faded to-day?" she asked again, and showed him the bouquet, which was quite withered.

"Do you know what is the matter with them?" said the student. "The flowers were at a ball last night, and that's why they hang their heads."

"But flowers can't dance!" said little Ida.

"Oh, yes!" said the student. "When it grows dark, and we are asleep, they jump merrily about; they have a ball almost every night."

"Can children go to this ball?"

"Oh, yes!" said the student; "little tiny daisies and the snow-drops."

"Where do the beautiful flowers dance?" asked little Ida.

"Have you not often been outside the town gate, near the big castle where the king lives in the summer, where the beautiful garden is with all the flowers? You have seen the swans which swim up to you when you give them bread-crumbs. Out there there are splendid balls, believe me."

"I was out in the garden there yesterday with my mother," said Ida; "but all the leaves were off the trees, and there are no longer any flowers there. Where are they? In the summer I saw so many!"

"They are in the castle," said the student. "You must know that as soon as the king and all the Court return to town the flowers immediately run out of the garden into the castle and enjoy themselves. You ought to see that: the two most beautiful roses seat themselves on the throne, and then they are king and queen; all the red cockscombs come and place themselves on each side and bow—they are the chamberlains. Afterwards all the pretty flowers arrive, and a great ball takes place. The blue violets represent little naval cadets; they dance with hyacinths and crocuses, which they address as 'Miss'; the tulips and the large tiger-lilies are old ladies, who see that they all dance well, and behave themselves."

"But," asked little Ida, "is nobody there who hurts the flowers because they dance in the king's castle?"

"The truth is, nobody knows about it," said the student. "Sometimes, of course, the old steward of the castle, who has to keep watch, comes during the night; he has a big bunch of keys, but as soon as the flowers hear the keys rattle they are quiet, and hide themselves behind the curtains, and only poke their heads out. 'I can smell that there are flowers here,' says the old steward, but he cannot see them."

"That's splendid!" said little Ida, and clapped her hands. "But should I not be able to see the flowers either?"

"Yes," said the student; "only remember—when you go there again to look through the window, then you will see them. I looked in to-day, and saw a large yellow lily resting on the sofa and stretching herself. She was a lady-in-waiting."

"Can the flowers from the Botanical Gardens also go there? Can they go such a long way?"

"Yes, certainly," said the student; "if they wish they can fly.

16

Have you not seen the pretty butterflies, red, yellow, and white? They look almost like flowers, and that is what they've been. They have flown off their stalks high into the air, and have beaten it with their petals as if they had little wings, and then they flew. And because they behaved themselves well they obtained permission to fly about in the daytime too, and had not to return home and sit still on their stalks; and thus the petals became in the end real wings. That you have seen yourself. It may be, however, that the flowers in the Botanical Gardens have never been at the king's castle, or do not know that there is such merriment out there at night. Therefore I will tell you how you can give a surprise to the professor of botany, who lives next door. You know him well, do you not? When you go into his garden you must tell one of the flowers that a large ball takes place at the castle every night; then the flower will tell all the others, and they will all fly away; and if the professor comes into the garden he will not find a single flower there, and he will be unable to understand what has become of them."

"But how can one flower tell the others? Flowers can't talk!"

"Of course they can't," said the student, "but then they make signs. Have you never seen that when the wind blows a little the flowers nod to one another and move all their green leaves? That they understand as well as us when we talk together."

"Can the professor understand their signs?" asked Ida.

"Certainly. One morning he came into the garden and saw a large stinging-nettle making signs with its leaves to a beautiful red carnation. It said: 'You are so pretty, and I love you with all my heart.' But the professor can't stand things of that sort, and beat the stinging-nettle at once on its leaves, which are its fingers; but then it stung him, and since that time he never dares touch a stinging-nettle again."

"That's amusing," said little Ida, laughing.

"How can one make a child believe such silly things!" said a tiresome privy councillor, who had come to pay a visit and was also sitting on the sofa. He could not bear the student, and always grumbled when he saw him cutting out the funny amusing figures: sometimes he cut out a man hanging on a gibbet and holding a heart in his hand, for he had been stealing hearts; sometimes an old witch, who was riding on a broomstick, and carrying her husband on her nose. But all this the old actuary could not stand, and then he gener-

"THE PROFESSOR CAN'T STAND THINGS OF THAT SORT"

ally said, as he did now: "How can one make a child believe such silly things? They are stupid fancies!"

But to little Ida what the student told her about the flowers seemed very amusing, and she thought a great deal about it.

The flowers hung their heads because they were tired of dancing all night; they were surely ill. So she took them to her other toys, which were kept on a nice little table, and the whole drawer was full of pretty things. In the doll's bed, her doll Sophy was sleeping, but little Ida said to her: "You must really get up now, Sophy, and be satisfied to lie in the drawer to-night. The poor flowers are ill, and they must lie in your bed; perhaps then they will recover!" And she took her out at once, and the doll looked very cross and did not say a single word, for she was angry that she could not keep her own bed.

Then Ida placed the flowers in the doll's bed, pulled the little counterpane over them, and said they must lie quietly, and she would make them some tea, so that they might get well again, and be able to get up in the morning. She drew the little curtains round the bed, lest the sun might shine in their eyes. She could not help thinking the whole evening about all the student had told her. And when she was going to bed herself she first looked behind the curtains, which hung before the window, where her mother's beautiful flowers stood, hyacinths and tulips, and she whispered in a low voice: "I know where you are going to-night—to the ball!" The flowers pretended not to understand her, and did not stir a leaf, but little Ida knew what she knew.

When she had gone to bed she lay for a long time thinking how delightful it would be to see the beautiful flowers dancing in the king's castle. "I wonder if my flowers have really been there?" Then she fell asleep. In the night she woke up again; she had been dreaming of the flowers and of the student whom the privy councillor had scolded. It was quite quiet in the bedroom where Ida slept; the night-light was burning on the table, and her father and mother were asleep.

"I wonder if my flowers are still lying in Sophy's bed!" she thought. "How I should like to know!" She raised herself a little and looked towards the door, which was ajar; in there lay her flowers and all her toys. She listened, and it seemed to her as if she heard someone in the room playing the piano, but very softly, and more beautifully than she had ever heard before. "I am sure all my flowers are dancing in there," she thought. "How much I should like to see them!" But she dared not get up for fear of waking her father and mother.

"Oh! I wish they would come in here!" she thought. But the

19

flowers did not come, and the music continued to play beautifully. At last she could bear it no longer—it was too beautiful. She crept out of her little bed, went softly towards the door, and peeped into the room. What an amusing sight she saw! There was no night-light in there, and yet it was quite light; the moon was shining on the floor; it was almost as light as day. All the hyacinths and tulips stood in two long rows in the room; not a single one remained on the window-sill, where only the empty pots were left. On the floor all the flowers danced very gracefully round one another, made figures, and held each other by their long green leaves while swinging round. At the piano sat a large yellow lily, which little Ida was certain she had seen in the summer, for she remembered distinctly that the student had said: "How much that lily is like Miss Lina!" But then they all laughed at him; but now it seemed to little Ida as if the flower was really like the young lady: it had just her manners when she played—sometimes she bent her yellow smiling face to one side, sometimes to the other, and nodded in time to the sweet music! No one noticed little Ida. Then she saw a big blue crocus jump on the table, walk straight to the doll's bed, and draw away the curtains; there were the sick flowers, but they got up at once and nodded to the others, to say that they wished to dance with them too. The old nutcracker in the shape of a man, whose lower jaw was broken off, got up and bowed to the beautiful flowers; they did not look at all ill now; they jumped down to the others and enjoyed themselves very much.

Then it seemed as if something fell from the table. Ida looked and saw the carnival birch-rod jump down, and it seemed as if it was one of the flowers. It looked very pretty, and a little wax doll with a broad-brimmed hat, such as the privy councillor usually wore, sat upon it. The carnival birch-rod hopped about among the flowers on its three red stilts, and stamped quite loudly, for it was dancing a mazurka, a dance which the other flowers were unable to manage, as they were too light and could not stamp.

The wax doll on the carnival birch-rod suddenly grew big, and, raising itself over the paper flowers which were on the rod, exclaimed: "How can one make a child believe such foolish things? They are stupid fancies!" And the wax doll looked exactly like the privy councillor—just as yellow and cross as he was. But the paper flowers hit him on his thin legs, and then he shrank up again and became quite a little wax doll. All this was very amusing to see, and little Ida could not help laughing. The carnival birch-rod continued to dance, and the privy councillor had to dance too. There was no getting out of it, whether he made himself tall or long or remained the little yellow wax doll with the broad-brimmed black hat. Then the other flowers, especially those which had rested in the doll's bed, interceded in his favour, and the carnival birch-rod gave in. At the same moment a loud knocking was heard in the drawer where Ida's doll Sophy lay with many other toys; the nutcracker in the shape of a man walked up to the edge of the table, laid itself down at full length, and began to open the drawer a little way. Sophy rose and glanced with astonishment all round. "I suppose there is a ball here to-night," she said. "Why has nobody told me of it?"

"Will you dance with me?" said the nutcracker.

"You are a nice one to dance with!" she said, and turned her back upon it.

Then she sat down on the edge of the drawer and thought that perhaps one of the flowers would ask her to dance, but none came. Then she coughed, "Hem! hem! hem!" but even in spite of this none appeared. Then the nutcracker began to dance by itself—not so badly, after all! As none of the flowers seemed to notice Sophy she let herself drop down from the drawer on the floor, to make a noise, All the flowers came running to her and inquired if she had hurt herself; they were all very polite to her, especially the flowers who had been in her bed. But she was not hurt, and Ida's flowers thanked her for the beautiful bed, and were very kind to her—took her into the centre of the room, where the moon was shining, and danced with her, while all the other flowers stood in a circle round them. Now Sophy was happy, and said they might keep her bed; she did not mind sleeping in the drawer.

But the flowers said: "You are very kind, but we cannot live any longer; we shall be dead by to-morrow. Tell little Ida to bury us in the garden, where she has buried the canary; then we shall wake up again next summer and be more beautiful than ever!"

"No, you must not die," said Sophy, and kissed them. Then the door flew open and many beautiful flowers came dancing in. Ida could not at all understand where they came from; surely they had come from the king's castle. Two beautiful roses with crowns on their heads walked in front; they were king and queen. Then came pretty stocks and carnations, bowing to all sides: they had brought music with them. Large poppies and peonies blew on pea-pods until they were quite red in the face. The blue hyacinths and the little white lilies of the valley tinkled as if they had bells. That was wonderful music! Then many other flowers came, and they all danced—blue violets, red daisies, and lilies of the valley. All the flowers kissed one another; it was lovely to watch. At last the flowers said "Good-night" to one another, and then little Ida stole back into her bed again, and dreamed of all she had seen. When she got up in the morning she quickly went to the little table to see if her flowers were still there. She drew the curtains from the little bed, and there they lay, all withered—much more so than the day before. Sophy was lying in the drawer where she had placed her, but she looked very sleepy.

"Can you remember what you have to tell me?" asked little Ida. But Sophy was dumb, and did not say a single word. "You are not good," said Ida. "Didn't they all dance with you?" Then she took a small paper box on which pretty birds were painted, opened it, and put the dead flowers in it. "This will be a pretty coffin for you," she said, "and when my Norwegian cousins come again they shall help me to bury you, out in the garden, that next summer you may grow again, and be prettier than ever!"

The Norwegian cousins were two lively boys called Jonas and Adolph; their father had given them two new crossbows, which they had brought with them to show Ida. She told them about the poor flowers, and asked them to help her to bury them. The two boys walked in front with their crossbows on their shoulders, while little Ida followed, carrying the pretty box with the dead flowers. In the garden they dug a little grave. Ida first kissed the flowers and then laid them with the box in the earth. Adolph and Jonas shot with their crossbows over the grave, for they had neither guns nor cannons.

THE GOBLIN AND THE PROVISION-
DEALER

THERE was a real student; he lived in an attic and owned nothing at all. There was also a real provision-dealer; he lived in a proper room, and he owned the whole house. The little goblin held on to him, for every Christmas Eve he always gave him a bowl of porridge with a big lump of butter in it. That the provision-dealer could give, and so the goblin lived in the provision-dealer's shop, and it was very comfortable. One evening the student came in by the back door to buy some candles and cheese. He had no one to send, and so he came himself. He got what he wanted, and the provision-dealer and his wife both nodded him a good evening. And she—she was a woman who could do more than merely nod; she was gifted with a tongue, if you like! The student nodded too, but suddenly stood still, reading the sheet of paper the cheese was wrapped up in. It was a leaf torn out of an old book, that ought never to have been torn up, an old book that was full of poetry.

"Here's some more of the same kind," said the provision-dealer; "I gave an old woman a few coffee-beans for it. If you give me two-pence you shall have the rest."

"Thanks!" said the student. "Give it me instead of the cheese; I can eat my bread and butter alone. It would be a sin to tear the book up into scraps. You are a fine man and a practical man, but you know as much about poetry as that tub there."

Now this was very rude, especially to the tub, but the provision-dealer laughed and the student laughed, for it was only said in fun. But the goblin was angry that anyone should dare to say such a thing to a provision-dealer who was a householder and who sold the best butter.

When night was come and the shop shut up, and all were in bed but the student, the goblin came out, went into the bedroom, and took madam's tongue away. She did not want it while she was asleep. And whatever object in the room he put it on acquired speech and voice, and told its thoughts and feelings just as well as madam. But only one object at a time could use it, which was a blessing; otherwise they would all have been speaking at once.

The goblin put the tongue on the tub, in which lay the old newspapers. " Is it really true," he asked, " that you don't know what poetry is? "

" Certainly I do," said the tub. " Poetry is something they always put at the bottom of newspapers, and which is sometimes cut out. I daresay I have a great deal more of it in me than the student, and yet I am only a simple tub compared with the provision-dealer."

Then the goblin placed the tongue on the coffee-mill. Mercy on us! how it rattled away! And he put it on the butter-cask, and on the till—all were of the same opinion as the waste-paper tub, and what the majority are agreed upon must be respected.

" Now I'll tell the student." And with these words the goblin stole quietly up the kitchen stairs to the attic where the student lived. He had a candle burning, and the goblin peeped through the keyhole and saw him reading in the torn book that he had got from the shop downstairs.

But how light it was in there! Out of the book shone a bright beam, which grew up into a thick stem and into a mighty tree, that rose and spread its branches over the student. Every leaf was fresh, and every blossom was a beautiful maiden's head, some with eyes dark and sparkling, others blue and wonderfully clear; every fruit was a shining star, and there was a sound of glorious singing.

No, such splendour the little goblin had never dreamed of, let alone seen or heard. He remained standing there on tiptoe, peeping and peeping till the light in the garret went out. Probably the student had blown it out and gone to bed, but the goblin remained standing there all the same, for he could still hear the sweet lovely singing—a beautiful lullaby for the student, who had lain down to rest.

" What a wonderful place this is! " said the goblin. " I never expected such a thing. I should like to live with the student." Then he thought, and thought it over again, but he sighed. " The student has no porridge," and he went away—yes, he went down again to the provision-dealer's. And it was a good thing too that he did come back, for the tub had almost worn out madam's tongue: it had already spoken out at one side all that was contained in it, and was just about to turn round to give it out from the other side too, when the goblin came and took the tongue back to madam. But from that time forth the whole shop, from the till down to the firewood, took its views from the tub; and all paid it so much respect, and had such confidence in it, that when the provision-dealer afterwards read the art and dramatic criticism in the newspaper of an evening they all believed it came from the tub.

But the little goblin no longer sat quietly listening to the wisdom and wit to be heard down there. No, as soon as the light began to glimmer out of the garret, he felt as if the rays were strong cables, drawing him up, and he was obliged to go and peep through the keyhole. Then a feeling of greatness came over him, such as we feel beside the rolling sea when the storm sweeps over it, and he burst into tears. He did not know himself why he wept, but a strange and very pleasant feeling was mingled with his tears. How wonderfully glorious it must be to sit with the student under that tree! But that could not be—he must content himself with the keyhole, and be glad of that. There he stood on the cold landing with the autumn wind blowing down from the trap-door in the loft; it was cold, so cold, but that the little fellow only felt when the light in the attic was put out and the music in the wonderful tree had died away. Ugh! Then he felt frozen, and he crept down to his warm corner again—it was cosy and comfortable there! And when Christmas came, and with it the porridge and the great lump of butter—why, then the provision-dealer was the master for him.

But in the middle of the night the goblin was awakened by a terrible noise and a banging at the shutters, against which the people outside were knocking as hard as they could. The night watchman blew his horn, for a great fire had broken out. Was it in the house itself, or at the neighbour's? Where was it? It was a dreadful moment.

The provision-dealer's wife was so bewildered that she took her gold earrings from her ears and put them into her pocket, so that she might save at least something; the provision-dealer made a dash for his bank-notes, and the maid for her silk shawl which she had managed to afford. Every one wanted to save the best they had; the goblin wanted to do that too, and in a few leaps he was up the stairs and in the room of the student, who was calmly standing at the open window gazing at the fire that raged in the house of the neighbour opposite. The little goblin seized the book from the table, put it into his red cap, and clasped it with both hands; the greatest treasure in the house was saved, and then he ran up and away, out upon the roof of the house, on to the chimney. There he sat in the light of the flames from the burning house opposite, both hands pressed over his red cap which held his treasure, and now he knew where his heart was and to whom he really belonged. But when the fire was extinguished, and the goblin again began to reflect calmly, well—

"I will divide myself between the two," he said. "I cannot give the provision-dealer up altogether because of the porridge!"

And that was only human after all. Most of us stick to the provision-dealer for the sake of the porridge.

THE UGLY DUCKLING

IT was delightful out in the country: it was summer, and the corn-fields were golden, the oats were green, the hay had been put up in stacks in the green meadows, and the stork went about on his long red legs and chattered Egyptian, for this was the language he had learned from his mother. Round the fields and meadows were great forests, and in the midst of the forests lay deep lakes. Yes, it was really delightful out in the country! In the midst of the sunshine there lay an old manor-house, with deep canals round it, and from the wall down to the water grew large burdocks, so high that little children could stand upright under the tallest of them. It was just as wild there as in the deepest wood. Here sat a duck upon her nest, for she had to hatch her ducklings, but she was almost tired out, for it took such a long time; and she so seldom had visitors. The other ducks liked better to swim about in the canals than to climb up to sit under a burdock and cackle with her.

At last one egg after another cracked open. "Piep! piep!" they cried; all the yolks had come to life, and little heads were peeping out.

"Quack! quack!" said the duck, and they all came out quack-ing as fast as they could, looking all round them under the green leaves, and the mother let them look as much as they wished, for green is good for the eyes.

"How wide the world is!" said the young ones, for they truly had much more room now than when they were in the eggs.

"Do you think this is the whole world?" said the mother. "That stretches far across the other side of the garden, quite into the parson's field; but I have never been there yet! I hope you are all here," she said, and she stood up. "No, I haven't got you all. The biggest egg is still there. How long is this going to last? I am getting tired of it." And she sat down again.

"Well, how goes it?" said an old duck, who had come to pay her a visit.

"It's taking so long with that one egg," said the duck sitting there. "It will not break. But look at the others! They are the prettiest ducklings I have ever seen! They are all just like their father, the rascal! He never comes to see me."

"Let me see the egg which will not break," said the old one. "Depend upon it, it is a turkey's egg! I was once cheated in that way, and had a lot of bother and trouble with the young ones, for they are afraid of the water. I could not get them into it. I quacked and pecked, but it was no use! Let me see the egg. Yes, that's a turkey's egg! Let it alone, and teach the other children to swim."

"I think I'll just sit on it a little longer," said the duck. "I've sat so long now that I may as well sit a few days more."

"As you please," said the old duck, and she went away.

At last the big egg broke. "Piep! piep!" said the little one, and crept out. It was very big and ugly. The duck looked at it.

"That's a terribly big duckling!" said she; "none of the others look like that: can it really be a turkey-chick? Well, we shall soon find that out! Into the water he shall go, even if I have to push him in myself!"

Next day the weather was splendidly bright, and the sun shone on all the green burdocks. The mother-duck went down to the canal, with all her little ones. Splash!—she sprang into the water. "Quack! quack!" she said, and one duckling after another plumped in. The water closed over their heads, but they came straight up again and swam capitally; their legs went of themselves, and there they were, all in the water, and the ugly grey duckling swimming with them.

"No, he's not a turkey," said she; "see how well he uses his legs, and how upright he holds himself! He's my own child! On the whole he's quite pretty, if only you look at him properly. Quack! quack! come along with me, and I'll lead you out into the world, and present you in the poultry-yard; but keep close to me, so that no one may tread on you, and take care of the cats!"

And so they came into the poultry-yard. There was a terrible riot going on there, for two families were quarrelling about an eel's head, and the cat got it after all.

"See, that's the way of the world!" said the mother-duck; and she whetted her beak, for she too wanted the eel's head. "Only use your legs," said she. "See that you bustle about, and bow your heads before the old duck yonder. She's the grandest of all of them here; she's of Spanish blood—that's why she's so fat, and, do you see, she has a red rag round her leg; that's something unusually fine, and the greatest distinction any duck can enjoy: it means that they don't want to lose her, and that she's to be recognized by man and beast. Stir yourselves—don't turn in your toes! A well-brought-up duck turns its toes right out, just like his father and mother—so! Now bend your necks and say ' Quack!' "

And so they did; but the other ducks round about looked at them, and said out loud:

"Look there! Now we're to have that lot too, as if there were not enough of us already! And—fie!—look how ugly that duckling is! We won't stand that!" And one duck flew straight at him, and bit him in the neck.

"Let him alone," said the mother; "he is doing no harm to any-one."

"Yes, but he's too big and so different," said the duck who had bitten him, "and therefore he must be pecked."

"Those are pretty children that mother has there!" said the old duck with the rag on her leg. "They're all pretty but that one; that's not a lucky one! I wish she could hatch him over again!"

"That cannot be, your Highness," said the duckling's mother. "He is not pretty, but he has a really good disposition, and swims as well as any other—yes, I may even say better! I think he will grow pretty, and may become smaller in time! He has lain too long in the egg, and therefore has not got the proper shape." And she stroked his neck and smoothed his feathers. "Moreover, he is a drake," said she, "and so it does not matter so much. I think he will be very strong, and make his way in the world!"

"The other ducklings are graceful enough," said the old duck. "Make yourself at home; and if you find an eel's head you may bring it me."

So now they felt at home. But the poor duckling which had crept last out of the egg, and looked so ugly, was bitten and pushed and made a fool of, as much by the ducks as by the chickens.

"He is too big!" they all said. And the turkey-cock, who had been born with spurs, and therefore thought himself an emperor, puffed himself up like a ship in full sail, and bore down upon him, and gobbled, and grew quite red in the face. The poor duckling did not know where to stand or where to go; he was quite miserable because he looked ugly, and was the butt of the whole yard.

So it went on the first day, and afterwards it became worse and worse. The poor duckling was hunted about by them all; even his brothers and sisters were quite cross with him, and said, " If only the cat would catch you, you ugly sight! " And his mother said, " If you were only far away! " And the ducks bit him, and the chickens pecked at him, and the girl who fed the poultry kicked at him with her foot.

Then he ran and flew over the hedge, and the little birds in the bushes flew up in fear.

" That is because I am so ugly! " thought the duckling; and he shut his eyes, but ran on farther; so he came out into the great moor, where the wild ducks lived. Here he lay the whole night long; he was so tired and sorrowful.

Towards morning the wild ducks flew up, and looked at their new comrade.

" What sort of a one are you? " they asked; and the duckling turned in every direction, and bowed to them as best he could. " You are remarkably ugly! " said the wild ducks. " But that's all the same to us, so long as you do not marry into our family! "

Poor thing! He certainly was not thinking of marrying, and only hoped to get leave to lie among the reeds and drink some of the marsh water.

Thus he lay two whole days, and then there came two wild geese, or, rather, ganders, for both were males. It was not long since each came out of the egg, and that's why they were so saucy.

" Listen, comrade," said one of them. " You're so ugly that I like you. Will you go with us, and become a bird of passage? Near here, in another moor, there are a few sweet lovely wild geese, all unmarried, and all able to say 'Quack!' You've a chance of making your fortune, ugly as you are! "

" Bang! bang! " sounded in the air above, and the two ganders fell dead in the swamp, and the water became blood-red. " Bang! bang! " it sounded again, and whole flocks of wild geese rose up

"WHY DO MY FLOWERS LOOK SO FADED TO-DAY?"

"Little Ida's Flowers"

WHEN NIGHT WAS COME AND THE SHOP SHUT UP

"Little Ida's Flowers"

from the reeds. And then there was another shot. A great hunt was going on. The hunters were lying in wait all round the moor—yes, some were even sitting up in the branches of the trees, which stretched far over the reeds. The blue smoke rose up like clouds among the dark trees and drifted far over the water; into the mud came the hunting dogs—splash, splash!—and the rushes and the reeds bent on every side. That was a fright for the poor duckling! He turned his head to put it under his wing, but at that moment a frightful great dog stopped close to the duckling. His tongue hung far out of his mouth and his eyes gleamed horribly; he thrust out his nose close to the duckling, showed his sharp teeth, and—splash, splash!—on he went, without touching him.

" Oh, thank heaven! " sighed the duckling. "I am so ugly that even the dog does not want to bite me! "

And so he lay quite still, while the shots rattled through the reeds, and gun after gun went off. At last, late in the day, all was quiet again; but the poor duckling did not dare to move; he waited several hours before he looked round him, and then made off out of the marsh as fast as he could. He ran on over field and meadow, and such a storm was blowing that it was difficult to get along at all.

Towards evening the duckling came to a miserable little peasant's hut. It was so tumbledown that it did not know which side to fall, and that's why it remained standing. The storm whistled so fiercely about the duckling that he was obliged to sit down to withstand it; and the tempest grew worse and worse. Then the duckling noticed that one of the hinges of the door had given way, and the door hung so askew that he could slip through the crack into the room; and so he did.

Here there lived a woman, with her tom cat and her hen. And the tom cat, whom she called Sonnie, could arch his back and purr, and he could even give out sparks, but for that one had to stroke his fur the wrong way. The hen had very little short legs, and therefore she was called Chickabiddy-shortlegs; she laid good eggs, and the woman loved her as her own child.

In the morning the strange duckling was noticed at once, and the tom cat began to purr, and the hen to cluck.

33

" What's all this? " said the woman, and looked about her; but she could not see well, and so she thought the duckling was a fat duck that had strayed in. " This is a rare catch! " she said. " Now I shall have duck's eggs. I hope it is not a drake. That we must find out! "

And so the duckling was taken on trial for three weeks; but no eggs came. And the tom cat was master of the house, and the hen was mistress, and always said, " We and the world! " for she thought they were half the world, and by far the better half too. The duckling thought it might be possible to hold another opinion, but the hen would not allow it.

" Can you lay eggs? " she asked.

" No."

" Then you'd better hold your tongue."

And the tom cat said, " Can you arch your back, and purr, and give out sparks? "

" No."

" Then you mustn't have any opinion of your own when sensible folk are talking."

And the duckling sat in a corner and was in a sad humour; then the fresh air and the sunshine streamed in; and he was seized with such a strange longing to swim on the water that he could not help telling it to the hen.

" What are you thinking of? " cried the hen. " You have nothing to do, that's why you have these fancies. Lay eggs or purr and they will pass away."

" But it is so delightful to swim on the water! " said the duckling, " so delightful to let it close over your head, and dive down to the bottom! "

" Yes, that must be a great pleasure truly," said the hen. " You must be going crazy. Ask the cat about it—he's the wisest creature I know—ask him if he likes to swim on the water or to dive under it: I won't speak of myself. Ask our mistress, the old woman; no one in the world is wiser than she. Do you think she has any longing to swim, and to let the water close over her head? "

" You don't understand me," said the duckling.

" We don't understand you? Then pray who will understand you? You surely don't pretend to be wiser than the tom cat and the old woman—to say nothing of myself. Don't be conceited, child, and be grateful for all the kindness that has been shown you. Have you not come into a warm room, and into company where you may learn something? But you are an idle chatterer, and it's no pleasure to be with you. You may believe me, I speak for your own good. I say unpleasant things to you, and that's the way you may always know your true friends! Just you learn to lay eggs, or to purr and give out sparks! "

" I think I'll go out into the wide world," said the duckling.

" Yes, do, by all means," said the hen.

And away went the duckling. He swam on the water and dived, but he was slighted by all the other creatures because of his ugliness.

Then autumn came. The leaves in the forest turned yellow and brown, the wind caught them so that they danced about, and the air turned very cold. The clouds hung low, heavy with hail and snow, and on the fence stood the raven and croaked, " Caw! caw! " from sheer cold; yes, it makes one shiver only to think of it. The poor duckling certainly had not a good time. One evening—the sun was just setting in all its beauty—there came a whole flock of great handsome birds out of the bushes. The duckling had never seen anything so beautiful. They were dazzlingly white, with long, slender necks. They were swans; they uttered a very peculiar cry, spread their lovely long wings, and flew away from that cold region to warmer lands, to open lakes. They rose so high, so high, that the ugly little duckling felt quite queer as he watched them. He turned round and round in the water like a wheel, stretched out his neck towards them, and uttered such a strange loud cry that he frightened even himself. Oh! he could not forget those beautiful, those happy birds; and as soon as he could see them no longer he dived right down to the bottom, and when he came up again he was quite beside himself. He knew not what birds they were, nor whither they were flying; but he loved them more than he had ever loved anyone

before. He was not at all envious of them. How could he think of
wishing for such loveliness as they had? He would have been quite
happy if only the ducks would have allowed him to be with them—
the poor ugly little thing!

And the winter grew so cold, so cold! The duckling was forced
to swim about in the water to prevent it from freezing all over;
but every night the hole in which he swam became smaller and
smaller. It froze so hard that the icy covering creaked; and the duckling had to use his legs all the time to keep the hole from freezing
up. At last he became exhausted, and lay quite still, and soon froze
fast into the ice.

Early in the morning a peasant came by and saw him. And he

went on to the ice, and took his wooden shoe and broke the ice to pieces, and carried the duckling home to his wife. There he came to again. The children wanted to play with him, but the duckling thought they would hurt him, and in his fright he fluttered up into the milk-pan, so that the milk splashed all over the room. The woman cried out and clapped her hands, at which the duckling flew into the butter-tub, and then into the meal-barrel and out again. What a sight he was then! The woman screamed, and struck at him with the fire-tongs; the children tumbled over one another in trying to catch the duckling; and they laughed and they screamed! Luckily the door stood open, and the poor creature was able to slip out among the shrubs into the newly fallen snow.

But it would be too sad to tell you all the misery and trouble the duckling had to bear through the hard winter. He was lying out on the moor among the reeds, when the sun began to shine warmly again. The larks were singing, and it was lovely springtime.

Then all at once the duckling flapped his wings: they beat the air more strongly than before, and bore him quickly away; and before he knew it he found himself in a large garden, where the apple-trees were in bloom, and lilacs scented the air and hung their long green branches down to the winding canals. Oh, here it was so beautiful, in the freshness of spring! and right in front of him from the thicket came three lovely white swans; they ruffled their feathers, and swam lightly over the water. The duckling knew the splendid creatures, and was seized with a strange sadness.

"I will fly to them, the royal birds! and they will kill me, because I, that am so ugly, dare to go near them. But that will not matter! Better be killed by them than snapped at by ducks, pecked by fowls, and kicked by the girl who takes care of the poultry-yard, and suffer hunger in winter!" And it flew into the water, and swam towards the beautiful swans; they saw him, and came sailing up with ruffled feathers. "Only kill me!" said the poor creature, and bent his head down to the water and awaited his death. But what did he see in the clear water? He saw below him his own image, but he was no longer a clumsy, dark grey bird, ugly and ungainly; he was himself a swan.

It matters little to be born in a duck-yard when one comes from a swan's egg!

He felt quite glad at all the trouble and misfortune he had suffered, now he realized his good fortune in all the beauty that surrounded him. And the big swans swam round him, and stroked him with their beaks.

Into the garden came some little children, and threw bread and corn into the water; and the youngest cried, "There is a new one!" and the other children shouted with joy, "Yes, a new one has come!" And they clapped their hands and danced about, and ran to their father and mother; and bread and cake were thrown into the water; and they all said, " The new one is the most beautiful of all! so young and handsome! " and the old swans bowed their heads to him.

Then he felt quite shy, and hid his head under his wings, for he did not know what to do; he was so happy, and yet not at all proud, for a good heart is never proud. He thought of how he had been persecuted and despised; and now he heard them all saying that he was the most beautiful of all beautiful birds. Even the lilac bent its branches straight down into the water before him, and the sun shone warm and mild. He ruffled his feathers and lifted his slender neck, and from his heart he cried joyfully:

" Of so much happiness I never dreamed when I was the ugly duckling! "

THE SHEPHERDESS
AND THE
CHIMNEY-SWEEP

HAVE you ever seen a really old cupboard, quite black with age, and carved with foliage and scrolls? Just such a one stood in a parlour; it was a legacy from the great-grandmother, and was covered from top to bottom with carved roses and tulips. There were the quaintest flourishes upon it, and from among these projected little stags' heads with antlers. In the middle of the cupboard an entire figure of a man had been carved. He was certainly ridiculous to look at, and he grinned, for you could not call it laughing; he had a goat's legs, little horns on his head, and a long beard. The children in the room always called him the Overandundergeneralwarcommandersergeant Billygoatslegs. That was a difficult name to pronounce, and there are not many who get this title; but to have carved him—that was certainly something. And there he was! He was always looking at the table under the looking-glass, for on this table stood a comely little shepherdess made of porcelain. Her shoes were gilt, her dress was adorned with a red rose, and besides this she had a golden hat and a shepherd's crook; she was lovely. Close by her stood a little chimney-sweep, as black as coal, and also made of porcelain. He was as clean and neat as anybody, for, as to his being a sweep, that was only what he was made to represent; the porcelain-makers might just as well have made a prince of him, if they had been so minded.

There he stood very prettily with his ladder, and his face as white and pink as a girl's, and that was really a fault, for a little blackened

40

he certainly ought to have been. He stood quite close to the shepherdess. They had both been placed where they stood, but as they had been placed there they had become engaged to each other, for they suited each other well. Both were young people, they were made of the same porcelain, were equally fragile.

Close to them stood another figure, three times as large as they were. This was an old Chinaman, who could nod. He was also made of porcelain, and said that he was the grandfather of the little shepherdess; but this he could not prove. He declared he had authority over her, and that therefore he had nodded to Overandundergeneralwarcommandersergeant Billygoatslegs, who was wooing the little shepherdess.

"Then you will get a husband," said the old Chinaman, "a husband who I verily believe is made of mahogany. He can make you Mrs Overandundergeneralwarcommandersergeant Billygoatslegs. He has the whole cupboard full of silver plate, which he keeps hidden in secret drawers."

"I won't go into the dark cupboard!" said the little shepherdess. "I have heard tell that he has eleven porcelain wives in there."

"Then you may become the twelfth," said the Chinaman. "This night, as soon as it rattles in the old cupboard, you shall be married, as sure as I am an old Chinaman!"

And with that he nodded his head and fell asleep. But the little shepherdess cried, and looked at her heart's beloved, the porcelain chimney-sweep.

"I want to beg of you," said she, "to go with me out into the wide world, for here we cannot stay!"

"I will do whatever you wish!" said the little chimney-sweep. "Let us start

41

directly! I think I can make a living by exercising my pro-
fession."

"If we were only safely down from the table!" said she. "I
shall not be happy until we are out in the wide world."

And he comforted her, and showed her how she must set her little
foot upon the carved border and the gilded foliage on the leg of
the table. He brought his ladder, too, to help her, and they were
soon together upon the floor. But when they looked up at the old
cupboard there was a great stir there. All the carved stags were
stretching out their heads, rearing up their antlers, and turning their
necks; and the Overandundergeneralwarcommandersergeant Billygoatslegs sprang high in the air, and shouted across to the old
Chinaman:

"Now they're running away! Now they're running away!"

At that they were rather frightened, and jumped quickly into the
drawer of the window-seat. Here there were three or four packs of
cards, which were not complete, and a little dolls' theatre, which
had been built up as well as it could be managed. A comedy was
being acted, and all the queens of diamonds and hearts, clubs and
spades, sat in the first row, fanning themselves with their tulips, and
behind them stood all the knaves, showing that they had a head both
above and below, as is usual in playing-cards. The comedy was
about two people who could not marry each other, and the shepherdess cried, because it was just like her own story.

"I cannot bear it!" said she. "I must get out of the drawer."

But when they got down on the floor, and looked up at the
table, the old Chinaman was awake, and was rocking his whole body
—although below he was all one lump.

"Now the old Chinaman's coming!" cried the little shepherdess,
and she fell down upon her porcelain knees, so frightened was she.

"I have an idea," said the chimney-sweep. "Shall we creep
into the great pot-pourri vase which stands in the corner? There we
can lie on roses and lavender, and throw salt in his eyes when he
comes."

"That will be of no use," said she. "Besides, I know that the old Chinaman and the pot-pourri vase were once engaged to each other, and a kind of liking always remains when people have once been on such terms. No, there's nothing left for us but to go out into the wide world!"

"Have you really courage to go out into the wide world with me?" asked the chimney-sweep. "Have you bethought how big it is, and that we can never come back here again?"

"Yes, I have," replied she.

And the chimney-sweep looked fixedly at her, and said:

"My way lies up the chimney. Have you really courage to creep with me through the stove—through the iron fire-box as well as up the flue pipe? Then we can get out into the chimney, and I know how to find my way there. We'll climb so high that they can't catch us, and at the very top there's a hole that leads out into the wide world."

And he led her to the door of the stove.

"It looks very black there," said she; but still she went with him, through the box and through the pipe, where it was pitch-dark night.

"Now we are in the chimney," said he; "and look, look! up there a beautiful star is shining!"

And it was a real star in the sky which shone straight down upon them, as if it would show them the way. And they crawled and they crept. It was a frightful way, and terribly steep, but he supported her and helped her up; he held her, and showed her the best places to place her little porcelain feet. And so they reached the top of the chimney, and upon that they sat down, for they were desperately tired, as they well might be.

The sky with all its stars was high above, and all the roofs of the town below them. They could see far around them, far out into the world. The poor shepherdess had never thought it would be like this. She leaned her little head against the chimney-sweep, and she wept so bitterly that all the gilt was washed off her girdle.

"This is too much," she said. "I cannot bear it! The world is too big! If I were only back upon the little table under the looking-glass! I shall never be happy until I am there again. I have followed

you out into the wide world, and now you may follow me back
home again if you really love me."

And the chimney-sweep spoke sensibly to her, spoke of the old
Chinaman and of Overandundergeneralwarcommandersergeant
Billygoatslegs, but she kissed her little chimney-sweep and sobbed
so bitterly that he could not help giving way to her, though it was
foolish.

And so with much difficulty they climbed down the chimney
again. And they crept through the pipe and the fire-box. That was
not pleasant at all. And at last they stood in the dark stove again.
There they listened behind the door, to find out what was going
on in the room. There it was quite still. They peeped out—ah!
there lay the old Chinaman in the middle of the floor. He had fallen
down from the table as he was pursuing them, and now he lay
broken into three pieces; his back had come off all in one piece,
and his head had rolled into a corner. The Overandundergeneralwarcommandersergeant Billygoatslegs stood where he had always stood,
and meditated.

" This is terrible! " said the little shepherdess. " The old grandfather has fallen to pieces, and it is our fault! I shall never survive it! "
And then she wrung her tiny little hands.

" He can be mended! " said the chimney-sweep. " He can easily
be mended! Don't be so hasty. If they cement his back together
and give him a good rivet in his neck he will be as good as new,
and may say many a disagreeable thing to us yet! "

" Do you think so? " said she.

So they climbed back upon the table where they used to stand.

" You see, this is as far as we have got," said the chimney-sweep;
" we might well have spared ourselves all our troubles! "

" If only old Grandfather could be riveted! " said the shepherdess.
" I wonder if that costs very much! "

And mended he was. The family had his back cemented and a
good rivet put in his neck; and he was as good as new, only he could
no longer nod.

" It seems you have become proud since you were broken to

pieces," said the Overandundergeneralwarcommandersergeant Billy-goatslegs. "I don't think there's so much to be proud of! Am I to have her, or am I not?"

And the chimney-sweep and the little shepherdess looked at the old Chinaman quite piteously, for they were afraid he might nod. But he could not do that, and it was irksome to him to tell a stranger that he always had a rivet in his neck; and so the little porcelain people remained together, and loved one another until they broke to pieces.

THE SNOW QUEEN

FIRST STORY

WHICH TREATS OF THE MIRROR AND THE BROKEN PIECES

WELL, now we're going to begin. When we are at the end of the story we shall know more than we do now, for he was a bad goblin! He was one of the very worst, for he was the devil. One day he was in a very good humour, for he had made a mirror which had this peculiarity, that everything good and beautiful that was reflected in it shrank into almost nothing, but that all that was worthless and ugly was magnified and looked even worse than before. The most lovely landscapes looked like boiled spinach, and the best of people looked hideous, or stood on their heads and had no bodies; their faces were so distorted that no one would know them, and if anybody had one freckle it was sure to spread all over his nose and mouth. That was most amusing, said the devil. When a good pious thought passed through anyone's mind it was shown again in the mirror, in such a way that the goblin-chief chuckled at his crafty invention. All who went to the goblin school—for he kept a goblin school—declared all round that a miracle had been worked. For at last, they asserted, one could see for the first time how the world and the people in it really looked. They ran about with the mirror, till at last there was not a land or a person that had not been seen in it distorted. Next they wanted to fly up to heaven with it, to scoff at the angels and the Lord. The higher they flew with the mirror, the worse it grinned, till they could scarcely hold it. Higher and higher they flew, nearer to God and the angels, and then the mirror trembled so terribly in its grinning that it slipped out of their hands and fell down to the earth, where it was shattered into a hundred million billion and more splinters. After that it caused greater misfortune than before, for some of the splinters were hardly as big as a grain of sand, and these flew about all over the world, and whenever they flew into anyone's eye they stuck there, and those people saw everything distorted, or had eyes only for the wrong side of a thing, for every little fragment had retained the same power as the whole looking-glass. A few people even got a tiny splinter of the mirror into their hearts, and that was terrible indeed, for such a heart became a block of ice. A few pieces of the glass were so large that they were used as window-panes, but it was a bad thing to look at one's friends through these panes; other pieces were made into spectacles, and when people put on these spectacles to see correctly and to be just, then things went all wrong; and then the Evil One laughed till his paunch shook: it delighted him so. But some little fragments of glass still floated about in the air. Now we shall hear!

SECOND STORY

A LITTLE BOY AND A LITTLE GIRL

IN the big town, where there are so many houses and people that there is not room enough for every one to have a little garden, and where most people therefore must be content with flowers in flower-pots, there were, however, two poor children who had a garden somewhat bigger than a flower-pot. They were not brother and sister, but they loved each other quite as much as if they had been. Their parents lived just opposite each other; they lived in two garrets, where the roof of one neighbour's house joined that of the other, with the gutter running between them. In each house was a little window. You had only to step across the gutter to get from one window to the other.

Outside each window the parents had placed a big wooden box, in which grew the vegetables that they used and a little rose-bush; there was one in each box, and they grew splendidly. The parents then thought of placing the boxes across the gutter, so that they nearly reached from one window to another, and looked just like two walls of flowers. Sweet peas hung over the boxes, and the rose-bushes sent out long shoots, which clustered round the windows and bent towards each other; it was almost like a triumphal arch of flowers and leaves. As the boxes were very high, and the children knew that they must not climb on them, they were often allowed to go out on to the roof behind the boxes, and to sit upon their little stools under the roses, and there they could play capitally.

In the winter there was an end of this amusement. The windows were sometimes frosted all over. But then they warmed coppers on the stove, and held the warm coins against the frosted pane; and this made a capital peep-hole, so round, so round! and out of each peeped a bright friendly eye, one from each window—it was the little boy and the little girl. His name was Kay and hers was Gerda.

In the summer they could get to each other at one jump, but in the winter they had to go down many stairs and up many stairs again, while the snow was falling outside.

"It is the white bees that are swarming," said the old grand-mother.

"Have they also a queen-bee?" asked the little boy, for he knew that there was one among the real bees.

"Yes, they have one," said grandmother. "She always flies where they swarm thickest. She is the largest of them all, and never settles on the earth, but flies up again into the black sky. Many a winter's night does she fly through the streets of the town, and looks in at the windows, and then they freeze fantastically and look like flowers."

48

" Yes, I've seen that ! " said both the children, and then they knew that it was true.

" Can the Snow Queen come in here? " asked the little girl.

" Let her try ! " said the boy; " I'll put her on the hot stove, and then she'll melt."

But the grandmother smoothed his hair, and told them some more tales.

In the evening, when little Kay was at home and half undressed, he climbed upon the chair by the window and looked out through the little hole. A few flakes of snow were falling outside, and one of them, the largest of all, settled on the edge of one of the flower-boxes. The snowflake grew larger and larger, till at last it became a maiden clothed in the finest white gauze, made of millions of star-like flakes. She was beautiful and delicate, but of ice—of blinding, sparkling ice. Yet she was alive; her eyes flashed like two bright stars, but there was no peace or rest in them. She nodded towards the window, and beckoned with her hand. The little boy was frightened, and jumped down from the chair, and the same moment it seemed as if a large bird flew by outside the window.

Next day it was clear and frosty, and then came the thaw, and with it the spring. The sun shone, the green shoots appeared, the swallows built their nests, the windows were opened, and the little children sat in their garden again, high up on the roof, at the top of the house.

How splendidly the roses bloomed that summer ! The little girl had learned a hymn in which there was something about roses; and she thought of her own roses; so she sang it to the little boy, and he sang too :

Roses fade and die, but we
Our Infant Lord shall surely see.

And the little ones held each other's hands, kissed the roses, and looked up at God's bright sunshine and spoke to it, as if the Christ-child were there. What lovely summer days those were ! How beautiful it was out there, by the sweet rose-bushes, which seemed as if they would never stop blooming !

Kay and Gerda sat and looked at the picture-book of beasts and

49

birds. It was then, exactly as the clock struck five in the great church tower, that Kay said:

" Oh! Something has stabbed my heart! And now something has got into my eye!"

The little girl put her arms round his neck. He blinked his eyes. But no, there was nothing at all to be seen.

" I think it is gone," said he; but it was not gone. It was one of those splinters of glass from the mirror—the goblin-mirror that we remember so well, the ugly glass that made everything great and good which was mirrored in it seem small and hideous, while the mean and the wicked things became distinct and large, and every fault was to be seen at once. Poor little Kay had also received a splinter right in his heart. And now that would soon become like a lump of ice. It did not hurt him any more, but the splinter was still there.

" Why are you crying?" he asked. " You look ugly like that. There's nothing the matter with me. Oh, fie!" he cried suddenly; " that rose is worm-eaten, and look—this one is quite crooked! They're ugly roses, after all—like the box they stand in!"

And he kicked the box with his foot, and tore both the roses off.

" Kay, what are you doing?" cried the little girl.

And seeing her dismay, he tore off another rose and jumped in at his own window, away from dear little Gerda.

When afterwards she came with her picture-book he said it was only fit for babies; and when grandmother told stories he was always sure to put in a *but*; and when he could manage it he would get behind her, put on a pair of spectacles, and talk just as she did; he could do it perfectly, and people laughed at him. Soon he could mimic the voice and walk of everybody in the street. Everything that was peculiar or ugly about them Kay would imitate. And people said, " He must certainly have a remarkable head, that boy!" But it was the glass that had got into his eye, the glass that had stuck in his heart, that caused all this, and even made him tease little Gerda, who loved him with all her heart.

His games now became quite different from what they were

before; they became quite sensible. One winter's day, when the snow was falling, he came out with a great burning-glass, held up the tail of his blue coat, and let the snowflakes fall upon it.

"Now look through the glass, Gerda," said he.

And every flake of snow was magnified, and looked like a splendid flower, or a star with ten points: it was lovely to see.

"Look, how clever!" said Kay. "That's much more interesting than real flowers; and there is not a single fault in them—they're quite regular until they begin to melt."

Soon after Kay came out with thick gloves on, and with his sledge on his back. He shouted into Gerda's ears, "I've got leave to go into the big square, where the other boys play," and off he went.

In the big square the boldest among the boys often tied their sledges to the country people's carts, and were dragged along a good way with them. It was great fun. At the height of their game there came along a big sledge. It was all painted white, and in it sat somebody wrapped in a rough white fur, and with a white rough cap on. The sledge drove twice round the square, and Kay managed to fasten his little sledge to it, and away he drove with it. It went faster and faster, straight into the next street. The driver turned round and nodded in a friendly way to Kay; it was just as if they knew one another: every time Kay wanted to cast loose his little sledge the stranger nodded again, and so Kay stayed where he was, and so they drove out at the town gate. Then the snow began to fall so fast that the boy could not see a hand's breadth before him, but still on he went. Then he hastily dropped the cord, so as to get loose from the big sledge, but it was no use, for his little sledge was fast bound to the other, and they went on like the wind. Then he called out loudly, but nobody heard him; and the snow fell fast and the sledge flew on; every now and then it gave a jump, and they seemed to be flying over hedges and ditches. The boy was quite frightened. He wanted to say "Our Father," but could remember nothing but the multiplication table.

The snowflakes became larger and larger; at last they looked like big white fowls. All at once they flew aside and the big sledge stopped, and the person who had driven it stood up. The fur and the cap were all made of snow; it was a lady, so tall and slender, and glittering white! It was the Snow Queen.

"We have travelled fast!" said she. "But you are shivering with cold! Creep under my bearskin."

And she put him beside her in her own sledge, and wrapped the fur round him, and he felt as if he was sinking into a snowdrift.

"Are you still cold?" she asked, and then she kissed him on the forehead.

Ugh! that was colder than ice; it went right through to his heart, half of which was already a lump of ice: he felt as if he was going to die—but only for a moment; and then he felt quite well again, and he did not notice the cold any more.

"My sledge! don't forget my sledge!"

That was the first thing he thought of; and it was bound fast to one of the white fowls, which flew behind them with the sledge upon its back. The Snow Queen kissed Kay once more, and then he had forgotten little Gerda, and his grandmother, and all at home.

"Now you shall have no more kisses," said she, "for if you did I should kiss you to death."

Kay looked at her. She was so beautiful, he could not imagine a more wise or lovely face; she did not appear to be made of ice now, as before, when she sat outside the window and beckoned to him. In his eyes she was perfect; he did not feel at all afraid. He told her he could do mental arithmetic as far as fractions, and that he knew the number of square miles and the number of inhabitants in all countries. And all the time she smiled, and then it seemed to him that what he knew was not enough, and he looked up into the great space, and she flew with him high up upon the black cloud, and the storm blew and whistled; it seemed as though the wind sang old songs. They flew over forests and lakes, over sea and land: beneath them roared the cold wind, the wolves howled, the snow glistened; above them flew black screaming crows; but above all the moon shone bright and clear, and Kay gazed at it through the long, long winter night; by day he slept at the feet of the Snow Queen.

THIRD STORY

THE FLOWER GARDEN OF THE WOMAN WHO
KNEW MAGIC

BUT how did it fare with little Gerda when Kay did not return? What could have become of him? No one knew; no one could give information. The boys could only say that they had seen him tie his little sledge to another very large one, which had driven along the street and out at the town gate. Nobody knew what had become of him; many tears were shed, and little Gerda cried long and bitterly. Then they said he was dead—he had been drowned in the river which flowed close by the town. Oh, those were long dark winter days indeed! Then came the spring, with its warm sunshine.

"Kay is dead and gone," said little Gerda.

"I don't believe it," said the sunshine.

"He is dead and gone," said she to the swallows.

"We don't believe it," they replied; and at last little Gerda did not believe it herself.

"I will take my new red shoes," she said one morning, "those that Kay has never seen; and then I will go down to the river, and ask it about him."

It was still very early; she kissed her old grandmother, who was asleep, took her red shoes, and went all alone out of the town gate to the river.

"Is it true that you have taken my little playmate? I will make you a present of my red shoes if you will give him back to me!"

And it seemed to her as if the waves nodded strangely; and then she took her red shoes, that she liked best of anything she possessed, and threw them both into the river; but they fell close to the bank, and the little wavelets bore them back to land again. It seemed as if the river would not take from her the dearest things she had because it had not got her little Kay. But she thought she had not thrown the shoes far enough out; so she climbed into a boat that lay among the reeds, and went to the farther end of the boat,

53

and threw the shoes into the water again; but the boat was not made fast, and at the movement she caused it drifted away from the shore. She noticed it, and hurried to get back, but before she reached the other end of the boat it was a yard from the bank, and was floating quickly away.

Then little Gerda was very much frightened, and began to cry; but no one heard her except the sparrows, and they could not carry her to land. They flew along the bank, and sang, as if to console her, "Here we are! here we are!" The boat drifted on with the stream, and little Gerda sat quite still, in her stockings. Her little red shoes floated along behind, but they could not catch up with the boat, which drifted faster.

It was very pretty on both sides. There were beautiful flowers, old trees, and slopes with sheep and cows; but not a human being was to be seen.

"Perhaps the river will carry me to little Kay," thought Gerda.

And then she became more cheerful, and stood up, and for many hours she watched the pretty green banks. At last she came to a big cherry orchard, where there was a little house with curious blue and red windows. It had a thatched roof, and in front stood two wooden soldiers, who presented arms to those who sailed past.

Gerda called to them, for she thought they were alive, but, of course, they did not answer. She came quite close to them; the river carried the boat into the shore.

Gerda called out still louder, and then there came out of the house an old, old woman leaning on a crutch: she had on a big sun-hat, painted with the most lovely flowers.

"You poor little child!" said the old woman. "How did you manage to come on the great strong river, and to float so far out into the wide world?"

And then the old woman went right into the water, hooked the boat with her crutch, drew it to land, and lifted little Gerda out. Gerda was glad to be on dry land again, though she felt a little afraid of the strange old woman.

"Come and tell me who you are, and how you came here,"

THE OLD WOMAN WENT RIGHT INTO THE WATER

said she. And Gerda told her everything; and the old woman shook her head, and said, "Hm! hm!" And when Gerda had told her everything, and asked if she had not seen little Kay, the woman said that he had not yet come by, but that he probably would soon come; she was not to be sorrowful, but taste her cherries and look at the flowers, for they were better than any picture-book, for each one of them could tell a story. Then she took Gerda by the hand and led her into the little house, and the old woman locked the door after them.

The windows were very high up, and the panes were red, blue, and yellow; the daylight shone in in a strange way, with all colours. On the table stood the finest cherries, and Gerda ate as many as she liked, for she had leave to do so. While she was eating them the old woman combed her hair with a golden comb, and the hair curled and shone like lovely gold round the sweet little face, which was round and as blooming as a rose.

"I have long wished for such a dear little girl as you," said the old woman. "Now you shall see how well we shall get on together."

And the more she combed little Gerda's hair, the more Gerda forgot her playmate Kay; for this old woman could work magic, but she was not a wicked witch. She only practised a little magic for her own amusement, and now only because she wanted to keep little Gerda. So she went into the garden, stretched out her crutch towards all the rose-bushes, and, beautiful as they were, they all sank into the black earth, and no one could tell where they had stood. The old woman was afraid that if Gerda saw roses she would think of her own, and remember little Kay, and run away.

Then she took Gerda out into the flower garden. What fragrance was there, and what loveliness! Every flower you could think of was there in full bloom; there were those of every season; no picture-book could be gayer and prettier. Gerda jumped for joy, and played till the sun went down behind the tall cherry-trees. Then she was put into a lovely bed with red silk pillows stuffed with blue violets, and she slept there, and dreamt as happily as a queen on her wedding-day.

Next day she could again play with the flowers in the warm sunshine; and thus many days went by. Gerda knew every flower; but, many as there were, it still seemed to her as if one were missing, but which one she did not know. One day she sat looking at the old woman's sun-hat with the painted flowers, and it happened that the prettiest of them all was a rose. The old woman had forgotten to remove it from her hat when she made the others sink into the ground. But so it always is when one does not keep one's wits about one.

" What, are there no roses here? " cried Gerda.

And she went among the beds, and searched and searched, but there was not one to be found. Then she sat down and cried; and her hot tears fell just upon a spot where a rose-tree lay buried, and when the warm tears moistened the earth the tree at once shot up again as blooming as when it had sunk; and Gerda embraced it, kissed the roses, and thought of the beautiful roses at home, and with them of little Kay too.

" Oh, how I have been wasting my time! " said the little girl, " I who ought to have been looking for little Kay! Do you know where he is? " she asked the roses. " Do you think he is dead? "

" He is not dead," said the roses. " We have been in the ground. All the dead people are there, but Kay is not there."

" Thank you," said little Gerda; and she went to the other flowers, looked into their cups, and asked, " Do you not know where little Kay is? "

But every flower stood in the sun thinking only of her own story or fairy-tale. Little Gerda heard many, many of them; but not one knew anything of Kay.

And what said the tiger-lily?

" Do you hear the drum ' rub-a-dub '? There are only three notes, always ' rub-a-dub '! Hear the funeral chant of the women! Hear the call of the priests! The Hindu woman stands in her long red robe on the funeral pile; the flames rise up round her and her dead husband; but the Hindu woman is thinking of the living one here in the circle, of him whose eyes burn hotter than flames, whose glances burn in her soul more ardently than the flames themselves which are soon to burn her body to ashes. Can the flame of the heart die in the flames of the funeral pile? "

"I don't understand that at all!" said little Gerda.

"That is my story," said the lily.

What says the convolvulus?

"Over the narrow mountain path hangs an old knight's castle:
the ivy grows thick over the crumbling red walls, leaf by leaf up to
the balcony, and there stands a beautiful girl. She leans over the
balustrade and gazes up the path. No rose on its stem is fresher than
she; no apple blossom wafted by the wind floats more lightly along.
How her costly silks rustle! 'Will he never come?'"

"Is it Kay you mean?" asked little Gerda.

"I am only talking of my own story—my dream," replied the
convolvulus.

What said the little snowdrop?

"Between two trees a board is hanging on ropes: it is a swing.
Two pretty little girls, with dresses as white as snow and green silk
ribbons on their hats, are sitting on it, swinging. Their brother, who
is bigger than they are, stands on the swing with his arm round the
rope to hold himself, for in one hand he has a little bowl, and in the
other a clay pipe: he is blowing soap-bubbles. The swing moves,
and the bubbles fly up with beautiful changing colours; the last one
still hangs from the bowl of the pipe, swayed by the wind. The swing
goes to and fro. A little black dog, light as the bubbles, stands up on
his hind legs and wants to be taken on to the swing. It goes on, and
the dog falls, and barks with anger: the bubble bursts. A swinging
board and a shimmering foam-picture—that is my song!"

"It may be very pretty, what you're telling me, but you speak so
mournfully, and you don't mention little Kay at all."

What do the hyacinths say?

"There were three beautiful sisters, transparent and delicate. The
dress of one was red, of the second blue, and of the third pure white.
Hand in hand they danced by the calm lake in the bright moonlight.
They were not elves—they were human-born. It was so sweet and
fragrant there! The girls disappeared in the forest, and the fragrance
became sweeter still. Three coffins, with the three beautiful maidens
lying in them, glided from the wood-thicket across the lake; the fire-

flies flew gleaming round them like little hovering lights. Are the dancing girls sleeping, or are they dead? The flower-scent says they are dead. The evening bell tolls their knell!"

"You make me quite sorrowful," said little Gerda. "Your scent is so strong, I cannot help thinking of the dead maidens. Ah! is little Kay really dead? The roses have been down beneath the ground, and they say no."

"Ding, dong!" rang the hyacinth bells. "We are not tolling for little Kay—we do not know him; we only sing our song, the only one we know."

And Gerda went to the buttercup, shining out among the green leaves.

"You are a little bright sun," said Gerda. "Tell me, if you know —where shall I find my playfellow?"

And the buttercup shone so gaily, and looked back at Gerda. What song could the buttercup sing? It was not about Kay.

"In a little courtyard God's bright sun shone warm on the first day of spring. The sunbeams glided down the white wall of the neighbouring house. Close by grew the first yellow flower, shining like gold in the bright sunbeams. An old grandmother sat out of doors in her chair; her pretty granddaughter, a poor maid-servant, had come home for a short visit: she kissed her grandmother. There was gold, heart's gold, in that blessed kiss, gold on the lips, gold on the ground, gold in the morning hour. See, that is my little story," said the buttercup.

"My poor old grandmother!" sighed Gerda. "Yes, she is surely longing for me and grieving for me, just as she did for little Kay. But I shall soon go home again and bring Kay with me. There is no use in my asking the flowers: they only know their own song, and give me no information." And then she tucked her little frock round her, that she might run the faster; but the jonquil struck her on the leg as she jumped over it, and she stopped to look at the tall flower, and asked, "Do you, perhaps, know anything?"

And she bent close down to the flower. And what did it say?

"I can see myself! I can see myself!" said the jonquil. "Oh!

oh! how sweet my scent is! Up in the little attic stands a little dancing girl half dressed. She stands sometimes on one foot, sometimes on both; she seems to tread on all the world. She's nothing but a delusion: she pours water out of a teapot on a bit of stuff—it is her bodice. ' Cleanliness is a good thing,' she says. Her white frock hangs on a hook; it has been washed in the teapot too, and dried on the roof. She puts it on and ties her saffron kerchief round her neck, and the dress looks all the whiter. Point your toes! Look how she seems to stand on a stalk! I can see myself! I can see myself!"

"I don't care at all about that!" said Gerda. "It is no use your telling me!"

And then she ran to the end of the garden. The door was locked, but she pressed against the rusty latch, and it gave way, the door sprang open, and little Gerda ran with bare feet out into the wide world. She looked back three times, but no one was there to come after her. At last she could run no more, and she sat down on a big stone; and when she looked round she saw that summer was over—it was late in the autumn. No one could know that in the beautiful garden, where there was always sunshine, and where the flowers of every season were always blooming.

"Alas! how I have lost my time!" said little Gerda. "It is already autumn! I must not stay any longer."

And she got up to go on. Oh, how sore and tired were her little feet! And all around looked so cold and bleak; the long willow leaves were quite yellow, and the mist dripped from the trees like rain; one leaf dropped after another—only the sloe still bore fruit, but the fruit was sour, and set the teeth on edge. Oh, how grey and gloomy it looked out in the wide world!

FOURTH STORY

THE PRINCE AND PRINCESS

GERDA had to rest again soon; and there hopped across the snow, just in front of where she was sitting, a big crow. It stopped a long time to look at her, nodding its head; and then it said, " Caw! caw! Goo' day! Goo' day!" It could not say it better, but it meant to be kind to the little girl, and asked where she was going all alone in the wide world. The word 'alone' Gerda understood very well, and felt how much it expressed; and she told the crow the whole story of her life and fortunes, and asked if it had not seen Kay.

And the crow nodded very gravely, and said:

" That may be! That may be!"

" What, do you believe so?" cried the little girl, and nearly smothered the crow, she kissed it so.

" Gently, gently!" said the crow. " I think I know: I believe it may be little Kay, but now he has certainly forgotten you for the Princess."

" Does he live with a princess?" asked Gerda.

" Yes; listen!" said the crow. " But it's so difficult for me to speak your language. If you know crows' language [1] I can tell it much better."

" No, I never learned it," said Gerda; " but my grandmother understood it, and could speak the language too. I only wish I had learned it."

" It doesn't matter," said the crow. " I will tell you as well as I can, but it will be rather badly."

And then the crow told her what it knew.

" In the country in which we now are there lives a princess who is quite wonderfully clever—but then she has read all the newspapers in the world, and has forgotten them again, she is so clever. Lately she was sitting on the throne—and that's not so very amusing, they say—and she began to hum a song, and it was just this,

Why shouldn't I be married?

' Wait—there's something in that!' said she. And at once she felt she wanted to get married, but she wished for a husband who could answer when he was spoken to, not one who only stood and looked

---

[1] Crows' language is a kind of gibberish children talk by adding syllables or letters to every word.

61

handsome, for that was wearisome. So she called all her maids of honour together, and when they heard what she wanted they were delighted. 'I like that, now,' said they; 'I thought the very same thing myself the other day.' You may be sure that every word I am telling you is true," said the crow. "I have a tame sweetheart who goes about freely in the castle, and she told me everything."

Of course, the sweetheart was a crow too, for birds of a feather flock together, and for a crow there is always another one.

"Newspapers were published directly, with a border of hearts and the Princess's initials. One could read in them that every young man who was good-looking might come to the castle and speak to the Princess, and the one who spoke in a way that showed he was quite at home there, and who spoke best, him would the Princess choose for her husband. Yes, yes," said the crow, "you can believe me. It's as true as I sit here. People came streaming in; there was a great crowding and running to and fro, but no one succeeded either on the first or second day. They could all speak well enough when they were out in the streets, but when they entered the palace gates, and saw the guards in silver, and at the top of the staircase the lackeys in gold, and the great lighted halls, they became confused. And when they stood in front of the throne where the Princess sat they could do nothing but repeat the last thing she said, and, of course, she did not care to hear her own words again. It was just as if the people in there had taken some sleeping powder and had fallen asleep till they got into the street again, for not till then were they able to speak. There stood a whole row of them, from the town gate to the palace. I went out myself to see it," said the crow. "They were hungry and thirsty, but in the palace they did not receive so much as a glass of lukewarm water. A few of the wisest had brought bread and butter with them, but they would not share with their neighbours, for they thought, 'Let him look hungry, and the Princess won't have him!'"

"But Kay, little Kay?" asked Gerda. "When did he come? Was he among the crowd?"

"Give me time! Give me time! We're just coming to him. It was on the third day that there came along a little person, without horse or carriage, walking quite merrily up to the castle. His eyes sparkled like yours, he had fine long hair, but his clothes were shabby."

"That was Kay!" cried Gerda, delighted. "Oh, then I have found him!" And she clapped her hands.

"He had a little knapsack on his back," said the crow.

"No, that must have been his sledge," said Gerda, "for he went away with a sledge."

"That may be so," said the crow, "for I did not look very closely. But this much I know from my tame sweetheart, that when he came in at the palace gate and saw the Life Guards in silver, and at the top of the staircase the lackeys in gold, he was not in the least abashed. He nodded, and said to them, 'It must be tiresome standing on the stairs—I'd rather go in.' The halls were ablaze with lights; privy councillors and excellencies walked about with bare feet, and carried golden vessels. It was enough to make anyone solemn! And his boots creaked dreadfully, but he was not at all frightened."

"That must have been Kay!" said Gerda. "I know he had new boots on; I've heard them creak in grandmother's room."

"Yes, certainly they creaked," said the crow. "And he went boldly in to the Princess herself, who sat on a pearl as big as a spinning-wheel; and all the maids of honour, with their maids and maids' maids, and all the cavaliers, with their gentlemen followers and their gentlemen's gentlemen, who themselves had a page apiece, were standing round; and the nearer they stood to the door, the prouder they looked. The gentlemen's gentlemen's pages, who always go in slippers, could hardly be looked at, so proudly did they stand in the doorway!"

"That must be terrible!" said little Gerda. "And yet Kay won the Princess?"

"If I had not been a crow I would have taken her myself, although I am engaged. They say he spoke as well as I do when I speak crows' language; so I heard from my tame sweetheart. He was merry and agreeable; he had not come to woo the Princess, but only to hear her wisdom; and he thought well of her, and she thought well of him again."

"Yes, that must have been Kay!" said Gerda. "He was so clever, he could do mental arithmetic up to fractions. Oh, won't you take me to the palace too?"

"Yes, that's easily said," replied the crow. "But how are we to manage it? I'll talk it over with my tame sweetheart; she can probably advise us; but this I must tell you—such a little girl as you are will never get leave to go right inside!"

"Oh, yes, I shall," said Gerda. "When Kay hears that I'm there he'll come out at once and fetch me."

"Wait for me over there at the stile," said the crow; and he wagged his head and flew away.

It was already late in the evening when the crow came back.

"Caw! caw!" said he. "I'm to greet you kindly from her, and here's a little loaf for you. She took it from the kitchen. There's bread enough there, and you must be hungry. You can't possibly get into the palace, for you are barefooted, and the guards in silver and the lackeys in gold would not allow it. But don't cry; you shall get in somehow. My sweetheart knows a little back staircase that leads up to the bedroom, and she knows where she can get the key."

And they went into the garden, into the great avenue, where the leaves were falling one after the other; and when the lights in the palace were put out one after the other, the crow led little Gerda to a back door, which stood ajar.

Oh, how Gerda's heart beat with fear and longing! It was just as if she had been going to do something wrong, and yet she only wanted to know if it was little Kay. Yes, it must be he. And she thought so earnestly of his clever eyes and his long hair: she could see how he smiled as he used to when they sat at home under the roses. He would surely be glad to see her; to hear what a long way she had come for his sake; and to know how sorry they had all been at home when he did not come back. Oh, what fear and what joy that was!

Now they were on the stairs. A little lamp was burning upon a cupboard, and in the middle of the room stood the tame crow,

KAY AND GERDA IN THEIR GARDEN HIGH UP ON THE ROOF
"The Snow Queen"

GERDA AND THE LITTLE ROBBER GIRL IN THE ROBBERS' CASTLE

"The Snow Queen"

turning her head on every side and staring at Gerda, who curtsied as her grandmother had taught her.

"My betrothed has spoken to me very favourably of you, my little lady," said the tame crow. "Your *vita*, as they call it, is really most touching. Will you take the lamp? Then I will go first. We will go straight along, for we shall meet nobody."

"I feel as if someone were coming after us," said Gerda, as she fancied something rushed by her. It seemed like a shadow on the wall; horses with flowing manes and thin legs, hunters, and gentle-men and ladies on horseback.

"They are only dreams," said the Crow. "They are coming to carry the nobles' thoughts out hunting. That's all the better, for you may look the more closely at them in bed. But I hope, when you are taken into favour and are honoured, that you will show a grateful heart."

"Of that we may be sure!" said the crow from the wood.

They came now into the first room; the walls were hung with rose-coloured satin embroidered with flowers; and here again the dreams came flitting by them, but they swept by so quickly that Gerda could not see the high-born lords and ladies. Each room was more splendid than the last; one was almost bewildered! And then they came to the bedchamber. Here the ceiling was like a great palm-tree with leaves of glass, of costly glass, and in the middle of the floor were two beds, each hung like a lily on a stalk of gold. One of them was white, and in that lay the Princess; the other was red, and in that it was that Gerda was to look for little Kay. She bent one of the red leaves aside, and she saw a brown neck. Oh, that was Kay! She called his name out loud, and held the lamp over him. The dreams rushed on horseback through the room again—he awoke, turned his head, and—it was not little Kay!

The Prince was like him only in the neck; but he was young and handsome, and the Princess peeped out, blinking, from the white lily bed, and asked what was the matter. Then little Gerda cried, and told them her whole story, and all that the crows had done for her.

"You poor little thing!" said the Prince and Princess.

And they praised the crows, and said that they were not angry with them at all, but they were not to do it again. However, they should be rewarded.

"Will you fly away free?" asked the Princess. "Or would you rather have permanent posts as Court crows, with the leavings of the kitchen as perquisites?"

And the two crows bowed, and begged for permanent posts, for they thought of their old age, and said, "It is so good to have something put by for the old man," as they put it.

And the Prince got up out of bed, and let Gerda sleep in it, and he could not do more than that. She folded her little hands, and thought, "How good men and animals are!" and then she shut her eyes and went quietly to sleep. All the dreams came flying by again, looking like God's angels, and they drew a little sledge, on which Kay sat and nodded; but all this was only a dream, and so it was gone again as soon as she awoke.

Next day she was clothed from top to toe in silk and velvet. She was invited to stay in the castle and enjoy herself, but she only begged them to give her a little carriage, and a horse, and a pair of little boots; and then again she would drive out into the wide world and find Kay.

And they gave her both boots and a muff, and she was prettily dressed; and when she was ready to start a new coach of pure gold was there for her before the door. Shining like a star on it was the coat of arms of the Prince and Princess. Coachman, footmen, and the postilions—for there were postilions too—all had golden crowns on their heads. The Prince and the Princess themselves helped her into the carriage, and wished her good luck. The forest crow, who was now married, accompanied her the first three miles. He sat by Gerda's side, for he could not bear riding backward. The other crow stood in the doorway, flapping her wings; she did not go with them, for she suffered from headache, that had come on since she had got her permanent appointment: she had had too much to eat. The coach was stocked with sugar-cakes, and under the seat there were ginger-nuts and fruit.

66

"THEY ARE ONLY DREAMS," SAID THE CROW

"Farewell! Farewell!" cried the Prince and Princess; and little Gerda wept, and the crow wept. And they went on like that for the first three miles, and then the crow said farewell too, and that was the saddest parting of all. And then he flew up into a tree, and beat his black wings as long as he could see the coach, which glittered like the bright sunshine.

FIFTH STORY

THE LITTLE ROBBER GIRL

THEY drove on through a dark forest, but the coach gleamed like a torch, that dazzled the robbers' eyes, and that they could not bear.

"It is gold! It is gold!" cried they, and rushed forward and seized the horses, killed the little postilions, the coachman, and the footmen, and then dragged little Gerda out of the carriage.

"She is fat—she is pretty—she has been fattened on nuts!" said the old robber woman, who had a long matted beard, and eyebrows that hung down over her eyes. "She's as good as a little fatted lamb! How well she will taste!"

And she drew out her shining knife, that glittered in a horrible way.

"Oh!" screamed the old woman at the same moment; for her ear was bitten by her own little daughter, who hung on her back and was as wild and savage as an animal. "You ugly brat!" said her mother, and she had not time to kill Gerda then.

"She shall play with me!" said the little robber girl. "She shall give me her muff and her pretty dress, and sleep with me in my bed!"

And then she bit her again, so that the woman jumped high in the air and turned about, and all the robbers laughed and said:

"Look how she dances with her young!"

"I will go in the carriage!" said the little robber girl.

And she would have her own way, for she was so spoiled and obstinate; and she and Gerda sat in the carriage, and off they drove over stock and stone deep into the forest. The little robber girl was as big as Gerda, but stronger and more broad-shouldered, and she had a dark skin. Her eyes were quite black, and they looked almost mournful. She took little Gerda round the waist, and said:

"They shall not kill you as long as I don't get angry with you. I suppose you are a princess?"

"No," replied Gerda. And she told all that had happened to her, and how fond she was of little Kay.

The robber girl looked at her earnestly, and gave a little nod with her head, and said:

"They shall not kill you even if I do get angry with you, for then I will do it myself."

And then she dried Gerda's eyes, and put her two hands into the beautiful muff that was so soft and warm.

Soon the coach stopped, and they were in the courtyard of a robber's castle. Its walls had cracked from the top to the bottom; ravens and crows flew out of the open holes, and big bulldogs—each of which looked as if he could devour a man—jumped high in the air, but they did not bark, for that was forbidden.

In the great old smoky hall a big fire was burning in the middle of the stone floor. The smoke went up to the ceiling, and had to find its own way out. A big cauldron of soup was boiling, and hares and rabbits were roasting on the spit.

"You shall sleep here to-night with me and all my little animals," said the robber girl.

They got something to eat and drink, and then went over into a corner, where there were lying some straw and some carpets. Overhead, sitting on laths and perches, were nearly a hundred pigeons. They all seemed to be asleep, but they moved a little when the two little girls came.

"They are all mine," said the little robber girl; and she quickly seized one of the nearest, held it by the feet, and shook it till it flapped its wings. "Kiss it!" she cried, and beat it in Gerda's face. "There sit rascals from the wood," she went on, pointing to a number of laths that had been nailed in front of a hole high up in the wall. "Those are wood rascals, those two; they fly away at once if one does not keep them properly shut up. And here's my old sweetheart

'Bae.'" And she dragged out by the horns a reindeer that was tied up and had a polished copper ring round its neck. "We have to keep him fast too, or he'd run away from us. Every evening I tickle his neck with my sharp knife, and that frightens him terribly!"

And the little girl drew a long knife out of a crack in the wall and let it slide over the reindeer's neck. The poor animal kicked out with its legs, and the robber girl laughed, and pulled Gerda into bed with her.

"Do you keep the knife with you while you're asleep?" asked Gerda, and looked at it rather frightened.

"I always sleep with my knife," replied the robber girl. "One never knows what may happen. But tell me once again what you told me before about little Kay, and why you went out into the wide world."

And Gerda told it all over again, and the wood pigeons cooed above them in their cage, and the other pigeons slept. The little robber girl put her arm round Gerda's neck, held her knife in the other hand, and slept so that anyone could hear her; but Gerda could not close her eyes at all—she did not know whether she was to live or die.

The robbers sat round the fire, sang, and drank, and the old robber woman turned somersaults. It was terrible for the little girl to see.

Then the wood pigeons said, "Coo! coo! We have seen little Kay. A white hen was carrying his sledge. He sat in the Snow Queen's carriage, which drove close by the forest as we lay in our nests. She blew upon us young pigeons, and all died except us two. Coo! coo!"

"What are you saying up there?" asked Gerda. "Where was the Snow Queen going? Do you know anything about it?"

"She was probably going to Lapland, for there there's always ice and snow. Ask the reindeer that is tied up by the rope."

"There there is snow and ice. There it is glorious and fine!" said the reindeer. "There one runs free in the wide glittering valleys! There the Snow Queen has her summer tent; but her stronghold is up nearer the North Pole, on the island they call Spitzbergen."

"Oh, Kay, little Kay!" sighed Gerda.

"You must lie still," said the robber girl, "or else you will feel the knife in your body."

In the morning Gerda told her all that the wood pigeons had said, and the robber girl looked very serious, and nodded her head, and said:

"That's all the same—that's all the same. Do you know where Lapland is?" she asked the reindeer.

"Who should know better than I?" said the animal, and its eyes shone in its head. "There was I born and bred! There have I leaped about over the snowfields!"

"Listen!" said the robber girl to Gerda. "You see all our men-folk have gone. Only mother is here still, and she'll stay; but towards noon she drinks out of the big bottle, and then she sleeps for a little; then I'll do something for you."

Then she sprang out of bed, and clasped her mother round the neck and pulled her beard, saying:

"Good morning, my own dear nanny-goat!" And her mother filliped her nose till it was red and blue; but that was all done out of pure love.

When the mother had drunk out of her bottle and was taking a little nap the robber girl went to the reindeer, and said:

"I should like very much to tickle you a few times more with the knife, for then you are so funny; but it's all the same. I'll loosen your rope and help you out, so that you may run to Lapland; but you must use your legs well, and carry this little girl to the palace of the Snow Queen, where her playfellow is. You've heard what she told me, for she spoke loud enough, and you were listening."

The reindeer jumped high for joy. The robber girl lifted little Gerda up, and had the sense to tie her on, and even to give her her own little cushion to sit on. "It's all the same," said she, "and there are your fur boots for you, for it's growing cold; but I shall keep the muff, for it's so very pretty. Still, you shall not freeze, for all that: here are my mother's big mittens—they'll reach right up to your elbows. Put them on! Now your hands look just like my ugly mother's!"

And Gerda wept for joy.

" I can't bear to see you whimpering," said the little robber girl. " You ought to be looking delighted! And here are two loaves and a ham for you, so you can't starve."

These were tied on the reindeer's back. The little robber girl opened the door, called in all the big dogs, and then cut the rope with her knife, and said to the reindeer:

" Now run, but take good care of the little girl! "

And Gerda stretched out her hands, with the big mittens, towards the little robber girl, and said, " Farewell! "

And off flew the reindeer over stumps and stones, away through the great forest, over marshes and steppes, as fast as it could go. The wolves howled and the ravens croaked. " Hiss! hiss! " it went in the air. It was as if the sky was red with fire.

" Those are my old Northern Lights," said the reindeer. " Look how they flash! " And then he ran on faster than ever, day and night. The loaves were eaten, and the ham too, and so they reached Lapland.

SIXTH STORY

THE LAPP WOMAN AND THE FINN WOMAN

AT a little hut they stopped. It was very humble; the roof sloped right down to the ground, and the door was so low that the family had to creep on their stomachs when they wanted to go in or out. No one was in the house but an old Lapp woman, cooking fish over an oil lamp; and the reindeer told her all Gerda's history, but his own first, for that seemed the more important, and Gerda was so numbed with cold that she could not speak.

" Oh, you poor creatures! " said the Lapp woman. " You've a long way to run yet! You must go more than a hundred miles into Finmark, for the Snow Queen is there, staying in the country, and burning blue lights every evening. I'll write a few words on a dried stockfish, for I have no paper, and I'll give you that to take to the Finn woman up there. She can give you better information than I."

And when little Gerda had been warmed, and had had something to eat and drink, the Lapp woman wrote a few words on a dried stockfish, bidding Gerda to take good care of it, tied her on the reindeer again, and away they went. Flash! flash! it went up in the sky. All night long burned the beautiful blue Northern Lights.

NO ONE WAS IN THE HOUSE BUT AN OLD LAPP WOMAN

And then they got to Finmark, and knocked at the chimney of the Finn woman, for she had no door at all.

There was such a heat inside that the Finn woman herself went about almost naked. She was little and very grimy. She at once loosened little Gerda's things and took off her mittens and boots, or else it would have been too hot for her. Next she laid a piece of

73

THE LAPP WOMAN WROTE A FEW WORDS ON A DRIED STOCKFISH

ice on the reindeer's head, and read what was written on the stock-fish. She read it three times, and then she knew it by heart, and put the fish into the soup-kettle, for it was good to eat, and she never wasted anything.

And then the reindeer told his own history first, and little Gerda's after, and the Finn woman blinked with her wise eyes, but said nothing at all.

"You are so clever," said the reindeer. "I know you can tie

all the winds of the world together with a bit of thread; if the skipper undoes one knot he has a good wind; if he undoes the second it blows hard; but if he undoes the third and the fourth there comes such a tempest that the forests are blown down. Will you not give the little girl a draught, so that she may get twelve men's strength, and overcome the Snow Queen?"

"Twelve men's strength!" said the Finn woman. "Much good that would be!"

And she went to a shelf and took down a great rolled-up skin, and unrolled it. Strange characters were written upon it, and the Finn woman read until the water ran down her forehead.

But the reindeer begged again so hard for little Gerda, and Gerda looked at the Finn woman with beseeching eyes so full of tears that she began to blink with her own, and drew the reindeer into a corner, and whispered to him, while she laid fresh ice upon his head:

"Little Kay is certainly at the Snow Queen's, and finds everything there to his taste and liking, and thinks it the best place in the world; but that is because he has a splinter of glass in his eye and a little grain of glass in his heart. These must be got out, or he will never be human again, and the Snow Queen will keep her power over him."

"But can't you give little Gerda something that will give her power to conquer all this?"

"I can give her no greater power than she has already. Don't you see how great that is? Don't you see how man and beast are obliged to serve her, and how with her bare feet she has got on so well in the world? She must not be told of her power by us: it is in her heart, and there it will remain, because she is such a dear innocent child. If she herself cannot reach the Snow Queen and remove the bits of glass from little Kay we can be of no use! Two miles from here the Snow Queen's garden begins; so far you can carry the little girl. Then set her down by the big bush with the red berries that stands in the snow. Don't stop there gossiping, but hasten back here again!"

75

And the Finn woman lifted little Gerda on to the reindeer, who ran off as fast as he could.

"Oh, I have left my boots! I have left my mittens!" cried Gerda, as soon as she felt the biting cold. But the reindeer dare not stop: he ran on till he came to the bush with the red berries. There he put Gerda down, and kissed her on the mouth. Big bright tears ran down the creature's cheeks; and then it ran back, as fast as it could. There stood poor Gerda without shoes, without gloves, in the midst of the terrible icy Finmark.

She ran on as fast as she could; then she was met by a whole regiment of snowflakes; but they did not fall from the sky, for that was quite bright, and shone with the Northern Lights. The snowflakes ran along the ground, and the nearer they came the larger they grew. Gerda still remembered how large and curious the snowflakes had appeared when she looked at them through the burning-glass. But here they were far larger and much more terrible—they were alive! They were the Snow Queen's advance guard and had the strangest shapes. Some looked like ugly great porcupines, others like knots of snakes, that stretched out their heads, and others like little fat bears,

76

whose hair stood on end. All were dazzling white: all were living snowflakes.

Then little Gerda said " Our Father "; and the cold was so great that she could see her own breath, which came out of her mouth like smoke. Her breath became thicker and thicker, and formed itself into little bright angels, who grew and grew as soon as they touched the earth. All had helmets on their heads and shields and spears in their hands. Their number increased more and more, and when Gerda had finished " Our Father " a whole legion stood round about her, and thrust their spears at the terrible snowflakes, so that these were shattered into a hundred pieces. Little Gerda could now go safely and fearlessly on her way. The angels chafed her hands and feet, and then she did not feel the cold so much, and hurried on to the Snow Queen's palace.

But now we will see what Kay is doing. He certainly is not thinking of little Gerda, and least of all that she is standing in front of the palace.

SEVENTH STORY

OF THE SNOW QUEEN'S CASTLE AND WHAT HAPPENED THERE AT LAST

THE walls of the palace were made of the drifting snow, and the windows and doors of the cutting winds. There were more than a hundred halls, all just as the snow had drifted. The largest of them extended for several miles; they were all lit up by the strong Northern Lights, and how wide and empty, how icy cold and glittering they all were! There never was any merriment there, not even a little bears' ball, at which the storm could have played the music, while the polar bears walked about on their hind legs and showed off their pretty manners; never any little games of kiss-in-the-ring or touch; never any little coffee parties among the young lady arctic foxes. Empty, vast, and cold were the halls of the Snow Queen. The Northern Lights flamed so brightly that they could be counted both when they were highest in the sky and when they were lowest. In the middle of this empty endless snow hall was a frozen lake. It had cracked into a thousand pieces, but each piece was so exactly like the rest that it was a perfect work of art. In the middle of the lake sat the Snow Queen when she was at home, and then she said that she sat in the mirror of understanding, and that this was the only one, and the best in the world.

Little Kay was quite blue with cold—indeed, nearly black; but he did not feel it, for she had kissed away his icy shiverings, and his heart was like a lump of ice. He was dragging some sharp flat pieces of ice to and fro, joining them together in all kinds of ways, for he wanted to make something out of them. It was just like when we have little tablets of wood and piece them together to form patterns which we call a Chinese puzzle. Kay was making patterns too—and very artistic ones. It was the ice game of reason. In his eyes the patterns were very remarkable and of the highest importance; that was because of the speck of glass in his eye. He laid out whole patterns, so that they formed words—but he could never manage to make the word he wanted—the word ' eternity.'

The Snow Queen had said: "If you can make that word you shall be your own master, and I will give you the whole world and a new pair of skates."

But he could not.

" Now I must fly away to warm countries," said the Snow Queen. " I will go and peep into the black cauldrons." She meant the burning mountains Etna and Vesuvius, as they are called. "I'll whiten them a little. That's necessary; it will be good for the lemons and the grapes."

And away flew the Snow Queen, and Kay sat all alone in the great empty mile-long ice hall and gazed at his pieces of ice, and thought and thought till cracks were heard inside him: one would have thought that he was frozen.

It was then that little Gerda entered the castle by the great gate. Here cutting winds kept guard, but she said the evening prayer, and the winds dropped as if they wanted to go to sleep; and she went

on into the great empty cold halls, and she saw Kay. She recognized him, and flew to him, and embraced him, and held him fast, and called out:

"Kay, dear little Kay! At last I have found you!"

But he sat quite still, stiff and cold. Then little Gerda wept hot tears, which fell upon his breast. They penetrated into his heart, they thawed the lump of ice, and melted the little piece of glass in it. He looked at her, and she sang the hymn:

> Roses fade and die, but we
> Our Infant Lord shall surely see.

Then Kay burst into tears. He wept so that the splinter of glass was washed out of his eye. And then he knew her, and cried joyfully: "Gerda, dear little Gerda! Where have you been all this time? And where have I been?" And he looked all around him. "How cold it is here! How empty and vast!"

And he held fast to Gerda, and she laughed and wept for joy. There was such joy that even the pieces of ice danced about them; and when they were tired and lay down again they formed themselves into the very letters the Snow Queen meant when she said that if he found them out he should be his own master, and she would give him the whole world and a new pair of skates.

And Gerda kissed his cheeks, and they became blooming. She kissed his eyes, and they shone like her own. She kissed his hands and feet, and he became well and merry. The Snow Queen might come home now; there stood his discharge, written in shining blocks of ice.

And they took each other by the hand and went out of the great palace. They talked of the grandmother, and of the roses on the roof; and wherever they went the winds sank to rest and the sun came out; and when they came to the bush with the red berries, the reindeer was standing there waiting. He had brought with him another young reindeer, whose udder was full, and who gave the children warm milk and kissed them on the mouth. Then they carried Kay and Gerda, first to the Finn woman, where they warmed themselves thoroughly in the hot room, and received instructions for their journey home, and then to the Lapp woman, who had made clothes for them and got their sledge ready for them.

The reindeer and the young one ran free by their side, and followed them as far as the boundary of the country, where the first green leaves were budding, and where they took leave of the two reindeer and the Lapp woman. "Farewell!" they all said. And once more they heard the birds twitter and saw the forest all decked with green buds, and out of it, on a splendid horse, which Gerda knew, for it had drawn her golden coach, a young girl came riding, with a bright red cap on her head and pistols in her belt. It was the little robber girl, who had grown tired of staying at home, and wished first to go north and, if she didn't like that, then somewhere else. She knew Gerda at once, and Gerda knew her too; it was a joyful meeting.

"You are a fine fellow to go gadding about!" she said to little Kay. "I should like to know whether you deserve that anybody should run to the end of the world after you!"

But Gerda patted her cheeks, and asked after the Prince and Princess.

"They've gone to foreign countries," said the robber girl.

"But the crow?" said Gerda.

"Why, the crow is dead," answered the other. "The tame sweetheart has become a widow, and goes about with a bit of black worsted round her leg. She complains most sadly, but it's all talk. But now tell me how you have fared, and how you got hold of him."

And Gerda and Kay told their story.

" Snip-snap-snurre-basselurre!" said the robber girl.

And she took them both by the hand, and promised that if she ever came through their town she would come and pay them a visit. And then she rode away into the wide world. But Gerda and Kay went hand in hand, and as they went the spring became lovely with flowers and verdure. The church bells rang, and they recognized the high steeples and the great town in which they lived. On they went to their grandmother's door, and up the stairs, and into the room, where everything stood in the same place as before. The big clock was going "Tick! tick!" and the hands moved; but as they went in through the door they noticed that they had become grown-up people. The roses out on the roof gutter were blooming at the open window, and there stood their little children's stools, and Kay and Gerda sat down each on their own, and held each other by the hand. They had forgotten the cold empty grandeur of the Snow Queen's castle like a heavy dream. Grandmother was sitting in God's bright sunshine, and read aloud from the Bible, " Except ye become as little children, ye shall in no wise enter into the kingdom of God."

And Kay and Gerda looked into each other's eyes, and all at once they understood the old hymn:

> Roses fade and die, but we
> Our Infant Lord shall surely see.

There they both sat, grown up and yet children—children at heart—and it was summer, warm lovely summer.

THE SWINEHERD

THERE was once a Prince who was not very rich and whose kingdom was very small, but still it was big enough for him to afford to marry, and married he wanted to be.

Now, it was certainly rather bold of him to say to the Emperor's daughter, " Will you have me? " But he did venture, for his name was famous far and wide, and there were hundreds of princesses who would have said, " Yes, thank you." But did *she* say so? Well, now we shall hear.

On the grave of the Prince's father there grew a rose-bush, a very beautiful rose-bush. It bloomed only every fifth year, and even then it bore only a single rose, but that was a rose! It was so sweet that whoever smelt it forgot all sorrow and trouble. And then he had a nightingale, which could sing as if all possible melodies dwelt in its little throat. This rose and this nightingale the Princess was to have, and so they were put into great silver caskets and sent to her.

The Emperor had the presents carried before him into the great hall where the Princess was playing at ' visiting ' with her maids of honour—they had nothing else to do—and when she saw the silver caskets, with the presents in them, she clapped her hands for joy.

" If only it were a little pussy-cat! " said she.

But there came out only the lovely rose.

" Oh, how prettily it is made! " said all the Court ladies.

" It is more than pretty," said the Emperor; " it is charming."

But the Princess touched it, and then she was almost ready to cry.

" Fie, papa! " she said; " it is not artificial—it's a *natural* rose! "

" Fie! " said all the Court; " it's a natural one! "

" Let us first see what is in the other casket before we get angry," said the Emperor. And then the nightingale came out; it sang so beautifully that for the moment they did not know what to say against it.

"*Superbe! charmant!*" said the maids of honour, for they all spoke French, each one worse than the other.

"How that bird reminds me of our late beloved Empress's musical box!" said an old cavalier. "Ah, yes! it is the same tone, the same expression!"

"Yes," said the Emperor; and he cried like a little child.

"I do hope it is not a real bird," said the Princess.

"Yes, it is a real bird," said those who had brought it.

"Yes! Then let the bird fly away," said the Princess; and she would on no account allow the Prince to come.

But the Prince was not to be discouraged. He stained his face brown and black, drew his hat down over his brows, and knocked at the door.

"Good day, Emperor!" he said. "Could I not be taken into service here in the castle?"

"Yes," said the Emperor, "but there are so many who wish for that. But let me see! I do want someone to look after the pigs, for we have many of them."

And so the Prince was appointed the imperial swineherd. He was given a miserable little room down by the pigsty, and there he had to stay. All day long he sat and worked, and by the evening he had made a neat little pot, with bells all round it, and when the pot boiled these bells rang out prettily and played the old tune:

> Ah, thou darling Augustin,
> All is lost, lost, lost!

But the most artful thing about it was that, by holding one's finger in the steam, one could at once smell what kind of dinner was being cooked at every stove in the town. That was quite another thing to the rose.

Soon the Princess came by with all her maids of honour, and when she heard the melody she stood still and looked quite pleased, for she too could play "Ah, thou darling Augustin." It was the only tune she could play, and then she played it with one finger.

"Why, that's what I play!" she said. "He must be a well-educated swineherd! Listen ! Go in and ask him what the instrument costs!"

So one of the maids of honour had to run in; but first she put on her clogs.

"What will you take for that pot?" said the maid of honour.

"I will have ten kisses from the Princess," said the swineherd.

"Heaven preserve us!" said the maid of honour.

"Well, I won't sell it for less," said the swineherd.

"Well, what did he say?" asked the Princess.

"I really cannot tell you," said the maid of honour. "It is so shocking!"

"Well, you can whisper it." And she whispered it. "He is very rude," said the Princess, and went away at once. But when she had gone a little way the bells sounded so prettily:

Ah, thou darling Augustin,
All is lost, lost, lost!

"Listen!" said the Princess. "Ask him will he take ten kisses from my maids of honour."

"No, thank you!" said the swineherd. "Ten kisses from the Princess, or I shall keep my pot."

"How tiresome!" cried the Princess. "But at least you'll have to stand round me, so that nobody sees."

And the maids of honour stood round her, and spread out their skirts, and so the swineherd had his ten kisses and she had the pot.

Then there was rejoicing! All the evening and all the day long the pot was kept boiling; there was not a kitchen in the whole town where they did not know what was being cooked, at the shoemaker's as well as the chamberlain's. The ladies danced with pleasure, and clapped their hands.

"We know who will have sweet soup and pancakes, and who has hasty pudding and cutlets; how interesting that is!"

"Highly interesting!" said the mistress of the robes.

"Yes, but hold your tongues, for I am the Emperor's daughter."

"Heaven preserve us!" they all said together.

The swineherd—that is to say, the Prince (but, of course, they did not know that he was not a real swineherd)—let no day pass without doing something, and so he made a rattle. When any one swung this rattle he could play all the waltzes, galops, and polkas that have been known since the beginning of the world.

"But that is *superbe*!" said the Princess, as she went past. "I have never heard anything finer. Listen! Just go in and ask what the instrument costs; but no more kisses!"

"He will have a hundred kisses from the Princess," said the maid of honour who had been in to ask.

"I think he must be mad!" said the Princess; and she went away; but when she had gone a little way she stopped. "One must encourage art," said she. "I am the Emperor's daughter! Tell him he shall have ten kisses, like the last time, and he may take the rest from my maids of honour."

"Ah, but we don't like it!" said the maids of honour.

"That's all nonsense!" said the Princess. "If I can kiss him you can too; remember, I give you your board and wages."

And so the maids of honour had to go down to him again.

"A hundred kisses from the Princess," said he, "or nothing!"

"Stand round me!" said she then; and all the maids of honour stood round her while he kissed her.

"What is that crowd down by the pigsty?" asked the Emperor, who had stepped out on the balcony. He rubbed his eyes, and put on his spectacles. "Why, those are the maids of honour up to their tricks! I shall have to go down to them!"

So he pulled up his slippers at the back, for he had shoes on that he had trodden down at the heels. Gracious me! how he hurried! As soon as he got down to the courtyard he went quite softly, and the maids of honour were too busy counting the kisses and seeing fair play—he shouldn't have too many, but not too few either—to notice the Emperor. Then he stood on tiptoe.

"What's all this?" said he when he saw them kissing, and he hit them on the head with his slipper, just as the swineherd was taking the eighty-sixth kiss.

" Be off! " said the Emperor, for he was angry.

And the Princess and the swineherd were both banished from his empire. So there she stood and cried, and the swineherd scolded, and the rain poured down.

" Oh, miserable wretch that I am! " said the Princess; " if only I had taken that handsome Prince! Oh, how unhappy I am! "

And the swineherd went behind a tree, washed the black and brown stains from his face, threw away the shabby clothes, and stepped forth in his princely garments, so handsome that the Princess could not help curtsying to him.

" I have come to despise you," said he. " You would not have an honest prince; you did not value the rose and the nightingale, but for a mere toy you kissed the swineherd, and now you must make the best of it! "

And so he went into his kingdom and shut and locked the door in her face. So now she might stand outside and sing:

Ah, thou darling Augustin,
All is lost, lost, lost!

THE BEETLE

THE emperor's favourite horse was shod with gold; he had a golden horseshoe on each foot.

But why was that?

He was a beautiful creature, with slender legs, bright, intelligent eyes, and a mane that hung down like a veil over his neck. He had carried his master through the smoke of gunpowder and the rain of bullets, and had heard the balls whistling past. He had bitten, kicked, and taken part in the fight when the enemy pressed forward, and, leaping with the emperor across the fallen horse of one of the foe, had saved the bright golden crown and the life of the emperor—and that was worth more than all the bright gold. And that is why the emperor's horse had golden horseshoes.

A beetle came creeping out. "First the great, then the small," said he; "but size is not everything." And with that he stretched out his thin legs.

"Well, what do you want?" asked the smith.

"Golden shoes," replied the beetle.

"Why, you must be out of your senses!" cried the smith. "You want golden shoes too?"

"Certainly—golden shoes!" said the beetle. "Am I not as good as that creature there, that is waited on, and brushed, and has food and drink put before him? Don't I belong to the imperial stables too?"

"But why has the horse golden shoes?" asked the smith. "Don't you understand that?"

"Understand? I understand that it is a personal slight for me," said the beetle. "It is done to vex me, and I will therefore go out into the wide world."

"Go along!" said the smith.

"You rude fellow!" said the beetle; and then he went out of

the stable, flew a short distance, and soon afterwards found himself in a beautiful flower-garden, fragrant with roses and lavender.

"Isn't it beautiful here?" asked one of the little lady-birds that were flying about with their red, shield-shaped, black-spotted wings. "How sweet it is here, and how lovely!"

"I have been used to better than that," said the beetle. "You call this beautiful? Why, there's not even a dunghill."

Then he went on, under the shadow of a big gilliflower, where a caterpillar was creeping along.

"How beautiful the world is!" said the caterpillar. "The sun is so warm, and everything so happy! And when one day I fall asleep and die, as they call it, I shall awake as a butterfly."

"What things you do fancy!" said the beetle. "To fly about as a butterfly! I come from the emperor's stable, but no one there—not even the emperor's favourite horse, that wears my cast-off golden shoes—fancies anything like that. Get wings! Fly! Well, we'll fly now!" And away flew the beetle. "I don't want to be vexed, but I am all the same," he said, as he flew off.

Soon afterwards he fell upon a great lawn; here he lay awhile, and pretended to be asleep, but at last he really dozed off.

Suddenly a heavy shower of rain fell from the clouds. The noise awoke the beetle, and he wanted to creep into the earth, but could not, for he was being turned over and over. First he was swimming on his stomach, then on his back, and flying was not to be thought of; he despaired of getting away from the place alive. So he lay where he lay, and remained there. When the rain had left off a little, and the beetle had blinked the water out of his eyes, he saw the gleam of something white; it was linen laid out to bleach. He reached it and crept into a fold of the damp linen. It was certainly not so comfortable here as in the warm dunghill in the stable, but nothing better happened to be at hand, and so he stayed where he was—stayed a whole day and a whole night, and the rain stayed too. Towards morning he crept out; he was greatly annoyed at the climate.

On the linen sat two frogs, their bright eyes sparkling with pure joy.

"This is glorious weather," said one. "How refreshing! And the linen keeps the water together so beautifully. My hind-legs are itching to swim."

"I should like to know," said the other, "whether the swallow which flies about so far has ever found a better climate than ours in her many travels abroad. So nice and damp! It is really like lying in a wet ditch. Whoever doesn't like this can't be said to love his native country."

"Have you then never been in the emperor's stable?" asked the beetle. "There the dampness is warm and fragrant; that's the climate for me! But you can't take it with you when you travel. Is there no dung-heap in the garden here, where people of rank, like myself, can feel at home and take up their quarters?"

The frogs either could not or would not understand him.

"I never ask twice!" exclaimed the beetle, after he had already asked three times and received no answer.

Thereupon he went a little farther, and came across a piece of broken pottery which should certainly not have been lying there, but which, as it lay, afforded a good shelter against wind and weather. Here lived several families of earwigs; they did not require much —only company. The females are full of tenderest maternal love, and every mother therefore praised her child as the most beautiful and cleverest.

"Our little son is engaged to be married!" said one mother. "Sweet innocence! It is his sole ambition to get into a parson's ear some day. He is so artless and lovable; his engagement will keep him steady. What joy for a mother!"

"Our son," said another mother, "had hardly crept out of the egg when he was off on his travels. He's all life and spirits; he'll run his horns off. What joy for a mother! Isn't it so, Mr Beetle?" They recognized the stranger by the cut of his wings.

"You are both right!" said the beetle, and then they begged him to enter the room—that is to say, to come as far as he could under the piece of pottery.

"Now you see my little earwig too," cried a third and a fourth mother. " They are the sweetest children, and very playful. They are never naughty, except when they occasionally have pains in their inside; unfortunately, one gets those only too easily at their age."

In this manner every mother spoke of her baby, and the babies joined in too, and used the little nippers that they have in their tails to pull the beetle by his beard.

" Yes, they're always up to something, the little rogues! " said the mothers, bubbling over with maternal affection. But this bored the beetle, and so he asked whether it was much farther to the dunghill.

" Why, that's out in the wide world, on the other side of the ditch," answered an earwig. " I hope none of my children will go so far—it would be the death of me."

" I'll try to get as far anyhow," said the beetle; and he went off without saying good-bye, for that is considered the most polite way. By the ditch he met several of his kind—all beetles.

" We live here! " they said. " We are very comfortable. May

we ask you to step down into the rich mud? The journey has no doubt been very fatiguing for you?"

"Very," said the beetle. "I have been exposed to the rain, and have had to lie on linen, and cleanliness always weakens me very much. I have pain, too, in one wing, through having stood in the draught under a broken piece of pottery. It is really quite a comfort to get once more among one's own kindred."

"Perhaps you come from the dung-heap?" asked the eldest.

"Oho! from higher places!" cried the beetle. "I come from the emperor's stable, where I was born with golden shoes on my feet. I am travelling on a secret mission, but you must not ask me any questions about it, for I won't betray the secret."

With that the beetle stepped down into the rich mud. There sat three young beetle maidens; they giggled, because they did not know what to say.

"They are all three still disengaged," said the mother; and the young beetle maidens giggled again, this time from bashfulness.

"I have not seen greater beauties in the imperial stables," said the beetle, taking a rest.

"Don't you spoil my girls for me, and don't speak to them unless you have serious intentions. But about that I have no doubt, and so I give you my blessing!"

"Hurrah!" cried all the other beetles, and our beetle was now engaged. The engagement was immediately followed by the wedding, for there was no reason for delay.

The following day passed very pleasantly, and the one after that fairly so; but on the third day the time had come to think of food for the wife, and perhaps even for the children.

"I have allowed myself to be taken in," thought the beetle. "Nothing is therefore left for me but to take others in, in return."

So said, so done. Away he went, and stayed out the whole day and the whole night—and his wife sat there, a lonely widow.

"Oh!" said the other beetles, "that fellow whom we received into our family is a thorough vagabond; he went away and left his wife sitting there, to be a burden upon us."

"Well, then she must be passed off as unmarried again, and stay here as my child," said the mother. "Fie on the villain who deserted her!"

In the meantime the beetle had gone on travelling, and had sailed across the watery ditch on a cabbage-leaf. In the morning two people came to the ditch; when they spied him they picked him up, turned him over and over, and looked very wise, especially one of them—a boy. "Allah sees the black beetle in the black stone and in the black rock. Isn't it written so in the Koran?" Then he translated the beetle's name into Latin, and enlarged upon its species and nature. The second person, an older scholar, was for taking him home with them. But the other said that they had specimens quite as good as that, and this, our beetle thought, was not a polite thing to say—so he suddenly flew out of the speaker's hand. His wings being now dry, he flew a pretty long distance and reached a hotbed, where, one of the windows of the glass-house being ajar, he slipped in comfortably and buried himself in the fresh manure.

"How delightful it is here!" he said.

Soon after he fell asleep, and dreamt that the emperor's favourite horse had fallen and had given him his golden horseshoes, with the promise to have two more made for him.

That was very acceptable. When the beetle awoke he crept out and looked about him. What splendour there was in the hothouse! In the background were palm-trees, growing to a great height; the sun made them look transparent, and under them what a wealth of verdure and bright flowers, red as fire, yellow as amber, and white as driven snow!

"There is an incomparable splendour in these plants," said the beetle. "How fine they will taste when they decay! This is a good larder! There must certainly be relatives of mine living here. I'll have a look round to see if I can find anyone to associate with. Proud I am, and that is my pride." And now he strolled about in the hothouse, and thought of his beautiful dream of the dead horse, and the golden horseshoes he had inherited.

Suddenly a hand seized the beetle, squeezed him, and turned him over and over.

THE BEETLE

The gardener's son and a little girl who played with him had come up to the hotbed, had spied the beetle, and wanted to have some fun with him. First he was wrapped up in a vine-leaf, and then put into a warm trousers pocket. There he cribbled and crabbled about with all his might; but for this he got a squeeze from the boy's hand, and that taught him to be quiet. Then the boy ran off to the great lake at the end of the garden. Here the beetle was put into an old, half-broken wooden shoe, in which a little stick was placed for a mast, and to this mast the beetle was bound by a woollen thread. Now he was a sailor and had to sail. The lake was not very large, but to the beetle it seemed an ocean; he was so terrified by it that he fell on his back and kicked out with his feet. The little ship sailed away, and the current of the water seized it. But when it went too far from the shore the little boy would turn up his trousers, go into the water, and fetch it back to the land. But at last, just as it was setting out to sea again in full sail, the children were called away for something important; they hastened to obey, and, running away from the lake, left the little ship to its fate. This drifted farther and farther away from the shore, and farther out into the open sea. It was terrible for the beetle, for he could not get away, being bound to the mast. Then a fly paid him a visit. " What lovely weather! " said the fly. " I'll rest here and bask in the sun; it's very pleasant for you here."

" You talk of what you don't understand! Don't you see that I'm tied fast? "

" But I'm not," said the fly, and flew off.

" Well, now I know the world," said the beetle. " It's a base world. I'm the only honest one in it. First they refuse me golden shoes; then I have to lie on wet linen and stand in a draught; and, to cap all, they fasten a wife on to me. Then, when I have taken a quick step out into the world, and learned how comfortable one can be there, and how it ought to be for me, up comes a human boy, binds me fast, and leaves me to the wild waves, while the emperor's favourite horse prances about in golden shoes. That vexes me most of all! But one must not count on sympathy in this world. My career is very interesting; but what's the use of that if nobody knows it? The world doesn't deserve to be made acquainted with my story, for it ought to have given me golden shoes in the emperor's stable when the emperor's favourite horse was being shod, and I stretched out my legs too. If I had received golden shoes I should have been an ornament to the stable; now the stable has lost me, the world has lost me—all is over!"

But all was not over yet. A boat, in which there were some young girls, came rowing up.

"Look, there's an old wooden shoe sailing along," said one of the girls.

"There's a little creature tied up in it!" cried another.

The boat came quite close to our beetle's little ship, and the young girls fished it up out of the water. One of them drew a small pair of scissors out of her pocket, cut the woollen thread without hurting the beetle, and when she got to the shore placed him in the grass.

"Creep, creep. Fly, fly—if thou canst," she said. "Freedom is a glorious thing."

The beetle flew up and went through the open window of a large building; there he sank down, tired and exhausted, upon the fine, soft long mane of the emperor's horse that was standing in the stables where both he and the beetle were at home. The beetle clung fast to the mane, sat there quite still for a short time, and recovered.

"Here I sit on the emperor's favourite horse—sit on him just like an emperor. But what was I going to say? Ah, yes! I remember. It's a good idea, and quite correct. Why does the emperor's horse have golden shoes? That's what the smith asked me. Now the answer is clear to me. The horse had golden horseshoes on my account!"

And now the beetle was in a good temper. "Travelling opens one's mind," he said.

The sun's rays came streaming into the stable upon him, and made things bright and pleasant.

94

" The world is not so bad after all, when you come to examine it," said the beetle; " but you must know how to take it."

Yes, the world was beautiful, because the emperor's favourite horse had only received golden shoes so that the beetle might become his rider. " Now I will go down to the other beetles and tell them how much has been done for me. I will relate to them all the disagreeable things I went through in my travels abroad, and tell them that I shall now remain at home till the horse has worn out his golden shoes."

SOUP FROM A SAUSAGE-PEG

I

"THAT was an excellent dinner yesterday," said an old mouse of the female sex to another who had not been present at the festive meal. "I sat number twenty-one from the old mouse-king; that was not such a bad place! Would you like to hear the menu? The courses were very well arranged: mouldy bread, bacon-rind, tallow candles, and sausage—and then the same things over again. It was just as good as having two banquets. Everything went on as jovially and as good-humouredly as at a family gathering. There was absolutely nothing left but the sausage-pegs. The conversation turned upon these, and at last the expression 'soup from sausage skins,' or, as the proverb runs in the neighbouring country, 'soup from a sausage-peg,' was mentioned. Now every one had heard of this, but no one had tasted such soup, much less prepared it. A very pretty toast to the inventor was drunk; it was said that he deserved to be made a Poor-Law Guardian. That was very witty, wasn't it? And the old mouse-king rose and promised that the young lady mouse who could prepare the said soup in the most tasty way should be his queen; he gave her a year and a day for the trial."

JUST AS THE SWINEHERD WAS TAKING THE EIGHTY-SIXTH KISS

''The Swineherd''

THE BANQUET WHERE THE REALLY GRAND COMPANY WERE ASSEMBLED
"The Elfin Hill"

"That wasn't bad!" said the other mouse. "But how is the soup prepared?"

"Ah! how is it prepared?" That was just what all the other lady mice, both young and old, were asking. They would all have liked to be queen, but they did not want to take the trouble to go out into the wide world to learn how to prepare the soup, and yet that was what would have to be done. But every one is not ready to leave home and family; and out in the world cheese-rinds are not to be had for the asking, nor is bacon to be smelt every day. No, one must suffer hunger, perhaps even be eaten up alive by a cat.

Such were probably the considerations by which the majority allowed themselves to be deterred from going out into the world in search of information. Only four mice gave in their names as being ready to start. They were young and active, but poor; each of them intended to proceed to one of the four quarters of the globe, and it would then be seen to which of them fortune was favourable. Each of the four took a sausage-peg with her, so that she might be mindful of her object in travelling; the sausage-peg was to be her pilgrim's staff.

They set out at the beginning of May, and not till the May of the following year did they return, and then only three of them; the fourth did not report herself, nor did she send any word or sign, notwithstanding that the day of trial had arrived.

"Yes, every pleasure has its drawback," said the mouse-king. Then he gave orders that all the mice for many miles round should be invited. They were to assemble in the kitchen, and the three travelled mice should stand in a row alone; a sausage-peg, hung with black crape, was erected in memory of the fourth, who was missing. No one was to give his opinion before the mouse-king had said what was to be said.

Now we shall hear!

97

II

WHAT THE FIRST LITTLE MOUSE HAD SEEN AND LEARNT ON HER TRAVELS

" When I went out into the wide world," said the little mouse, " I thought, as a great many do at my age, that I already knew all there was to be known. But that was not so; years must pass before one gets as far as that. I went straight to the sea. I went off in a ship that sailed to the north. I had been told that a ship's cook must know how to make the best of things at sea, but it is easy to make the best of things if one has plenty of sides of bacon and great tubs of salt pork and mouldy flour; one has delicate living there, but one does not learn how to make soup from a sausage-peg. We sailed on for many days and nights; the ship rocked fearfully, and we did not get off without a wetting either. When we at last reached our destination I left the vessel; it was up in the far north.

" It is a strange thing to leave one's own corner at home, to sail in a ship which is only a kind of corner too, and then suddenly to find oneself more than a hundred miles away in a strange land. I saw great trackless forests of pines and birches that smelt so strong that I sneezed and thought of sausages. There were great lakes there too. The waters when looked at quite close were clear, but from a distance they appeared black as ink. White swans lay upon them; they lay so still I thought they were foam, but when I saw them fly and walk I recognized them. They belong to the same race as the geese; one can easily see that by their walk—no one can deny his descent. I kept to my own kind. I associated with the forest and field mice, who, by the way, know very little, especially as regards cooking, and yet that was just what I had gone abroad for. The idea that soup might be made from a sausage-peg seemed to them so extraordinary that it at once spread from mouth to mouth through the whole wood. That the problem could ever be solved they thought an impossibility, and least of all did I think that there, and the very first night too, should I be initiated into the manner of preparing it.

It was the height of summer, and that, said the mice, was why the forest smelt so strongly, why the herbs were so fragrant, the lakes so clear and yet so dark, with the swans floating upon them.

" On the edge of the wood, surrounded by three or four houses, a pole as high as the mainmast of a ship had been set up, and from the top of it hung wreaths and fluttering ribbons—it was a maypole. Lads and lasses danced round the tree, and sang as loudly as they could to the music of the fiddler. All went merrily in the sunset and by moonlight, but I took no part in it—what has a little mouse to do with a May-dance? I sat in the soft moss and held my sausage-peg fast. The moon threw its rays just upon a spot where stood a tree covered with such exceedingly fine moss that I may almost say it was as fine and soft as the mouse-king's fur; but it was green, and that is good for the eyes.

" All at once the most charming little people came marching out. They did not reach higher than my knee, and though they looked like human beings they were better proportioned. They called themselves elves, and wore fine clothes of flower-leaves trimmed with the wings of flies and gnats, which did not look at all bad. Directly they appeared they seemed to be looking for something—I did not know what; but at last some of them came up to me, the chief among them pointing to my sausage-peg, and saying, ' That is just the kind of one we want! It is pointed—it is excellent! ' And the more he looked at my pilgrim's staff the more delighted he became.

" ' To lend,' I said, ' but not to keep.'

" ' Not to keep! ' they all cried; then they seized the sausage-peg, which I let go, and danced off with it to the spot with the fine moss, where they set it up in the midst of the green. They wanted to have a maypole too, and that which they now had seemed cut out for them. Then it was decorated; what a sight that was!

" Little spiders spun golden threads round it, and hung it with fluttering veils and flags, so finely woven and bleached so snowy white in the moonshine that it dazzled my eyes. They took the colours from the butterflies' wings and strewed these over the white

linen, and flowers and diamonds gleamed upon it so that I did not
know my sausage-peg again; there was certainly not another maypole in the whole world like that which had been made out of it.
And now at last came the real great party of elves. They wore no
clothes at all—it could not have been more genteel. I was invited
to witness the festivities, but only at a certain distance, for I was too
big for them.

"Then began a wonderful music! It seemed as if thousands of
glass bells were ringing, so full, so rich that I thought it was the
singing of the swans; I even thought I heard the voice of the cuckoo
and the blackbird, and at last the whole wood seemed to join in.
There were children's voices, the sound of bells, and the song of
birds; the most glorious melodies and all that was lovely came out
of the elves' maypole—it was a whole peal of bells, and yet it was
my sausage-peg. That so much could have been got out of it I
should never have believed, but it no doubt depends upon what
hands it gets into. I was deeply moved; I wept, as a little mouse
can weep, for pure joy.

"The night was far too short, but up yonder they are not any
longer about that time of year. In the morning dawn the light

breezes sprang up, the surface of the woodland lake became ruffled, and all the dainty floating veils and flags floated in the air. The wavy garlands of spiders' web, the hanging bridges and balustrades, or whatever they are called, vanished as if they were nothing. Six elves carried my sausage-peg back to me, asking me at the same time whether I had any wish that they could fulfil. So I begged them to tell me how to make soup from a sausage-peg.

"'How we do it?' asked the chief of the elves, smiling. 'Why, you have just seen it. You hardly knew your own sausage-peg again.'

"'They only mean that for a joke,' I thought, and I told them straight away the object of my journey, and what hopes were entertained at home respecting this brew. 'What advantage,' I asked, 'can accrue to the mouse-king and to the whole of our mighty kingdom by my having witnessed this splendour? I can't shake it out of the sausage-peg and say, "Look, here is the sausage-peg; now comes the soup!" That would be a kind of dish that could only be served up when people had had enough.'

"Then the elf dipped his little finger in the cup of a blue violet and said to me, 'Pay attention! Here I anoint your pilgrim's staff, and when you return home and enter the mouse-king's castle touch the warm breast of your king with it, and violets will spring forth and cover the whole of the staff, even in the coldest winter-time. And with that I think I have given you something to take home with you, and even a little more!'"

But before the little mouse said what this "a little more" was she touched the king's breast with her staff, and in truth the most beautiful bunch of violets burst forth. They smelt so strongly that the mouse-king immediately ordered the mice who stood nearest the chimney to put their tails into the fire to make a smell of burning, for the scent of the violets was not to be borne, and was not of the kind they liked.

"But what was the 'more' of which you spoke?" asked the mouse-king.

"Well," said the little mouse, "that is, I think, what is called 'effect.'" And thereupon she turned the sausage-peg round, and, behold, there was no longer a single flower to be seen upon it; she held only the naked peg, and this she lifted like a conductor's baton.

"'Violets,' the elf told me, 'are to look at, to smell, and to touch. Hearing and taste, therefore, still remain to be considered.'" Then the little mouse beat time, and music was heard—not such as rang through the forest at the elves' party, but such as is to be heard in the kitchen. What a sound of cooking and roasting there was! It came suddenly, as if the wind were rushing through all the victuals, and as if the pots and kettles were boiling over. The fire-shovel hammered upon the brass kettle, and then—suddenly all was quiet again. The low subdued singing of the tea-kettle was heard, and it was wonderful to listen to: they could not quite tell whether the kettle was beginning to boil or leaving off. The little pot bubbled and the big pot bubbled, and one took no notice of the other, and it seemed as if there was no rhyme nor reason in the pots. Then the little mouse waved her baton more and more wildly—the pots foamed, threw up big bubbles, boiled over; the wind roared and whistled through the chimney—ugh! it became so terrible that the little mouse even lost her stick.

"That was a heavy soup!" said the mouse-king. "Isn't the dish coming soon?"

"That is all," answered the little mouse, with a bow.

"All! Well, then, let us hear what the next has to say!" said the king.

III

What the Second Little Mouse had to tell

"I was born in the castle library," said the second mouse. "I and several members of our family have never had the good fortune to get into the dining-room, let alone the larder; it was only on my travels and here to-day that I saw a kitchen. Indeed, we often had to suffer hunger in the library, but we acquired much knowledge. The rumour of the royal prize offered to those who could make soup from a sausage-peg reached our ears, and then my old grandmother brought out a manuscript that she could not read herself, but which she had heard read out, and in which was written: 'If one is a poet, one can make soup from a sausage-peg.' She asked me whether I was a poet. I felt that I was innocent in that respect, and she said that then I must go out and manage to become one. I again asked what I was to do, for it was quite as difficult for me to find that out as to make the soup. But my grandmother had heard a good deal read out, and she said three things above all were necessary: 'Understanding, imagination, and feeling. If you can manage to attain these three you are a poet, and then the matter of the sausage-peg will be an easy one for you.'

"I departed, and marched towards the west, out into the wide world, to become a poet.

"Understanding is of the most importance in everything—that I knew; the other two qualities are held in much less esteem, and I therefore went in quest of understanding first. Yes, where does it dwell? 'Go to the ant and learn wisdom,' said a great king of the Jews; that I had learnt in the library. So I did not stop till I came to the first great ant-hill, and there I lay upon the watch to become wise.

"The ants are a very respectable little people; they are understanding all through. Everything with them is like a well-worked sum in arithmetic that comes right. To work and to lay eggs, they say, means both to live and to provide for posterity, and so that is what they do. They divide themselves into clean and dirty ants; the ant-queen is number one, and her opinion the only correct one. She contains the wisdom of all the world, and it was important for me to know that. She spoke so much, and it was so clever, that it seemed to me like nonsense. She said that her ant-hill was the highest thing in the world, though close beside it stood a tree which was higher, much higher—it was not to be denied, and so nothing was said of that. One evening an ant had lost herself on the tree and had crawled up the trunk—not so far up as the crown, but still higher than any ant had reached till then; and when she turned round

103

and came home again she told of something far higher that she had come across out in the world. But this all the ants thought an insult to the community, and the ant was therefore condemned to be muzzled and to be kept in solitary confinement for life. But shortly afterwards another ant came across the same tree and made the same journey and the same discovery. She spoke about it with delibera-tion, but unintelligibly, as they called it; and as she was, besides, a much-respected ant and one of the clean ones she was believed; and when she died an egg-shell was erected to her memory, for they had a great respect for the sciences. I saw," continued the little mouse, " that the ants always ran about with their eggs on their backs. One of them once dropped her egg, and though she took great pains to pick it up again she did not succeed. Just then two others came up, who helped her with all their might, so that they nearly dropped their own eggs in doing so. But then they immediately stopped in their efforts, for one must think of oneself first—and the ant-queen declared that in this case both heart and understanding had been shown. ' These two qualities,' she said, ' give us ants a place in the first rank among all reasoning beings. We all possess understanding in a high degree, and I have the most of all.' And with that she raised herself on her hind-legs, so that she could not fail to be recognized. I could not be mistaken : I swallowed her. ' Go to the ants to learn wisdom '—now I had the queen!

"I now went closer to the large tree I have already mentioned several times. It was an oak, with a tall trunk and a full, wide-spreading crown, and was very old. I knew that here dwelt a living being, a woman called a dryad, who is born with the tree and dies with it. I had heard of this in the library. Now I beheld such a tree, and one of these oak-maidens. She uttered a terrible cry when she saw me so close to her. Like all women, she was very much afraid of mice; but she had more cause to be so than others, for I could have gnawed the tree through on which her life depended. I spoke to the maiden in a friendly, cordial way, and inspired her with courage; she took me in her dainty hand, and when I had told her why I had gone out into the wide world she promised me that very evening I should probably have one of the two treasures of which I was still in quest. She told me that Phantasy was her intimate friend, that he was as handsome as the God of Love, and that he rested many an hour under the leafy branches of the tree, which then rustled more strongly than ever over the two. He called her his dryad, she said, and the tree his tree; the beautiful gnarled oak was just to his taste, the roots spread themselves deeply and firmly in the ground, and the trunk and the crown rose high up into the fresh air; they knew the driving snow, the keen winds, and the warm sunshine, as these should be known. 'Yes,' continued the Dryad, 'the birds up there in the crown sing and tell of foreign countries they have visited, and on the only dead bough the stork has built his nest— that is very ornamental, and one hears a little, too, about the land of the pyramids. All this pleases Phantasy, but it is not enough for him; so I myself have to tell him about the life in the woods, and have to go back to my childhood's days when I was young and the tree was frail, so frail that a stinging-nettle overshadowed it; and I have to tell everything till now that the tree has grown big and strong. Now sit you down under the green thyme yonder and pay attention; and when Phantasy comes I'll find some opportunity to tweak his wings and pull out a little feather. Take the feather—no better one has been given a poet for a pen—and it will suffice you!

"And when Phantasy came the feather was pulled out, and I seized it," said the little mouse. "I put it in water and held it there till it got soft. It was very hard to digest even then, but still I nibbled it up at last. It is very easy to gnaw oneself into being a poet, though there are many things that one has to swallow. Now I had two— understanding and imagination—and through these two I knew that the third was to be found in the library; for a great man has said and written that there are novels which exist purely and solely to relieve people of their superfluous tears, and are therefore a kind of sponge to suck up the feelings. I remembered a few of those books which had always looked particularly appetizing, and were well thumbed and greasy; they must have absorbed an infinite deal of emotion.

"I betook myself back to the library, and devoured, so to speak,

105

a whole novel—that is, the soft or essential part of it; but the crust, the binding, I left. When I had digested it, and another one besides, I noticed what a stirring there was inside me, and I devoured a piece of a third novel. And now I was a poet. I said so to myself, and told it to others too. I had headache and stomach-ache, and I don't know what aches I didn't have. Then I began to think what stories might be made to refer to a sausage-peg, and a great many pegs and sticks and staves and splinters came into my thoughts—the ant-queen had possessed an extraordinary understanding. I remembered the man who put a white stick into his mouth by which he could make both himself and the stick invisible. I thought of wooden hobby-horses, of stock rhymes, of breaking the staff over anyone, and of goodness knows how many expressions of that kind concerning staves, sticks, and pegs. All my thoughts ran upon pegs, sticks, and staves, and if one is a poet—and that I am, for I have tortured myself till I have become one—one must be able to make poetry on these things too. I will therefore be able to serve you up a peg—that is, a story—every day in the week; yes, that is my soup!"

SHE HAD BEEN RUNNING DAY AND NIGHT

"Let us hear what the third one has to say!" ordered the mouse-king.

"Peep! peep!" was heard at the kitchen door, and a little mouse—it was the fourth of the mice who had competed for the prize, the one whom the others believed to be dead—shot in like an arrow. She knocked the sausage-peg with the crape right over. She had been running day and night, had travelled on the railway by goods train, having watched her opportunity, and yet she had arrived almost too late. She pressed forward, looking very crumpled. She had lost her sausage-peg, but not her voice, for she began to speak at once, as

if they had been waiting only for her and wanted to hear her only—
as if everything else in the world was of no consequence whatever.
She spoke at once, and went on till she had said all she had to say.
She appeared so unexpectedly that no one had time to object to her
speech while she was speaking. Let us hear what she said.

IV

WHAT THE FOURTH MOUSE HAD TO TELL, BEFORE THE THIRD ONE HAD SPOKEN

"I immediately betook myself to the largest town," she said;
" the name has escaped me—I have a bad memory for names. From
the railway-station I was taken with some confiscated goods to the
town-hall, and when I arrived there I ran into the gaoler's dwelling.
The gaoler was talking of his prisoners, especially of one who had
uttered some hasty words. About these words other words had been
spoken, and then again others, and these again had been written
down and recorded.

" ' The whole thing is soup from a sausage-peg,' said the gaoler;
' but the soup may cost him his neck!'

" Now this gave me some interest in the prisoner," said the little
mouse, " so I seized an opportunity and slipped in to him; there is
a mouse-hole behind every locked door! The prisoner looked very
pale, and had a long beard and large sparkling eyes. The lamp
flickered and smoked, and the walls were so used to that that they
grew no blacker for it. The prisoner was scratching pictures and
verses in white upon the black, but I did not read them. I believe
he was finding it very dull, and I was a welcome guest. He lured
me with bread-crumbs, and with whistling and gentle words. He
was very glad to see me; I gradually began to trust him, and we
became friends. He shared his bread and water with me, gave me
cheese and sausage, and I lived well; but I must say that after all it
was principally the good company that kept me there. He let me
run about on his hand, on his arm, and right up his sleeve; he let

107

me creep about in his beard, and called me his little friend. I really began to like him—such things are mutual! I forgot what I had gone out into the wide world to seek, and left my sausage-peg in a crack in the floor; it lies there still. I wanted to stay where I was; if I went away the poor prisoner would have no one at all, and that is too little in this world. I stayed, but he did not. He spoke to me very sadly the last time, gave me twice as much bread and cheese as usual, and threw me kisses; he went and never came back. I don't know his history. 'Soup from a sausage-peg,' the gaoler had said, and to him I now went. He certainly took me in his hand, but he put me into a cage, into a treadmill. That's awful! One runs and runs and gets no farther, and is only laughed at.

"The gaoler's daughter was a most charming little girl, with a head of curls like the finest gold, and such joyous eyes and such a smiling mouth! 'You poor little mouse,' she said, and, peeping into my hateful cage, she drew out the iron pin, and I sprang down upon the window-sill and so out upon the gutter of the roof. Free! free! I thought only of that, and not of the object of my travels.

"It was dark—night was drawing near. I took up my lodgings in an old tower where a watchman and an owl dwelt. I trusted neither, and least of the two the owl. That animal is like a cat, and possesses the great failing of eating mice; but one may be mistaken, and that I was. She was a respectable, highly educated old owl; she knew more than the watchman, and quite as much as I. The owl children made a fuss about everything. 'Don't make soup from a sausage-peg,' the old one would say; those were the harshest words she could bring herself to utter, such tender affection did she cherish for her own family. Her behaviour inspired me with such confidence that I sent her a 'peep' from the crack where I sat. This confidence pleased her very much, and she assured me that I should be under her protection, and that no animal would be allowed to do me harm. She would eat me herself in winter, she declared, when food got scarce.

"She was in every way a clever woman; she explained to me that the watchman could only shriek through the horn that hung loose at his side, saying, ' He is terribly conceited about it, and thinks he is an owl in the tower. He wants to look big, but is very little! Soup from a sausage-peg!'

"I begged the owl to give me the recipe for the soup, and then she explained it to me. ' Soup from a sausage-peg,' she said, ' is only a human expression, and can be used in different ways. Every one thinks his own way is the most correct, but the whole thing really means nothing.'

"' Nothing!' I exclaimed. I was struck. The truth is not always agreeable, but truth is above everything, and the old owl said so too. So I thought it over, and soon perceived that if I brought home that which is above everything I should bring far more than soup from a sausage-peg. And thereupon I hastened away, so that I might get home in time and bring the highest and best, that which is above everything—the truth. The mice are an enlightened little people, and the mouse-king is above them all. He is capable of making me queen —for the sake of truth!"

"Your truth is a lie!" said the mouse who had not yet spoken. "I can prepare the soup, and I will prepare it too."

V

How it was prepared

"I didn't travel," said the third mouse; "I remained in the country, and that's the right thing to do. There is no necessity to travel—one can get everything just as good here. I remained; I did not get my information from supernatural beings, did not gobble it up, nor yet learn it from owls. I have evolved mine from my own thoughts. Now just you get the kettle put upon the fire. That's it. Now some water poured into it! Quite full—up to the brim! So— now more fuel! Let it burn up, so that the water boils—it must boil over and over! That's it! Now throw the peg in. Will the king now be pleased to dip his tail into the boiling water and stir it with that tail? The longer the king stirs, the stronger the soup will

become. It costs nothing. It requires no other ingredients—only stirring!"

" Can't anyone else do that?" asked the king.

" No," said the mouse. " It is only the king's tail that contains the power."

And the water boiled and spluttered, and the mouse-king placed himself close to the kettle—there was almost danger attached to it— he put out his tail, as the mice do in the dairy when they skim a pan of milk and then lick their creamy tails. But he only put his tail in as far as the hot steam, then he quickly sprang down from the hearth.

" It's understood, of course, that you are to be my queen!" he cried; " but we'll leave the soup till our golden wedding. In this way the poor of my kingdom, who will have to be fed then, will have something to look forward to with pleasure, and for a long time, too."

Then they held the wedding. But several of the mice said, as they were returning home, " That was really not to be called soup from a sausage-peg after all, but rather soup from a mouse's tail." This and that of what had been told they thought very good; but the whole thing might have been different. " Now I would have told it so—and so—and so——! "

These were the critics, and they are always so wise—afterwards.

This story went out all over the wide world, and opinions differed about it, but the story itself remained as it was. And that is the best thing in both great things and small, even with regard to soup from a sausage-peg—not to expect any thanks for it.

THE ELFIN HILL

SOME large lizards were running nimbly about in the clefts of an old tree; they could understand each other very well, for they spoke lizard language.

"How it is rumbling and buzzing in the old elfin hill!" said one lizard. "I've not been able to close my eyes for two nights because of the noise! I might just as well lie and have toothache, for then I can't sleep either!"

"There's something going on in there!" said another lizard. "They let the hill stand on four red posts till cock-crow, to have it regularly aired, and the elfin girls have learnt new dances with some stamping in them! There's something going on."

"Yes, I have talked with an earthworm of my acquaintance," said the third lizard. "The earthworm came straight out of the hill, where he had been grubbing in the ground night and day: he had heard a great deal. He can't see, poor creature, but he understands how to wriggle about and listen. They expect visitors in the elfin hill—visitors of rank, but who they are the earthworm could not tell, and perhaps, indeed, he did not know. All the will-o'-the-wisps are ordered to hold a torch dance, as it is called; and the silver and gold, of which there is plenty in the elfin hill, is being polished and put out in the moonshine."

"Who may these strangers be?" asked all the lizards. "What can be going on? Hark, how it hums and how it rumbles!"

At the same moment the elfin hill opened, and an old elfin maiden, hollow at the back, but for the rest very respectably dressed, came tripping out. She was the old elfin king's housekeeper. She was a distant relative of the family, and wore an amber heart on her forehead. Her legs moved so rapidly—trip, trip! Gracious!—how she could trip!—straight down to the moor, to the night raven.

"You are invited to the elfin hill this evening," said she, "but

"YOU ARE INVITED TO THE ELFIN HILL THIS EVENING," SAID SHE

will you do me a great service and undertake the invitations? You ought to do something, as you don't keep house yourself. We shall have some very distinguished friends, troll-folk who have something to say; and so the old elfin king wants to make a display."

" Who's to be invited? " asked the night raven.

" To the grand ball all the world may come, even human beings, if they can talk in their sleep, or can do something in our way. But for the banquet the company is to be strictly select; we shall only have the most distinguished. I had a dispute with the elfin king, for in my opinion we could not even admit ghosts. The merman and his daughters must be invited first. They may not be much pleased to come on dry land, but they shall have a wet stone to sit upon, or something still better, and then I think they won't refuse for this once. All the old trolls of the first class, with tails, and the wood demon and his gnomes we must have; and then I think we may not leave out the grave pig, the death horse, and the church dwarf, though they certainly belong to the clergy, who are not of our class. But that's only their vocation; they are closely related to us and frequently pay us visits."

" Caw! " said the night raven, and flew off at once to give the invitations.

The elfin girls were already dancing on the elfin hill, and they danced with long shawls woven of mist and moonshine, and that looks very pretty for those who like that sort of thing. In the middle of the elfin hill was the great hall, splendidly decorated. The floor had been washed with moonshine, and the walls rubbed with witches' fat, so that they shone in the light like tulips. In the kitchen plenty of frogs were roasting on the spit, snail-skins with little children's fingers, and salads of mushroom spawn, wet mice's snouts, and hemlock; beer brewed by the marsh witch, sparkling saltpetre wine from grave cellars—all very substantial eating. Rusty nails and church window glass were among the sweets.

The old elfin king had his golden crown polished with powdered slate pencil; it was slate pencil from the first form, and it's very difficult for the elfin king to get first form slate pencil! In the bed-

THE ELFIN GIRLS WERE ALREADY DANCING ON THE ELFIN HILL

room curtains were hung up, and fastened with snail-slime. Yes, there was indeed a rumbling and jostling there!

" Now we must perfume the place by burning horsehair and pig's bristles, and then I think I shall have done my part," said the old elfin maiden.

" Father dear," said the youngest daughter, " may I hear now who our distinguished guests are to be? "

" Well," said he, " I suppose I must tell you now. Two of my daughters must be prepared to be married! Two will certainly be married. The old goblin from Norway, he who lives in the old Dovrefjeld, and possesses many strong castles on the rocky hills, and a gold mine which is better than anyone thinks, is coming with his two sons, who both want to choose a wife. The old goblin is a true old honest Norwegian veteran, merry and straightforward. I know him from old days, when we drank with one another. He came here to fetch his wife; now she is dead—she was a daughter of the King of the Chalk-cliffs of Möen. He took his wife on tick, as the saying is. Oh, how I am longing for the old Norwegian gnome! His sons, they say, are rather rude, forward youngsters, but perhaps people do them wrong, and they'll be right enough when they grow older. Let me see that you can teach them manners! "

" And when will they come? " asked one of his daughters.

" That depends on wind and weather," said the elfin king. " They travel economically: they come when there's a chance of a ship. I wanted them to go across Sweden, but the old one did not like that way. He does not advance with the times, and I don't like that."

Just then two will-o'-the-wisps came hopping up, one quicker than the other, and so one came first.

" They're coming! They're coming! " they cried.

" Give me my crown, and let me stand in the moonshine," said the elfin king.

And the daughters lifted up their shawls and bowed down to the ground.

There stood the old goblin from Dovre, with a crown of hardened icicles and polished fir cones. Moreover, he wore a bearskin and great warm boots. His sons, on the contrary, went bare-necked, and with no braces, for they were strong men.

"Is that a hill?" asked the younger of the boys, and he pointed to the elfin hill. "Up in Norway we should call it a hole."

"Boys!" said the old man, "a hole goes in, a hill goes up. Have you no eyes in your heads?"

The only thing they wondered at down here, they said, was that they could understand the language without difficulty.

"Don't give yourself airs!" said the old man. "One would think you were not full-fledged."

And then they went into the elfin hill, where the really grand company were assembled, and that in such haste that one might almost say they had been blown together. But for each it was nicely and prettily arranged. The sea folk sat at table in big wash-tubs: they said it was just as if they were at home. All showed good table manners except the two small Northern trolls, and they put their legs up on the table; but they thought that everything became them.

"Feet off the table!" said the old goblin, and they obeyed, but not immediately. The ladies who sat next to them they tickled with pine cones that they had brought with them, and then took off their boots to be more at their ease, and gave them to the ladies to hold, but their father, the old Dovre goblin, was quite different; he told such fine stories of the imposing Norwegian rocks, and of the waterfalls which rushed down white with foam with a noise like thunder and the sound of organs; he told of the salmon that leap up the rushing streams when the nixie plays upon her golden harp; he told of shining winter nights, when the sledge bells are jingling, and the lads skate with burning torches over the clear ice, which is so transparent that they can see the fishes start beneath their feet. Yes, he could tell it so finely that one saw and heard what he described. It was just as if the sawmills were going, as if the servants and maids were singing songs and dancing the halling dance. Hurrah! All at once the old goblin gave the old elfin girl a smacking kiss! That *was* a kiss! And yet they were not related to each other at all!

Then the elfin maidens had to dance, first in the usual way and then with stamping steps, and that suited them well; then came the artistic and solo dance. Gracious! How they could stretch their legs! Nobody knew where they began and where they ended, which were their arms and which their legs—they were all mixed up like wood shavings; and then they whirled round till the death horse turned giddy and was obliged to leave the table.

"Prrrr!" said the old goblin. "That's good fun for the legs! But what else can they do besides dancing, stretching their legs, and making a whirlwind?"

"That you shall soon know!" said the elfin king.

And he called out the youngest of his daughters. She was as dainty and light as moonshine; she was the most delicate of all the sisters. She took a white shaving in her mouth, and disappeared—that was her gift.

But the old goblin said he should not like his wife to possess this gift, and he did not think that his boys would either.

The second could walk beside her own self, just as if she had a shadow, and that is what the troll-folk never have.

The third daughter was of quite another kind; she had learned in the brewhouse of the marsh witch, and understood how to lard elder-tree logs with glow-worms.

"She will make a good housewife," said the old goblin; and then he winked a health to her with his eyes, for he did not want to drink too much.

Next came the fourth elfin girl; she had a big golden harp to play upon, and when she struck the first string all lifted up their left feet, for the trolls are left-legged, and when she struck the second chord all had to do what she wished.

"That's a dangerous woman!" said the old goblin; but both his sons went out of the hill, for they had had enough of it.

"And what can the next daughter do?" asked the old goblin.

"I have learned to love everything that is Norwegian," said she, "and I will never marry unless I can go to Norway."

But the youngest sister whispered to the old king, "That's only because she has heard in a Norwegian song that when the world sinks

SHE TOOK HIM BY THE WRIST, AND HE LAUGHED TILL HE CLUCKED

down the cliffs of Norway will remain standing like monuments, and so she wants to get there, because she is afraid of sinking down too."

"Ho! ho!" said the old goblin. "Is that the meaning of it? But what can the seventh and last do?"

"The sixth comes before the seventh!" said the elfin King, for he could count. But the sixth would not come out.

"I can only tell people the truth!" said she. "Nobody cares for me, and I have enough to do to sew my shroud."

Now came the seventh and last, and what could she do? Why, she could tell stories, as many as ever she wished!

"Here are all my five fingers," said the old goblin. "Tell me one for each!"

And she took him by the wrist, and he laughed till he clucked, and when she came to the ring finger, which had a golden ring round its waist, just as if it knew there was to be a wedding, the old goblin said:

"Hold fast what you have: the hand is yours; I'll have you for a wife myself!"

And the elfin girl said that the story of the ring finger and of little Peter Playman, the fifth, were still to be told.

"We'll hear those in winter," said the goblin, "and we'll hear about the pine-tree, and the birch, and the fairies' presents, and the crackling frost. You shall tell your tales, for no one up there knows how to do that well; and then we'll sit in the stone rooms where the pine logs burn, and drink mead out of the golden horns of the old Norwegian kings—the Neckan has given me a couple; and when we sit there, and the nixie comes on a visit, she'll sing you all the songs of the saeter girls. That will be merry. The salmon will leap in the waterfall against the stone walls, but they cannot come in."

"Yes, it's very good living in dear old Norway; but where are my boys?"

Yes, where were the boys? They were running about in the fields, and blowing out the will-o'-the-wisps, which had come so kindly for the torch dance.

"What's all this romping about?" said the old goblin. "I have taken a mother for you, and now you may take one of the aunts."

But the lads said that they would rather make a speech and drink good fellowship—they did not want to marry; and they made speeches, and drank brotherhood, and tipped up their glasses on their nails, to show they had emptied them. Afterwards they took their coats off and lay down on the table to sleep, for they did not stand on ceremony. But the old goblin danced about the room with his young bride, and he changed boots with her, for that's more fashionable than exchanging rings.

"The cock is crowing," said the old elfin girl who kept house. "Now we must shut the shutters, so that the sun may not burn us."

And the hill shut itself up.

But outside the lizards ran up and down in the cleft tree, and one said to the other:

"Oh, how much I like that old Norwegian goblin!"

"I like the boys better," said the earthworm. But he could not see, the miserable creature.

THE STEADFAST TIN SOLDIER

THERE were once five-and-twenty tin soldiers, who were all brothers, as they were cast from an old tin spoon. They all carried their guns on their shoulders and looked straight forward, and they all had the same smart uniform, red and blue. The first words which they heard upon seeing the light of day, when the lid was taken off the box in which they were packed, were, "Tin soldiers!" These words were uttered by a little boy who had received them as a birthday present, and clapped his hands for joy; he then put them in rank and file on the table. One soldier looked exactly like another: only one, who had been cast last of all, when there was not enough tin left, was not like his brothers, for he had only one leg; nevertheless, he stood just as firmly on his one leg as the others on two; and he was the very one who became famous.

On the table where they were placed were many other toys; but what caught the eye most of all was a pretty castle of paper. Through its little windows one could look into the rooms. Before the castle stood little trees round a clear lake, which was made by a little looking-glass. Swans made of wax were swimming on it and were reflected in it. All this was very pretty, but the prettiest of all was a little lady who stood in the open door of the castle; she was cut out of paper, but she had a frock of the whitest muslin on, and a piece of narrow blue ribbon was fixed on her shoulders like a scarf, and on it was fixed a glittering tinsel rose, as large as her whole face. The little lady stretched out both arms, for she was a dancer; and as she had lifted one leg high up, so that the tin soldier could not see it, he thought she had only one leg like himself.

"That's the wife for me," he thought; "but she is very grand; she lives in a castle, while I have only a box, which I share with four-and-twenty; that is no place for her. But I must make her acquaintance." And then he laid himself at full length behind a snuff-box which was on the table; there from his place he could see the little dainty lady, who continued to stand on one leg without losing her balance.

At night all the other tin soldiers were put back into their box, and the people of the house went to bed. Now the toys began to play, to pay visits, to make war, and to go to balls. The tin soldiers rattled in their box, for they wished to take part in the games, but they could not raise the lid. The nutcrackers turned somersaults, the slate-pencil amused itself on the slate; they made so much noise that the canary woke up and began to talk, and even in verse. The tin soldier and the dancer were the only ones who remained in their places. She was standing on tiptoe with her arm stretched out; he stood firmly on his one leg, never taking his eyes away from her for a moment. When the clock struck twelve suddenly the lid of the snuff-box flew open; there was no snuff in it, but a small black troll, a jack-in-the-box, who did the trick.

"Tin soldier," said the troll, "will you keep your eyes to yourself?"

The tin soldier pretended not to hear it.

" All right; wait till to-morrow," said the troll.

When morning came and the children were up the tin soldier was placed on the window-sill; all at once, whether it was the troll or the draught, the window flew open and the soldier fell headlong down into the street from the third story. That was a terrible fall! With his one leg in the air, he stood on his helmet, while his bayonet stuck in the ground between the paving stones. The servant and the little boy came down at once to look for him; but although they were so close to him that they almost trod upon him, they did not find him. If the tin soldier had cried out, " Here I am!" they would surely have found him; but he did not consider it proper to call out aloud, because he was in uniform.

Then it began to rain, first very little, but soon more, till it became a heavy shower. When the rain had ceased two street boys came by.

" Look, there is a tin soldier!" said one of them. " Let's give him a sail! "

So they made a boat out of a piece of newspaper, put the tin soldier in it, and let him float down the gutter; both the boys ran by the side and clapped their hands. Heaven preserve us! What waves there were in the gutter, and such a strong current too, for the rain had been pouring down in torrents. The paper boat rocked up and down; sometimes it turned round so quickly that the tin soldier trembled; but he remained firm, he did not move a muscle, and looked straight forward, holding his gun on his shoulder. All at once the boat was driven into a long drain, and there it became as dark as it had been in his box.

" Where am I going to? " he thought. " This is the fault of the black troll. Ah! if only the little lady sat here with me in the boat, then I should not mind how dark it was."

Then there came a big water-rat which lived in the drain.

" Have you got a pass? " asked the rat. " Give me your pass! "

But the tin soldier kept silent and held his gun tighter than before.

The boat rushed on; the rat followed, gnashing its teeth, and crying out to the chips of wood and straws: "Stop him, stop him! He has not paid the toll! he has not shown his pass!"

The current became stronger and stronger; the tin soldier could already see the light of day where the drain ended; but he also heard a roaring noise, strong enough to frighten a brave man. Just think: there, where the drain ended, the water rushed into a big canal, for him as dangerous as for us to be carried over a big waterfall. He was already so close to it that to stop was impossible. The boat dashed on; the poor tin soldier held himself as stiff as he could; nobody

125

could say of him that he had blinked an eye. The boat rapidly whirled round three or four times, and was filled with water to the very brim; it must sink. The tin soldier stood up to his neck in water; deeper and deeper sank the boat, more and more soaked became the paper; then the water closed over the soldier's head. He thought of the sweet little dancer whom he should never see again, and there sounded in his ear:

> Farewell, soldier, true and brave,
> Nothing now thy life can save.

Then the paper boat fell to pieces, and the tin soldier, sinking into the water, was snapped up by a big fish.

It was very dark indeed inside the fish, much darker than in the drain, and it was awfully narrow too, but the tin soldier remained firm, and lay down full length, holding his gun firmly on his shoulder.

The fish rushed about and made the most extraordinary movements; at last it became quiet; it seemed as if a flash of lightning passed through it, the broad daylight appeared, and a voice shouted, " The tin soldier! " The fish had been caught and taken to market; there it had been sold and brought to the kitchen, where the cook had just cut it open with a big knife. With two fingers she took the tin soldier round the middle, and carried him upstairs, to show everybody the wonderful man who had been travelling about in a fish's stomach; but the tin soldier was not proud. They put him on the table, and there—what strange things happen in this world!—he was in the self-same room where he had been before! He saw the same children and the same toys were on the table; there was also the pretty castle, with the dear little dancer. She stood still on one leg and held the other high up in the air: she too was steadfast. The tin soldier was very much touched, and he nearly shed tin tears, but that was not becoming for a soldier. He looked at her, but said nothing. Suddenly one of the little boys took up the tin soldier and threw him into the stove, without giving any reason for this strange conduct! Again it must have been the fault of the troll in the snuff-

box! The tin soldier stood there in the strong light and felt an un-
bearable heat, but whether this heat was caused by the real fire or
by love he did not know. His colours had vanished, but nobody
could say if that happened during his journey or if grief was the
cause of it. He looked at the little lady and she looked at him, and
he felt that he was melting, but still he stood upright with his gun
in his arm. All at once a door flew open, the wind took the dancer
and she flew like a sylph into the stove to the tin soldier, blazed up,
and was gone in a moment. The tin soldier melted down into a
lump, and when the servant cleared out the cinders next morning
she found him in the shape of a little tin heart. Of the little dancer
only the tinsel rose was left, and that was burnt as black as coal.

OLE LUKÖJE

THERE is no one in the world who knows so many stories as Ole Luköje. He can tell them beautifully!

Towards evening, when the children are still sitting nicely at table or on their stools, then comes Ole Luköje. He comes up the stairs so quietly, for he always walks in his socks; he opens the doors gently, and—whish! he squirts sweet milk into the children's eyes in tiny drops, but still quite enough to prevent them from keeping their eyes open and therefore from seeing him. He steals behind them, and blows softly on their necks, and this makes their heads heavy.

"HE SAYS YOU MAY GO AND OPEN THE CHEST IN THE CORNER AND YOU
WILL SEE THE DEVIL CROUCHING INSIDE IT"

"Little Claus and Big Claus"

IN THE MIDST OF THE TREE SAT A KINDLY LOOKING OLD WOMAN

"Elder-Tree Mother"

OLE LUKÖJE

Oh, yes, but it does not hurt them, for Ole Luköje is the children's friend; he only wants them to be quiet, and that they are not until they have been put to bed.

They are to be quiet only that he may tell them stories.

When the children are asleep Ole Luköje sits down upon the bed. He has fine clothes on; his coat is of silk, but it is impossible to say what colour it is, for it shines green, red, and blue, according as he turns. Under each arm he carries an umbrella; the one with pictures on it he opens over good children, and then they dream the most beautiful stories all night; but the other, on which there is nothing at all, he opens over naughty children, and then they sleep as though they were deaf, so that when they awake in the morning they have not dreamed the least thing.

Now we shall hear how for one whole week Ole Luköje came to a little boy named Hjalmar every evening, and what he told him. There are seven stories, for there are seven days in the week.

MONDAY

"Listen now!" said Ole Luköje in the evening, when he had put Hjalmar to bed. "I'll just make things look nice."

And all the flowers in the flower-pots grew into large trees, stretching out their long branches across the ceiling and along the walls, so that the whole room looked like a beautiful arbour; and all the branches were full of flowers, every flower being finer than a rose, and smelling sweetly. If anyone had wanted to eat them they were sweeter than jam. The fruits shone like gold, and there were cakes simply bursting with currants. It was marvellous. But at the same time a terrible wail was heard coming from the table drawer where Hjalmar's school-books lay.

"Whatever is the matter?" said Ole Luköje, going to the table and opening the drawer. It was the slate, upon which a terrible riot was going on, because a wrong figure had got into the sum, so that it was nearly falling to pieces; the slate pencil hopped and skipped at the end of its string, as if it were a little dog, and would have liked to put the sum right, but it could not. And from Hjalmar's copy-book there also came the sounds of woe, terrible to hear. On every page there stood at the beginning of each line a capital letter, with a small one next to it; that was for a copy. Now, next to these stood some other letters which Hjalmar had written, and these thought

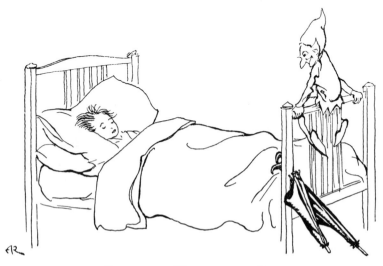

"LISTEN NOW!" SAID OLE LUKÖJE

they looked just like the first two. But they lay there as if they had fallen over the pencil lines upon which they ought to have stood.

"Look!—this is the way you ought to hold yourselves up," said the copy. "Look!—slanting like this, with a powerful flourish."

"Oh, we should like to," said Hjalmar's letters; "but we can't—we are too weak!"

"Then you must have a powder," said Ole Luköje.

"Oh, no," they cried, and stood up so straight that it was a pleasure.

"Well, we cannot tell any stories now!" said Ole Luköje; "I must drill them. One, two! one, two!" And in this way he

130

drilled the letters. They stood up quite straight, and looked as nice as only a copy can do. But when Ole Luköje had gone, and Hjalmar looked at them in the morning, they were just as weak and miserable as before.

TUESDAY

As soon as Hjalmar had gone to bed Ole Luköje touched all the pieces of furniture in the room with his little magic squirt; whereupon they immediately began to chatter.

And they all talked about themselves except the spittoon, which stood there silent and angry at their being so vain as to talk only about themselves, to think only about themselves, and to take no notice whatever of the spittoon, which stood modestly in the corner and let itself be spat at.

Over the chest of drawers hung a large picture in a gilt frame; it was a landscape. In it one could see lofty old trees, flowers in the grass, and a wide river flowing round about a wood, past many castles, and far into the wide sea.

Ole Luköje touched the picture with his magic squirt, and the birds immediately began to sing, the branches of the trees to wave, and the clouds to drift across it; one could see their shadows passing over the landscape.

Then Ole Luköje lifted little Hjalmar up to the frame, and Hjalmar put his feet into the picture, right into the high grass; and there he stood. The sun shone down upon him through the branches of the trees. He ran to the water and sat himself in a little boat which was lying there; it was painted red and white, the sails shone like silver, and six swans, all with golden crowns round their necks and a bright blue star on their heads, drew the boat along, past the green wood where the trees tell of robbers and witches, and where the flowers speak of the dainty little elves and of what the butterflies have told them.

Most lovely fishes, with scales like silver and gold, swam after the boat. Now and then they took a jump, making the water splash, and birds, red and blue, small and large, flew in two long rows after them.

The gnats danced, and the cockchafers said, " Boom! boom!" They all wanted to follow Hjalmar, and each had a story to tell.

That really was a pleasant voyage! At times the woods were thick and dark, at times full of sunlight and flowers, like the most beautiful garden. There were great castles built of glass and of marble, and on the balconies stood princesses, who were all little girls whom Hjalmar knew very well, and with whom he had formerly played. They stretched out their hands, holding out to him the prettiest sugar-pigs that any cake-woman could sell. Hjalmar caught hold of one end of a sugar-pig as he sailed by, and the princess also held on tightly, and each got a piece of it; she got the smaller, Hjalmar the bigger. At every castle little princes kept guard. They shouldered their golden swords and showered down raisins and tin soldiers; they were real princes.

Sometimes Hjalmar sailed through forests, sometimes through great halls or through the middle of a town; he also came to the town where his nursemaid lived, who had carried him when he was quite a little boy and who had always been so fond of him, and she nodded and beckoned to him, and sang the pretty little verse which she had herself written and sent to Hjalmar:

"I think of thee full many a time,
  Hjalmar, my own dear boy;
Thy little mouth, thy rosy cheeks,
  How oft I kissed with joy.
I heard thee lisp thy first sweet words,
  Yet must I say good-bye;
May heaven bless thee here on earth,
  Dear angel from on high!"

And all the birds sang too, the flowers danced on their stalks, and the old trees nodded as if Ole Luköje were also telling them stories.

WEDNESDAY

How the rain was pouring down outside! Hjalmar could hear it in his sleep, and when Ole Luköje opened one of the windows the water came up to the window-sill. It formed quite a lake, and a splendid ship was lying close to the house.

"Would you like to sail with me, little Hjalmar?" said Ole Luköje. "You can reach foreign countries to-night, and get back here by the morning."

Then Hjalmar suddenly found himself dressed in his Sunday clothes on board the beautiful ship. The weather at once became fine, and they sailed through the streets, cruised round the church, and were soon on a great stormy sea. They sailed until they lost sight of land, and saw a flock of storks which were also coming from home and going to warm countries. They were flying in a line one after another, and had already come very far. One of them was so tired that his wings could scarcely carry him any longer; he was the last in the line, and was soon left a long way behind, till at last he sank with outspread wings lower and lower. He flapped his wings once or twice more, but it was of no use; first he touched the rigging of the ship with his feet. Then he slid down from the sail, and bump!—at last he stood on the deck.

The cabin-boy took him and put him into the hen-house with the chickens, ducks, and turkeys; there stood the poor stork, a prisoner among them.

"Look at the fellow!" said all the fowls, and the turkey-cock puffed himself out as much as he could, and asked him who he was. The ducks waddled backward and jostled each other, quacking, "What a fool! What a fool!" And the stork told them about the heat of Africa, and the pyramids, and about the ostrich who runs across the desert like a wild horse; but the ducks did not understand him, and nudged each other, saying: "I suppose we all agree that he is very stupid?"

"Of course he is very stupid," said the turkey; and then he gobbled. So the stork was silent and thought of his Africa.

"What beautifully thin legs you have," said the turkey-cock. "What do they cost a yard?"

"Skrat, skrat, skrat!" grinned all the ducks; but the stork pretended not to have heard it.

"You might laugh anyhow!" said the turkey-cock to him; "for it was very wittily said. But perhaps it was too deep for you! Ha! ha! He is not very clever. We will keep to our interesting selves." And then he gobbled, and the ducks quacked "Gik, gak! gik, gak!" It was terrible how funny they found it!

But Hjalmar went to the hen-house, opened the door, and called the stork, who hopped out to him on the deck. He had now had a good rest, and he seemed to nod to Hjalmar, as if to thank him. He then spread his wings and flew to the warm countries; but the hens clucked, the ducks quacked, and the turkey-cock turned red as fire in the face.

"To-morrow we shall make soup of you," said Hjalmar; and with that he awoke and found himself in his little bed. It was a strange journey upon which Ole Luköje had taken him that night.

THURSDAY

"Do you know what?" said Ole Luköje; "only don't be frightened, and you will see a little mouse here." And he held out his hand with the pretty little animal in it. "She is come to invite you to a wedding. There are two little mice here who are going to enter the married state to-night. They live under the floor of your mother's larder, which must be a fine place to dwell in."

"But how can I get through the little mouse-hole in the floor?" asked Hjalmar.

"Let me look after that," said Ole Luköje. "I will soon make you small." And then he touched Hjalmar with his little magic squirt, and he grew smaller and smaller, until at last he was not so big as a

135

finger. "Now you can borrow the clothes of the tin soldier; I think they will fit you, and it looks well to wear uniform when you are in company."

"So it does," said Hjalmar, and in the blink of an eye he was dressed like the prettiest little tin soldier.

"Will you be good enough to sit in your mother's thimble?" said the little mouse. "Then I shall have the honour of drawing you along."

"Gracious! And will you yourself take so much trouble, madam?" said Hjalmar; and in that way they drove to the mouse's wedding.

At first they came to a long passage under the floor, just high enough to enable them to drive along with the thimble, and the whole passage was illuminated with rotten wood.

"Doesn't it smell delightful here?" asked the mouse, who was drawing him along. "The passage is smeared with bacon-rind. There can be nothing nicer!"

Then they came to the hall where the wedding was to take place. On the right-hand side stood all the little lady mice, and they whispered and giggled as though they were having rare fun; on the left stood all the gentlemen mice, stroking their whiskers with their paws. In the middle of the hall could be seen the bride and bridegroom standing in the hollowed-out rind of a cheese; they were kissing each other in a shocking way before the eyes of all, for they were already betrothed and on the point of being married.

More and more strangers kept coming; the mice were almost treading each other to death, and the bridal pair had placed themselves right in the doorway, so that it was impossible to go out or in. The whole room, like the passage, had been smeared with bacon-rind, and that was all the refreshments there were; for dessert, however, a pea was shown, in which a mouse of the family had bitten the name of the bridal pair—that is to say, of course, only the initials. But what a novel idea it was!

All the mice agreed that it was a splendid wedding, and that the conversation had been most agreeable.

Then Hjalmar drove home again. He had certainly been in distinguished society, but he had also had to huddle himself up a good deal, to make himself small, and to wear a tin soldier's uniform.

FRIDAY

"It is unbelievable how many grown-up people there are who would only be too pleased to have me," said Ole Luköje. "Particularly those who have done something bad. 'Dear little Ole,' they say to me, 'we cannot close our eyes, and so we lie awake the whole night and see all our wicked deeds sitting like ugly little trolls on the bedstead, and squirting hot water over us; we wish you would come and drive them away, so that we could get a good sleep.' Then they sigh deeply. 'Indeed, we would willingly pay for it! Good night, Ole—the money is on the window-sill.' But I don't do it for money," said Ole Luköje.

"What are we going to do to-night?" asked Hjalmar.

137

"Well, I don't know whether you would like to go to another wedding to-night; it is of quite a different kind to last night's. Your sister's big doll—the one that looks like a man and is called Hermann—is going to marry the doll Bertha. Besides this it is the bride's birthday, and therefore they will receive a great many presents."

"Yes, I know that," said Hjalmar. "Whenever the dolls want new clothes my sister lets them have a birthday or a wedding. That has happened quite a hundred times already."

"Yes, but to-night is the hundred-and-first wedding, and when a hundred-and-one is reached everything is over. That is why this one will be such a grand affair. Only just look!"

And Hjalmar looked upon the table. There stood the little doll's house with lights in the windows, and all the tin soldiers presenting arms in front of it. The bride and bridegroom were sitting on the floor and leaning against the leg of the table. They seemed very thoughtful, and for this they had perhaps good cause. Ole Luköje, dressed in Grandmother's black gown, married them. When the ceremony was over all the furniture in the room began to sing the following beautiful song, written by the lead pencil. It went to the air of the soldiers' tattoo:

> We'll sing our song out like the wind,
>   Long live the bridal pair!
> Though both so dumb, so stiff and blind,
>   Of leather made, they'll wear.
> Hurrah! hurrah! though deaf and blind,
> We'll sing it out in rain and wind.

And now came the presents; they had, however, declined to accept any eatables, love being enough for them to live on.

"Shall we take a country house or travel abroad?" asked the bridegroom. To settle this, the swallow, who had travelled a great deal, and the old hen, who had hatched five broods of chicks, were asked for their advice.

The swallow spoke of the beautiful warm countries, where the grapes grow large and full, where the air is so mild and the mountains have such colours as are never seen in our country.

"But still they have not our curly-kale," said the hen. "I was once in the country for a whole summer with all my chicks; there was a sand-pit, into which we might go and scrape up, and then we were admitted to a garden full of curly-kale. Oh, how green it was! I cannot imagine anything nicer!"

"But one cabbage stalk is just like another," said the swallow; "and then we very often have bad weather here."

"Well, one gets used to that," said the hen.

"But it is cold here, and it freezes."

"That is good for cabbages," said the hen. "Besides, it can be warm here too. Didn't we have a summer, four years ago, that lasted five weeks? It was almost too warm to breathe. And then we have not poisonous animals, as they have there; and we are free from robbers. He must be a wicked man who does not think that our country is most beautiful. He really does not deserve to be here."

And then the hen wept. "I have travelled too. I rode for more than twelve miles in a coop. Travelling is by no means a pleasure."

"Yes, the hen is a sensible woman," said the doll Bertha. "I don't in the least care for travelling over mountains myself, for you only go up and down again. No, we will go into the gravel-pit outside the gate and walk in the cabbage garden."

And so it was settled.

SATURDAY

"Shall I hear any stories to-night?" asked little Hjalmar, as soon as Ole Luköje had sent him to sleep.

"We have no time for any this evening," said Ole Luköje, opening his beautiful umbrella over him. "Just look at these Chinamen!"

The umbrella looked like a big Chinese bowl with blue trees and pointed bridges, and with little Chinamen nodding their heads.

"We must have the whole world cleaned up by to-morrow morning," said Ole Luköje, "for it is a holiday—it is Sunday. I will go to the church steeple and see whether the little church goblins are polishing the bells, so that they may sound sweetly. I will go out into the fields and see whether the wind is blowing the dust off the grass and the leaves; and, what is the biggest job of all, I must fetch down the stars to polish them. I take them in my apron; but first each one must be numbered, and the holes in which they are fixed must also be numbered, so that they may be put back in their right places. They would otherwise not hold fast, and we should have too many falling stars, one tumbling down after another.

"Look here! Do you know, Mr Ole Luköje," said an old portrait which hung on the wall in Hjalmar's bedroom, "I am Hjalmar's great-grandfather? I thank you for telling the boy tales; but you must not put wrong ideas into his head. The stars cannot be taken down and polished. The stars are worlds, just like our earth, and that is the beauty of them."

"Thanks shall you have, you old great-grandfather!" said Ole

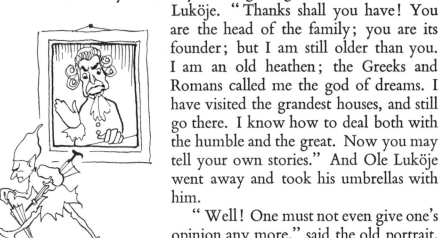

Luköje. "Thanks shall you have! You are the head of the family; you are its founder; but I am still older than you. I am an old heathen; the Greeks and Romans called me the god of dreams. I have visited the grandest houses, and still go there. I know how to deal both with the humble and the great. Now you may tell your own stories." And Ole Luköje went away and took his umbrellas with him.

"Well! One must not even give one's opinion any more," said the old portrait. And so Hjalmar awoke.

OLE LUKÖJE

SUNDAY

"Good evening!" said Ole Luköje. Hjalmar nodded and jumped up to turn his great-grandfather's portrait to the wall, so that it could not interrupt, as it did yesterday.

"You must tell me some stories about the five green peas who lived in one pod, about the leg of the cock which went courting the leg of the hen, and about the darning-needle who was so grand that she fancied she was a sewing-needle."

"You can have too much of a good thing," said Ole Luköje. "You know very well that I prefer showing you something. I will show you my brother. He also is called Ole Luköje, but he never comes to anyone more than once, and when he does come to them he takes them with him on his horse and tells them stories. He only knows two; one is so extremely beautiful that no one in the world can imagine anything like it; the other is most awful and horrible—it cannot be described."

Then Ole Luköje lifted little Hjalmar up to the window, saying: "Now you will see my brother, the other Ole Luköje. They call him Death. Do you see—he does not look so bad as in the picture-books, where they make him out to be a skeleton. No, it is silver embroidery on his coat; it is a splendid hussar uniform; a black velvet mantle floats behind him over the horse. See at what a gallop he rides."

And Hjalmar saw how this Ole Luköje rode away, taking both

young and old upon his horse. Some he placed before him and others behind, but he always asked first:

" How is your report for good behaviour? "

" Good! " they all replied.

" Yes, but let me see it myself," said he; and then each one had to show him the book. All those who had ' very good ' and ' excellent' were placed in front upon the horse and heard the delightful story; but those who had ' pretty good ' and ' middling ' had to get up behind and listen to the horrible story. They trembled and cried, and wanted to jump off the horse, but could not do so, for they had suddenly grown fast to it.

" But Death is a most beautiful Ole Luköje," said Hjalmar. " I am not afraid of him."

" Nor should you be! " said Ole Luköje. " Only take care that you get good reports! "

" Well, that's instructive," mumbled the great-grandfather's portrait. " It is of some use to give one's opinion occasionally."

And so he felt satisfied.

And that is the story of Ole Luköje. Perhaps he will tell you some more to-night himself.

LITTLE CLAUS AND BIG CLAUS

THERE lived two men in one village, and they had the same name —both were called Claus; but one had four horses, and the other only a single horse. To distinguish them from each other, folk called him who had four horses Big Claus and the one who had only a single horse Little Claus. Now we shall hear what happened to each of them, for this is a true story.

The whole week through Little Claus was obliged to plough for Big Claus, and to lend him his one horse; then Big Claus helped him out with all his four, but only once a week, and that was on Sunday. Hurrah! how Little Claus cracked his whip over all five horses, for they were as good as his own on that one day. The sun shone gaily, and all the bells in the church tower were ringing to church. The people were all dressed in their best, and were going, with their hymn-books under their arms, to hear the parson preach, and they saw Little Claus ploughing with five horses. And he was so pleased that he cracked his whip again and again, and cried, " Gee up, all my horses!"

" You must not say that," said Big Claus, " for only the one horse is yours."

But when some more people went by to church Little Claus forgot that he was not to say this, and he cried, " Gee up, all my horses!"

" Now, I tell you, you must stop it," said Big Claus, " for if you say it again I shall hit your horse on the head, so that he will fall down dead, and then that will be the end of him!"

" I will certainly not say it any more," said Little Claus.

But when some people came by soon after and nodded " Good day " to him he was so pleased, and thought it looked so fine, after all, to have five horses to plough his field, that he cracked his whip again, and cried out, " Gee up, all my horses!"

"I'll 'gee up' your horses for you!" said Big Claus. And he took a mallet and hit the only horse of Little Claus on the head, so that he fell down, and was dead instantly.

"Oh, now I haven't any horse at all!" said Little Claus; and he began to cry.

But after a while he flayed the horse, and let the hide dry in the wind, and put it in a sack and hung it over his shoulder, and went to the town to sell his horse's skin.

He had a very long way to go, and was obliged to pass through a great dark wood, and the weather became dreadfully bad. He went quite astray, and before he got into the right way again it was evening, and it was too far to get to the town or back home again before nightfall.

Close by the road stood a large farmhouse. The shutters were closed outside the windows, but the light could still be seen shining out over the top of them.

"I may be able to get leave to stop here for the night," thought Little Claus; and he went and knocked.

The farmer's wife unlocked the door; but when she heard what he wanted she told him to go away, as her husband was not at home, and would not let her admit strangers.

"Then I shall have to lie out here," said Little Claus. And the farmer's wife shut the door in his face.

Close by stood a great haystack, and between this and the farmhouse was a little shed with a flat thatched roof.

"I can lie there," said Little Claus, when he looked up at the roof; "that is a capital bed. I suppose the stork won't fly down and bite me in the legs." For a living stork was standing on the roof, where it had its nest.

Now Little Claus climbed up to the roof of the shed, where he lay down, and turned about to settle himself comfortably. The wooden shutters did not cover the windows to the top, and he could look straight into the room. There was a big table, with the cloth laid, and wine and roast meat and a lovely fish upon it. The farmer's wife and the sexton were seated at table, and nobody besides. She was filling his glass, and he was sticking his fork into the fish, for that was his favourite dish.

"If one could only get some too!" said Little Claus, and he stretched out his head towards the window. Heavens! what a splendid cake he saw there! Yes, certainly, that *was* a feast.

Now he heard someone riding along the highroad. It was the woman's husband, who was coming home. He was a good man enough, but he had the strange peculiarity that he could never bear to see a sexton. If a sexton appeared before his eyes he got very angry. And that was the reason why the sexton had called on the wife to wish her "Good day" when he knew that her husband was not at home; and the good woman had put the best fare she had before him. But when they heard the man coming they were frightened, and the woman begged the sexton to creep into a big empty chest which stood there. And he did so, for he knew the husband could not bear the sight of a sexton. The woman quickly hid all the excellent meat and wine in her baking-oven; for if her husband had seen that he would have been sure to ask what it meant.

"Ah, yes!" sighed Little Claus up on the shed when he saw all the good fare put away.

"Is there anyone up there?" asked the farmer; and he looked up and saw Little Claus. "What are you lying up there for? Better come down indoors with me."

And Little Claus told him how he had lost his way, and asked leave to stay there for the night.

"Yes, certainly," said the farmer; "but first we must have something to live upon."

The woman received them both very kindly, spread the cloth on a long table, and gave them a great dish of groats. The farmer was hungry, and ate with a good appetite, but Little Claus could not help thinking of the lovely roast meat, fish, and cake which he knew were in the oven. Under the table, at his feet, he had laid the sack with the horse's hide in it; for, as we know, he had left home to sell it in the town. He could not relish the groats at all, so he trod upon the sack with his foot, and the dry skin inside creaked quite loud.

"Hush!" said Little Claus to his sack, at the same time treading on it again till it squeaked louder than before.

"Why, what have you in your sack?" asked the farmer.

"Oh, that's a magician," said Little Claus. "He says we are not to eat groats, for he has conjured the oven full of roast meat, fish, and cake."

"Wonderful!" said the farmer; and he opened the oven door in a hurry, and found all the dainty food which his wife had hidden there, but which, as he thought, had been conjured there by the wizard under the table. The woman dared not say anything, but put the things at once on the table; and so they both ate of the meat, the fish, and the cake. Then Little Claus again trod on his sack and made the hide creak.

"What does he say now?" asked the farmer.

"He says," said Claus, "that he has conjured three bottles of wine for us too, and that they are standing there in the corner behind the oven."

So the woman was obliged to bring out the wine which she had hidden, and the farmer drank it, and became very merry. He would have been very glad to have such a conjurer as Little Claus had there in the sack.

"Can he conjure up the devil?" asked the farmer. "I should like to see him, for now I am merry."

"Oh, yes," said Little Claus, "my conjurer can do anything that I ask of him—can you not?" he asked, and trod on the hide till it squeaked. "Do you hear? He answers yes. But the devil is very ugly to look at; we had better not see him."

"Oh, I'm not at all afraid. Pray, what will he look like?"

"Well, he'll look the very image of a sexton!"

"Ha!" said the farmer, "that *is* ugly! You must know, I can't bear the sight of a sexton. But it doesn't matter now, for I know that he's the devil, so I shall easily stand it. Now I have got up my courage, but do not let him come too near me."

"Now I will ask my conjurer," said Little Claus; and he trod on the sack and held his ear down.

" What does he say? "

" He says you may go and open the chest that stands in the corner, and you will see the devil crouching inside it; but you must hold the lid so that he doesn't slip out."

" Will you help me to hold it? " said the farmer. And he went to the chest where the wife had hidden the real sexton, who now lay inside, very much frightened. The farmer opened the lid a little way and peeped in under it.

" Hu! " he cried, and sprang backward. " Yes, indeed, now I've seen him, and he looked exactly like our sexton. Oh, it was dreadful!"

After this he had to drink again. So they sat and drank until late into the night.

" That conjurer you must sell to me," said the farmer. " Ask for him what you will! I'll give you a whole bushel of money for him, at once!"

" No, that I can't do," said Little Claus! " Only think how much use I can make of this conjurer."

" Oh, I should so much like to have him! " said the farmer; and he went on begging.

" Well," said Little Claus at last, " as you have been so kind as to give me shelter for the night I will let it be so. You shall have the conjurer for a bushel of money, but I must have the bushel heaped up."

" That shall you have," said the farmer. " But you must take the chest away with you as well. I will not keep it in my house another hour. One cannot tell—perhaps he may be there still."

Little Claus gave the farmer his sack with the dry hide in it, and got in exchange a whole bushel of money, and that heaped up. The farmer also gave him a big wheelbarrow on which to carry off his money and the chest.

" Farewell! " said Little Claus; and he went off with his money and the big chest, in which the sexton was still sitting.

On the other side of the wood was a wide, deep river. The water rushed along so rapidly that one could scarcely swim against the stream. A fine new bridge had been built over it. Little Claus stopped on the middle of the bridge, and said quite loud, so that the sexton could hear it:

" Oh, what shall I do with this stupid chest? It's as heavy as if stones were in it. I shall only get tired out if I drag it any farther, so I'll throw it into the river. If it swims home to me, well and good; and if it does not it will be no great matter."

And he took the chest with one hand and lifted it up a little, as if he meant to throw it into the river.

" No! let be! " cried the sexton from within the chest. " Let me out first! "

" Hu! " said Little Claus, pretending to be frightened, " he's in there still! I must make haste and throw him into the river, so that he may be drowned."

" Oh, no! oh, no! " screamed the sexton. " I'll give you a whole bushel of money if you'll let me go."

" Why, that's another thing! " said Little Claus; and he opened the chest.

The sexton crept quickly out, pushed the empty chest into the water, and went to his house, where Little Claus received a whole bushel of money. He had already received one from the farmer, and so now he had his whole wheelbarrow full of money.

" See, I've been well paid for the horse," he said to himself when he had got home to his own room and was emptying all the money into a heap in the middle of the floor. " That will vex Big Claus when he hears how rich I have grown through my one horse, but I won't tell him about it outright."

So he sent a boy to Big Claus for the loan of a bushel measure.

" What can he want with it? " thought Big Claus. And he smeared some tar underneath the measure, so that some part of whatever was measured should stick to it. And so it happened, for when he got the measure back there were three new silver shillings sticking to it.

" What's this? " cried Big Claus; and he ran off at once to Little Claus. " Where did you get all that money from? "

" Oh, that's for my horse's skin. I sold it yesterday evening."

" That's really being well paid," said Big Claus. He ran home in a hurry, took an axe, and killed all his four horses; then he flayed them, and drove off to the town with their hides.

"Hides! hides! Who'll buy any hides?" he cried through the streets.

All the shoemakers and tanners came running, and asked how much he wanted for them.

"A bushel of money for each!" said Big Claus.

"Are you mad?" said they all. "Do you think we have money by the bushel?"

"Hides! hides!" he cried again; and to all who asked him what the hides cost he replied, "A bushel of money."

"He wants to make fools of us," they all said together. And the shoemakers took their straps, and the tanners their aprons, and began to beat Big Claus.

"Hides! hides!" they shouted mock-ingly after him. "Yes, we'll tan your hide for you till the blood runs. Out of the town with you!" And Big Claus made off at top-speed, for he had never before had such a thrashing in his life.

"Well," said he, when he got home, "Little Claus shall pay for this. I'll kill him for it."

Now at Little Claus's house the old grandmother had died. She had been very cross and unkind to him, but still he was very sorry, and took the dead woman and put her in his warm bed to see if she would not come to life again. There he meant her to lie all night, and he himself would sit in the corner and sleep on a chair, as he had often done before. As he sat there in the night the door opened, and Big Claus came in with his axe. He knew where Little Claus's bed stood, and, going straight to

149

it, he hit the old grandmother on the head, thinking she was Little
Claus.

"There now!" said he. "You shall not make a fool of me any
more." And so he went home again.

"That's a bad fellow, that man," said Little Claus. "He wanted
to kill me. It was a good thing for my old granny that she was dead
already, or else he would have taken her life."

So he dressed his old grandmother in her Sunday clothes, borrowed
a horse of his neighbour, harnessed it to the cart, and sat the old
grandmother up against the back seat, so that she could not fall out
when the cart started off. And off they drove through the wood. As
the sun rose they came to an inn. There Little Claus pulled up, and
went in to get something to eat.

The innkeeper was very, very rich; he was a very good man too,
but as hot-tempered as if he was full of pepper and snuff.

"Good morning," said he to Little Claus. "You've put on your
Sunday clothes early to-day."

"Yes," said Little Claus. "I am going to town with my old
grandmother; she's sitting out there in the wagon. I can't bring her
into the room—will you take her a glass of mead? But you must
speak pretty loud, for she can't hear well."

"Yes, that I will," said the innkeeper. And he poured out a big
glass of mead, and went out with it to the dead grandmother, who
had been propped up in the wagon.

"Here's a glass of mead from your son," said the innkeeper. But
the dead woman said not a word, but sat quite still. "Don't you
hear?" cried the innkeeper, as loud as he could. "Here is a glass of
mead from your son!"

Once more he bawled out the same thing, and yet again, but as she
did not move he flew into a passion, and threw the glass in her face, so
that the mead ran down over her nose, and she tumbled backwards into
the wagon, for she had only been propped up, and not bound fast.

"Hallo!" cried Little Claus, as he rushed out of the door and
seized the innkeeper by the throat. "You've killed my grandmother
now! See, there's a big hole in her forehead."

"Oh, what a misfortune!" cried the innkeeper, wringing his hands. "That all comes of my hot temper. Dear Little Claus, I'll give you a whole bushel of money, and have your grandmother buried as if she were my own; only keep quiet, or they will cut my head off, and that is so unpleasant!"

So Little Claus again received a whole bushel of money, and the innkeeper buried the old grandmother as if she had been his own. And when Little Claus came home with all his money he at once sent his boy to Big Claus to ask to borrow a bushel measure.

"How is this?" said Big Claus. "Have I not killed him? I must go myself and see to this." And so he went over himself with the bushel to Little Claus.

"Now, where did you get all that money from?" he asked; and he opened his eyes wide when he saw it all together.

"You killed my grandmother, and not me," replied Little Claus; "and I've been and sold her, and got a whole bushel of money for her."

"That's really being well paid," said Big Claus; and he hastened home, took an axe, and killed his own grandmother forthwith, put her on a wagon, drove off to the town with her, to where the apothecary lived, and asked him if he would buy a dead person.

"Who is it, and where did you get him from?" asked the apothecary.

"It's my grandmother," said Big Claus. "I've killed her to get a bushel of money for her."

"Heaven save us!" cried the apothecary. "You're raving! Don't say such things, or you may lose your head." And he told him earnestly what a bad deed he had done, and what a bad man he was, and that he ought to be punished. And Big Claus was so frightened that he sprang out of the apothecary's shop straight into his wagon, whipped up the horses, and drove off home. But the apothecary and all the people thought him mad, and so they let him drive wherever he liked.

"You shall pay for this!" said Big Claus when he got out upon the highroad. "Yes, you shall pay me for this, Little Claus!" And directly he got home he took the biggest sack he could find, and went over to Little Claus's, and said, " Now, you've tricked me again! First I killed my horses and then my old grandmother! And it's all your fault, but you shall never trick me any more." And he seized Little Claus round the body and pushed him into the sack, and took him upon his back, and shouted out to him, " Now I am going to drown you."

It was a long way he had to go before he came to the river, and Little Claus was no light weight to carry. The road passed close by a church: the organ was playing, and the people were singing so beautifully! So Big Claus put down his sack, with Little Claus in it, close to the church door, and thought it would be a very good thing to go in and hear a psalm before he went farther. Little Claus could not get out, and all the people were in church, and so he went in.

" Oh, dear! oh, dear! " sighed Little Claus in the sack. And he turned and twisted, but he found he could not loosen the cord. Soon there came by an old drover with snow-white hair, and a great staff in his hand. He was driving a whole herd of cows and oxen before him, and they stumbled against the sack in which lay Little Claus and knocked it over.

" Oh, dear! " sighed Little Claus. " I'm so young still, and so soon going to heaven! "

" And I, poor fellow," said the drover, " am so old already, and yet I can't get there! "

" Open the sack," cried Little Claus; " creep into it instead of me, and you will soon get to heaven."

"With all my heart," said the drover; and he untied the sack, out of which Little Claus jumped quickly.

" But will you look after the cattle? " said the old man, and he crept into the sack, whereupon Little Claus tied it up, and went his way with all the cows and oxen.

Soon after Big Claus came out of the church. He took the sack on his shoulders again, but it seemed to him as if the sack had become lighter, for the old drover was not more than half as heavy as Little Claus.

" How light he is to carry now! Yes, that is because I have heard a psalm."

So he went on to the river, which was deep and broad, threw the sack with the old drover in it into the water, and called after him, thinking that it was Little Claus, " You lie there! Now you shan't trick me any more! "

Then he went homeward; but when he came to a place where two roads crossed there he met Little Claus driving all his cattle.

" What's this? " cried Big Claus. " Have I not drowned you? "

" Yes," said Little Claus, " you threw me into the river less than half an hour ago."

" But wherever did you get all those fine beasts from? " asked Big Claus.

" They are sea-cattle," said Little Claus. " I'll tell you the whole story—and thank you for drowning me, for now I'm at the top of the tree. I am really rich! I was so frightened when I lay in the sack, and the wind whistled about my ears when you threw me from the bridge into the cold water! I sank to the bottom immediately; but I did not hurt myself, for the most beautiful soft grass grows down there. Upon that I fell; and immediately the sack was opened, and the loveliest maiden, with snow-white clothes and a green wreath upon her wet hair, took me by the hand, and said, ' Are you come, Little Claus? Here you have some cattle to begin with. A mile farther along the road there is a whole herd more, which I will give to you.' And then I saw that the river formed a great highway for the people of the sea. Along its bed they were walking and driving straight from the sea, right up into the land, to where the river ends. It was all covered with flowers and the freshest grass; the fishes which swam in the water darted past my ears, like the birds in the air. What nice people there were there, and what fine cattle grazing in the hills and valleys! "

" But why did you come up again to us so quickly? " asked Big Claus. " I should not have done so, if it is so beautiful down there."

" Why," said Little Claus, " that was just good policy on my part. You heard me tell you that the sea-maiden said, ' A mile farther along

153

the road '—and by the road she meant the river, for she can't go anywhere else—' there is a whole herd of cattle for you.' But I know
what bends the stream makes—sometimes this way, sometimes that;
it's a long way to go round. No, it can be done in a shorter way by
coming up to the land and driving across the fields to the river again.
In this manner I save myself almost half a mile, and get all the quicker
to my sea-cattle!"

"Oh, you are a lucky man!" said Big Claus. "Do you think I
should get some sea-cattle too if I went down to the bottom of the
river?"

"Yes, I think so," said Little Claus. "But I cannot carry you in
the sack as far as the river; you are too heavy for me! But if you will
go there, and creep into the sack yourself, I will throw you in with a
great deal of pleasure."

"Thanks!" said Big Claus; "but if I don't get any sea-cattle
when I am down there I shall beat you, you may be sure!"

"Oh, no; don't be so fierce!"

And so they went together to the river. When the cattle, which
were thirsty, saw the stream they ran as fast as they could to get at
the water.

"See how they hurry!" cried Little Claus. "They are longing to
get back to the bottom."

"Yes, but help me first," said Big Claus, "or else you'll get a
thrashing!"

And so he crept into the great sack, which had been laid across the
back of one of the oxen.

"Put a stone in, I'm afraid I shan't sink else," said Big Claus.

"There's no fear of that," said Little Claus. Still, he put a big
stone into the sack, tied the rope tightly, and gave it a push. Plump!
Into the river went Big Claus, and sank at once to the bottom.

"I'm afraid he won't find any cattle!" said Little Claus; and then
he drove home those he had.

THE TINDER-BOX

A SOLDIER was marching along the highroad—left, right! left, right! He had a knapsack on his back and a sword at his side. He was returning from war, and was now on his way home.

When he had gone some distance he met an old witch. She was dreadfully ugly; her underlip was hanging down upon her breast.

She said, "Good evening, soldier! What a fine sword you have, and what a big knapsack! You are a true soldier! Now you shall have as much money as ever you wish for."

"Thank you, old witch," replied the soldier.

"Do you see that big tree?" said the witch, pointing out a tree which stood not far from them. "It is hollow inside! You must climb right up to the top, and then you will see a hole; through this hole you can let yourself down and get deep into the tree. I will tie a rope round your waist, so that I can pull you up when you call out to me."

"What shall I do down in the tree?" asked the soldier.

"Fetch money!" said the witch. "You must know that you will find a great hall at the bottom of the tree; it is quite light, for there are more than a hundred lamps burning down there. You will then see three doors; you can open them—the keys are in the locks. If you enter the first room you will find in the middle of the floor a large wooden chest and a dog sitting on it that has a pair of eyes as big as teacups. Never mind him! I will give you my blue-checked apron, which you must spread on the floor; then go quickly, seize the dog and place him on my apron, open the chest, and take out of it as much money as you like. It is all copper; if you would rather have silver, you must go into the second room. There you will see a dog with eyes as big as mill-wheels. But do not be afraid; put him on my apron and take the money. If, however, you wish to have gold, you can have that too, and as much as you can carry, if you go into the third room. But the dog sitting on that box has eyes as big as the Round Tower of Copenhagen: he *is* a dog, I can tell you, but you need not fear him. Only put him on my apron and he will not hurt you, and you can take as much gold as you like out of the chest."

" That is not so bad," said the soldier. " But what do you expect me to give you in return? For you will not do all this for nothing, I'll be bound."

"Yes," replied the witch. "I shall not ask you for a single penny. I only want you to bring up for me an old tinder-box which my grandmother forgot last time she was down there."

" Well, then, tie the rope round my waist," said the soldier.

" Here it is," said the witch, " and here is my blue-checked apron."

The soldier then climbed up the tree, let himself down into it by the rope, and found himself, as the witch had told him, in the great hall where the many lamps were burning.

He opened the first door. Ugh! there sat the dog with the eyes as big as teacups staring at him.

" You are a fine fellow," said the soldier, placed him on the apron of the witch, and took as many coppers as his pockets would hold. Then he locked the chest, put the dog upon it, and went on to the second room. Aha! there was the dog with the eyes as large as mill-wheels.

" Don't you stare at me so hard," said the soldier; " you might strain your eyes," and he put the dog on the witch's apron. When he saw the silver in the chest he threw away all the coppers he had taken, and filled his pockets and his knapsack with silver. Then he went into the third room. That was dreadful! The dog there had really two eyes as big as the Round Tower, and they went round in his head like wheels.

" Good evening," said the soldier, and touched his cap, for he had never in his life seen a dog like this. When he had looked at him for a bit he thought, " That'll do," lifted him down on to the floor, and

"I'LL DRAW MY SWORD AND CUT YOUR HEAD OFF!"

opened the chest. Good heavens! what a lot of gold there was! There was enough gold to buy the whole of Copenhagen and all the sugar-pigs from the cake-women, as well as all the tin soldiers, whips, and rocking-horses in the world. Yes, there was plenty of money there, sure enough! The soldier quickly threw away all the silver with which he had filled his pockets and his knapsack, and took gold instead. He crammed his pockets and his knapsack and even his cap and his boots with gold, so that he could scarcely walk. Now he really had a lot of money.

He placed the dog again on the chest, shut the door, and called up through the tree:

" Now pull me up, old witch."

" Have you found the tinder-box?" asked the old witch.

" Upon my soul," said the soldier, " I had really forgotten it." And he went back and fetched it. The old witch pulled him up, and soon he was again standing on the highroad, with his pockets, boots, knapsack, and cap full of gold.

" What will you do with the tinder-box?" asked the soldier.

" That's no business of yours," said the witch. " You have got your money. Give me the tinder-box."

" Sniksnak!" replied the soldier. " Tell me quick what you are going to do with it, or I'll draw my sword and cut your head off!"

" No," said the witch.

Then the soldier cut her head off. There she lay! And he tied all his gold up in her apron, slung it like a bundle on his shoulders, put the tinder-box into his pocket, and went straight to the town.

It was a fine town. He put up at the best inn, asked for the very best rooms and for his favourite dishes; for he was rich, now he had so much gold.

The servant who had to clean his boots thought they were rather shabby old things for such a rich gentleman, for he had not yet bought a new pair. Next day, however, he bought decent boots and fine clothes. And now our soldier had become a fine gentleman, and people told him all about the grand things in their town, and about the King, and what a beautiful princess his daughter was.

"Where can one see her?" asked the soldier.

"She cannot be seen at all," they all said. "She lives in a strong copper castle with many towers, surrounded by high walls! Nobody but the King himself can go in and out, for it has been foretold that she will marry a private soldier, and that the King will not hear of!"

"I should very much like to see her," thought the soldier, but there was no way of getting permission for that.

He began to lead a merry life, went to the play, drove in the royal park, and gave largely to the poor, and that was very good of him, for well he knew from former days what it meant to be without a single penny. He was now rich, had fine clothes, and soon found many friends, who all told him that he was a rare one and a true cavalier; all this pleased the soldier greatly. But, as each day he spent a good deal of money without receiving any, he had soon nothing but twopence left. So he had to give up the elegant rooms which he occupied and live at the top of the house in a little garret, he had to black his own boots, and to mend them himself with a darning-needle, and none of his former friends came to see him, for there were so many stairs to climb.

One dark evening he could not even buy a candle—when suddenly he remembered that there was a little stump of candle in the tinder-box which he had fetched out of the hollow tree with the help of the witch. He got out the tinder-box with the candle-end in it, and the instant he struck the flint and the sparks began to fly the door burst open and the dog with the eyes as large as teacups which he had seen down under the tree stood before him, and asked: "What are your lordship's commands?"

"What's this?" said the soldier. "That is a capital tinder-box if I can get whatever I wish for with it. Get me some money," he said to the dog. The dog was gone like lightning; but in a moment he was back again, with a large bag of coppers in his mouth.

In this way the soldier learned what a wonderful tinder-box he had. If he struck once, there came the dog from the chest containing the copper; if he struck twice, the dog who had the silver came; and if he struck three times, the dog who sat on the chest containing the gold made his appearance. So the soldier moved back into the elegant rooms, and wore his fine clothes again. All his former friends knew him once more, and made much of him.

One day the soldier thought, " It is very strange that nobody can get a sight of the Princess! All agree in saying that she is so beautiful; but what is the use of that if she has to stay for ever in the big copper castle with its many towers? Can I never manage to get to see her? Where is my tinder-box?" And he struck a spark, and there at once stood the dog with a pair of eyes as big as teacups.

"It is midnight, I know," said the soldier, "but I should very much like to see the Princess just for one moment."

The dog was out of the room in an instant, and before the soldier had time to think he was back again with the Princess. There she was, fast asleep on the dog's back, and she was so lovely that nobody could help seeing at once that she was a real princess. The soldier could not help it—he had to kiss her, for he was a true soldier.

Then the dog ran back with the Princess; but next morning, when the King and Queen were having their cup of tea, she told them that she had had a very strange dream during the night of a dog and a soldier; she had been riding on the dog and the soldier had kissed her.

"That's a pretty tale," said the Queen.

So next night one of the old Court ladies had to watch by the bed of the Princess to see whether it was really a dream, or what else it could be.

The soldier had such a longing to see the Princess again that at night he again sent for the dog, who went and fetched her and ran off with her as fast as he could. But the old lady put on water-boots and followed, running as fast as he did. When she saw them disappear into a large house she took a piece of chalk and made a large white cross on the door, and thought, "Now I shall know the house again." Then she returned home and went to bed. The dog soon brought the Princess back; and when he saw the white cross on the house where the soldier lived he took a bit of chalk too and made crosses on all the doors in the town. And that was very clever of him, for now the lady could not find the right door, as there were crosses on all of them.

160

Early next morning the King, the Queen, the lady, and all the officers of the Court went to see where the Princess had been.

"There is the house," said the King, when he saw the first door with a white cross.

"No; there it is, my dear husband," said the Queen, who saw a second door with a white cross.

"But there is one, and there is another," said all, and wherever they looked they saw white crosses on the doors. They soon saw that it would be useless to search any more.

But the Queen was a very clever woman; she could do more than merely ride in a carriage. She took her big golden scissors, cut a large piece of silk into squares, and made a nice little bag of it, and this she filled with fine buckwheat groats. Then she tied it to the Princess's back, and cut a little hole in it, so that the buckwheat could run out all along the road the Princess was taken.

At night the dog came again, took the Princess on his back, and ran with her to the soldier, who was deeply in love with her, and who only wished that he was a prince, that he might make her his wife.

The dog did not notice how the buckwheat was strewed all the way from the castle up to the soldier's window, where he climbed up the wall with the Princess. Next morning the King and Queen saw well enough where their daughter had been taken to, and the soldier was at once arrested and thrown into prison.

There he sat. Oh, how dark and dismal it was! He was told, "To-morrow you will be hanged." That was not pleasant to hear, and the worst of it was that he had left his tinder-box at the inn.

In the morning he could see through the iron bars how the people were hurrying out of the town to see him hanged. He heard the drums and saw the soldiers march past. All the world was going, and among them was a shoemaker's apprentice in his leather apron and slippers, who ran so fast that one of his slippers came off and flew against the wall, close under the window where the soldier sat behind the iron bars.

"Hi! You cobbler's boy! Don't be in such a hurry!" cried the soldier. "They can't do anything until I arrive. But if you would run to the place where I used to live and fetch me my tinder-box I will give you twopence! But you must put your best foot foremost!"

The boy, who was very anxious to have the money, fetched the tinder-box, handed it to the soldier, and—yes, now we shall see what happened.

Outside the town they had erected a high gibbet; soldiers and many thousands of people stood round it. The King and the Queen were sitting on a magnificent throne opposite the judges and Council.

The soldier was already standing on the top of the ladder, and they were just going to put the rope round his neck when he said he knew that it was the custom to grant a last request to a poor criminal before he suffered death, and he should very much like to smoke a pipe—the last he would ever have a chance of smoking in this world.

The King would not refuse this favour, and the soldier took up his tinder-box and struck—"One, two, three." And suddenly there stood all the dogs—the first with eyes as big as teacups, the second with eyes as big as mill-wheels, and the third with eyes as big as the Round Tower.

"Help me now, so that I shan't be hanged!" said the soldier.

Then the dogs rushed at the judges and the councillors, took one up by the legs, another by the nose, and threw them many fathoms high into the air, so that they fell down and were smashed to pieces.

"Let me be!" said the King; but the biggest of the dogs seized both him and the Queen and threw them up after the others.

Then the soldiers became frightened, and all the people cried out, "Little soldier, you shall be our King and marry the beautiful Princess!"

Then they seated the soldier in the King's carriage, and the three dogs danced in front of it and cried, "Hurrah!" The boys whistled on their fingers, and the soldiers presented arms. The Princess came out of the copper castle and became Queen, and she liked it very much.

The wedding festivities lasted eight days; the dogs sat at table and stared with all their eyes.

THUMBELISA

THERE was once a woman who wished for a tiny little child, but she did not know where she could get one. So she went to an old witch and said:

"I do so long for a little child! Can you not tell me where I can get one?"

"Oh! that can easily be managed," said the witch. "Here is a barley-corn for you; it is not the kind that grows in the country-man's field, or that the chickens get to eat. Set that in a flower-pot, and you shall see what you shall see."

"Thank you," said the woman; and she gave the witch a shilling, went home, and planted the barley-corn, and immediately there grew up a big handsome flower, which looked like a tulip; but the leaves were tightly closed, as though it was still a bud.

"That is a beautiful flower," said the woman; and she kissed its pretty yellow and red leaves. But just as she kissed it the flower opened with a pop. It was a real tulip, one could see that; but in the middle of the flower upon the green velvet stamens there sat a little tiny girl, so fine and graceful, and scarcely half a thumb's length in height, and therefore she was called Thumbelisa.

A neat polished walnut-shell served Thumbelisa for a cradle, blue violet-leaves were her mattresses, with a rose-leaf for a coverlet. There she slept at night, but in the daytime she played upon the table, where the woman had put a plate with a wreath of flowers round it, whose stalks stood in water; on the water was floating a large tulip-leaf, and on this Thumbelisa could sit, and sail from one side of the plate to the other, and she had two white horsehairs to row with. That was pretty indeed! She could also sing, and, oh, so delicately and sweetly that the like had never been heard before.

Once, as she lay at night in her pretty bed, there came an old toad hopping through the window, in which one pane was broken. The toad was very ugly, big, and damp; it hopped right down on to the table, where Thumbelisa lay sleeping under the red rose-leaf.

"That would be a lovely wife for my son," said the toad; and she picked up the walnut-shell in which Thumbelisa lay asleep and hopped with it through the window down into the garden.

There there ran a great broad brook; but the margin was swampy

"DON'T SPEAK SO LOUD, OR SHE WILL WAKE UP"

and soft, and here the toad dwelt with her son. Ugh! he was ever so ugly and foul, and looked just like his mother. "Koaks, koaks! brekke-ke-keks!" That was all he could say when he saw the graceful little maiden in the walnut-shell.

"Don't speak so loud, or she will wake up," said the old toad. "She might run away from us, for she is as light as swansdown. We will put her out in the brook upon one of the broad water-lily leaves. That will be just like an island for her, she is so small and light! Then she can't run away while we put the best room under the marsh in order, where you are to live and keep house together."

Out in the brook there grew a great many water-lilies with broad green leaves, which looked as if they were floating on the water. The leaf which was farthest out was also the largest of all, and to that the old toad swam out and laid the walnut-shell upon it with Thumbelisa. The poor little mite woke very early in the morning, and when she saw where she was she began to cry most bitterly, for there was water on all sides of the big green leaf, and she could not get to the land at all. The old toad sat down in the marsh, decking out her room with rushes and yellow water-weeds—it was to be made very pretty for the new daughter-in-law; then she swam out, with her ugly son, to the leaf where Thumbelisa was standing. They had come to fetch her pretty bed, to put it in the bridal chamber before she went in there herself. The old toad bowed low before her in the water, and said:

" See, here is my son; he will be your husband, and you will live so happily together in the marsh."

" Koaks, koaks! brekke-ke-keks!" That was all her son could say.

Then they took the delicate little bed and swam away with it; but Thumbelisa sat all alone upon the green leaf and cried, for she did not want to live at the nasty toad's, and have her ugly son for a husband. The little fishes swimming in the water below had seen the toad, and they had heard what she said; and so they lifted up their heads out of the water, for they wanted to see the little girl. As soon as they saw her they thought she was so pretty that they felt very sorry she should have to go down to the ugly toad. No, that must never be! They all collected in the water round the green stalk which held the leaf on which she stood, and with their teeth they gnawed through the stalk, and so the leaf floated down the stream. And away went Thumbelisa with it, far away where the toad could not get at her.

Thumbelisa sailed by many towns, and the little birds that sat in the bushes saw her, and sang, " What a lovely little maiden!" The leaf swam away with her, farther and farther; so Thumbelisa travelled to foreign lands.

A sweet little white butterfly kept fluttering round her, and at last settled on the leaf. He had taken a fancy to Thumbelisa, and she was very glad too, for now the toad could not reach them; and it was so beautiful where she was sailing—the sun shone upon the water, that glittered like shining gold. She took her sash and bound one end of it to the butterfly, and the other end of the ribbon she fastened to the leaf. It now glided on much faster, and she with it, for she stood upon the leaf.

Just then there came a big cockchafer flying past, and saw her, and in a moment he seized her slender waist in his claws, and flew with her up into a tree. The green leaf went swimming down the stream, and the butterfly with it, for he was fastened to the leaf and could not get away.

Mercy! how frightened poor little Thumbelisa was when the cockchafer flew with her up into the tree! But most of all she was sorry for the pretty white butterfly she had bound fast to the leaf, for if he could not free himself he would starve. The big cockchafer, however, did not trouble himself at all about this. He sat down with her upon the biggest green leaf of the tree, gave her the sweet part of the flowers to eat, and declared that she was very pretty, though she was not at all like a cockchafer. Afterwards all the other cockchafers who lived in the tree came to pay a visit. They looked at Thumbelisa, and the young lady cockchafers turned up their feelers and said:

" Why, she has no more than two legs!—that is most ungainly."

" She has not any feelers! " said they.

" Her waist is quite slender—fie! she looks like a human creature —how ugly she is! " said all the lady cockchafers.

And yet Thumbelisa was very beautiful! Even the cockchafer who had carried her off saw that; but when all the others said she was ugly he believed it at last, and would not have her at all—she might go where she liked. Then they flew down with her off the tree, and set her upon a daisy, and she cried, because she was so ugly that the cockchafers would have nothing to say to her; and yet she was the loveliest little being one could imagine, and as tender and fair as the most beautiful rose-leaf.

The whole summer through poor Thumbelisa lived quite alone in the great wood. She plaited herself a bed out of blades of grass, and

166

hung it up under a large burdock leaf, so that she was protected from the rain. She sucked the honey out of the flowers for food, and drank the dew that stood every morning upon the leaves. Thus the summer and the autumn passed away, but then came the winter, the cold, long winter. All the birds who had sung so sweetly to her flew away; trees and flowers shed their leaves; the great burdock under which she had lived shrivelled up, and there was nothing left of it but a yellow withered stalk; and she was dreadfully cold, for her clothes were torn, and she herself was so frail and small—poor Thumbelisa!— she was nearly frozen. It began to snow, and every snowflake that fell upon her was like a whole shovelful thrown upon one of us, for we are big, and she was only an inch long. Then she wrapped herself up in a dry leaf, but that would not keep her warm, and she shivered with cold.

Just outside the wood she came to a great cornfield, but the corn was gone long ago, only the naked dry stubble stood up out of the frozen ground. This was just like a great forest for her to struggle through. Oh, how she shivered with cold! Then she came to the door of a field-mouse. This was a little hole under the stubble. There the field-mouse lived, warm and comfortable, and had a whole room-ful of corn, and a fine kitchen and larder. Poor Thumbelisa stood at the door just like a poor beggar girl, and begged for a little bit of barley-corn, for she had not had the smallest morsel to eat for two days.

"You poor little creature," said the field-mouse—for really she was a good old field-mouse—" come into my warm room and have some food with me!"

As she was pleased with Thumbelisa, she said, "If you like you may stay with me through the winter, but you must keep my room clean and neat, and tell me stories, for I am very fond of them."

And Thumbelisa did as the kind old field-mouse bade her, and had a very good time of it.

"Now we shall soon have a visitor," said the field-mouse. "My neighbour is in the habit of visiting me once a week. He is even better off than I am; has large rooms, and goes about in such a beautiful black velvety fur. If you could only get him for a husband you would be well provided for, but he cannot see. You must tell him all the prettiest stories you know."

But Thumbelisa did not care about this; she thought nothing of the neighbour, for he was a mole. He came and paid a visit in his black velvet coat. The field-mouse told her how rich and how wise he was, and how his house was more than twenty times larger than hers, that he had learning, but that he did not like the sun and beautiful flowers, and sneered at them, for he had never seen them.

Thumbelisa had to sing, and she sang both *Cockchafer, fly, fly away!* and *The Monk goes to the Field.* Then the mole fell in love with her, because of her beautiful voice, but he said nothing, for he was a prudent man.

A short time before he had dug a long passage through the earth from his own house to theirs; and Thumbelisa and the field-mouse had leave to walk there as much as they wished. But he begged them not to be afraid of the dead bird which was lying in the passage. It was a whole bird, with wings and a beak. It must have died only a short time before, when the winter began, and was now buried just where the mole had made his passage.

The mole took a piece of decayed touchwood in his mouth, for that glimmers like fire in the dark, and then he went first and lighted them through the long dark passage. When they came where the dead bird lay the mole thrust up his broad nose against the ceiling and pushed the earth up, so that a great hole was made, through which the daylight could shine down. In the middle of the floor lay a dead swallow, his beautiful wings pressed close against his sides, and his head and feet drawn back under his feathers; the poor bird had certainly died of cold. Thumbelisa was very sorry for this, for she was very fond of all the little birds, who had sung and twittered so prettily for her through the summer; but the mole gave him a push with his crooked legs, and said, " Now he won't pipe any more. It must be miserable to be born a little bird! I'm thankful that none of my children can be that! Such a bird has nothing but his ' tweet-weet,' and has to starve in the winter! "

"Yes, you may well say that, as a clever man," observed the field-mouse. " Of what use is all this ' tweet-weet' to a bird when the winter comes? He must starve and freeze. But they say that's very grand!"

Thumbelisa said nothing; but when the two others had their backs turned she bent down, put the feathers aside which covered his head, and kissed him upon his closed eyes.

" Perhaps it was he who sang so prettily for me in the summer," she thought. "How much pleasure he gave me, the dear, beautiful bird!"

The mole now stopped up the hole through which the daylight shone, and showed the ladies home. But at night Thumbelisa could not sleep at all; so she got up out of her bed, and plaited a large beautiful carpet of hay, and took it and spread it over the dead bird, and laid some soft cotton-wool which she had found in the field-mouse's room at the bird's sides, so that he might lie warm on the cold ground.

" Farewell, you pretty little bird!" said she. "Farewell! And thanks for your beautiful song in the summer, when all the trees were green, and the sun shone warmly upon us." And then she laid her head on the bird's breast; but the next moment she was startled to hear something beating inside the bird. It was the bird's heart. The bird was not dead; he was only lying there torpid, and now he had been warmed, and came to life again.

In autumn all the swallows fly away to warm countries; but if one happens to be left behind it becomes so cold that it falls down as if dead, and lies where it fell, and then the cold snow covers it over.

Thumbelisa trembled all over, she was so startled; for the bird was big, big compared with her, who was only an inch in height. But she took courage, laid the cotton-wool closer round the poor bird, and brought a leaf of mint that she had used as her own coverlet, and laid it over the bird's head.

The next night she stole out to him again, and now he was alive, but so weak that he could only open his eyes for a moment and look at Thumbelisa, who stood before him with a bit of decayed wood in her hand, for she had no other light.

"I thank you, you pretty little child," said the sick swallow to her. "I feel so beautifully warm! Soon I shall get my strength back again, and I shall be able to fly again, out in the warm sunshine."

"Oh," she said, "it is so cold outside. It snows and freezes. Stay in your warm bed, and I will nurse you."

Then she brought the swallow water in the petal of a flower, and he drank it, and told her how he had torn one of his wings in a thorn bush, and so had not been able to fly as fast as the other swallows, which had sped far, far away to warm countries. So at last he had fallen to the ground, but he could remember nothing more, and did not know at all how he had come where she had found him.

The whole winter he remained there, and Thumbelisa took care of him and grew very fond of him. Neither the field-mouse nor the mole heard anything about it, for they did not like the poor swallow. As soon as the spring came and the sun warmed the earth the swallow bade Thumbelisa farewell, and she opened the hole which the mole had made in the ground above. The sun shone in upon them brightly, and the swallow asked if Thumbelisa would go away with him; she could sit upon his back, and they would fly away far into the green forest. But Thumbelisa knew that the old field-mouse would be grieved if she left her like this.

"No, I cannot!" said Thumbelisa.

"Farewell, farewell, you good, pretty girl!" said the swallow; and he flew out into the sunshine. Thumbelisa looked after him, and the tears came into her eyes, for she had become so fond of the poor swallow.

"Tweet-weet! tweet-weet!" sang the bird, and flew into the green forest. Thumbelisa felt very sad. She was not allowed to go out into the warm sunshine. The corn which was sown in the field over the house of the field-mouse had grown high into the air; it was quite a thick wood for the poor little girl, who was only an inch in height.

"You must get your outfit ready to be married this summer,"

said the field-mouse to her, for their neighbour, the tiresome mole in the black velvet coat, had proposed for her. " You must have both woollen and linen! You shall have things to wear, and to lie upon too, when you are the Mole's wife! "

Thumbelisa had to spin, and the mole hired four spiders to weave for her day and night. Every evening the mole paid her a visit; and he was always saying that when the summer should end the sun

would not shine nearly so hot, for that now it burned the earth almost as hard as stone. Yes, when the summer was over then he would keep his wedding day with Thumbelisa. But she was not glad at all, for she did not like the tiresome mole. Every morning when the sun rose, and every evening when it went down, she stole out of the door, and when the wind blew the corn aside, so that she could see the blue sky, she thought how bright and beautiful it was out here, and wished heartily to see her dear swallow again. But he did not come back any more; he must have flown far away into the beautiful green forest. When autumn came Thumbelisa had all her outfit ready.

" In four weeks you shall have your wedding! " said the field-mouse to her.

But Thumbelisa cried, and said she would not have the tiresome mole.

" Stuff and nonsense ! " said the field-mouse. " Don't be obstinate, or I'll bite you with my white tooth. He is a very fine man to marry. The Queen herself has not such a black velvet fur, and his kitchen and cellar are full. Be thankful to get him ! "

So the wedding was to take place. The mole had already come to fetch Thumbelisa; she was to live with him deep under the ground, and never to come out into the warm sunshine, for he did not like it. The poor little child was very sorrowful; she had now to say farewell to the beautiful sun, which at least she had been allowed by the field-mouse to see from the threshold of the door.

" Farewell, thou bright sun ! " she said, and stretched up her arms to it, as she walked a little way from the field-mouse's house, for now the corn had been reaped, and only the dry stubble stood in the fields. " Farewell, farewell ! " said she, and she threw her little arms round a small red flower close by her. " Give my love to the dear swallow from me, if you see him again."

" Tweet-weet ! tweet-weet ! " A voice suddenly sounded over her head. She looked up; it was the swallow, who was just flying by. As soon as he saw Thumbelisa he was very glad; and she told him how unwilling she was to have the ugly mole for her husband, and that she would have to live deep under the earth, where the sun never shone. She could not help crying about it.

" The cold winter is coming now," said the swallow; " I am going to fly far away to warm countries. Will you come with me? You can sit upon my back. Tie yourself on with your sash, and we will fly away from the ugly mole and his dark room, far away over the mountains to warm countries where the sun shines brighter than here, where it is always summer, and there are lovely flowers. Only fly with me, you dear little Thumbelisa, you who saved my life when I lay frozen in the dark, earthy passage."

" Yes, I will go with you ! " said Thumbelisa, and she seated herself on the bird's back, with her feet on his outspread wing, and tied her sash fast to one of his strongest feathers. Then the swallow flew high up into the air over forest and sea, high up over the great mountains, where the snow always lies; and Thumbelisa froze in the cold air, but then she crept under the bird's warm feathers, and only stuck out her little head to see all the beauty beneath her.

At last they reached the warm countries. There the sun shone much brighter than here, the sky seemed twice as high, on the hedges grew the most beautiful blue and green grapes, lemons and oranges hung in the woods, the air was fragrant with myrtles and balsams, and on the roads the loveliest children ran about, playing with the large gay butterflies. But the swallow flew still farther, and it became more and more beautiful. Under the magnificent green trees by the blue lake stood a palace of dazzling white marble, of the olden time. Vines wound themselves round the lofty pillars, and at the top were many swallows' nests, in one of which lived the swallow who carried Thumbelisa.

" That is my house," said the swallow; " but if you will choose for yourself one of the lovely flowers that are growing there I will put you into it, and you shall be as happy as you could wish."

" That would be delightful," said she, and clapped her little hands.

A great white marble pillar lay there which had fallen to the ground and broken into three pieces; but between these grew the most beautiful big white flowers. The swallow flew down with Thumbelisa, and sat her upon one of the broad leaves. But what was her surprise! There sat a little man in the middle of the flower, as white and transparent as if he had been made of glass; he had the loveliest gold crown on his head, and beautiful bright wings on his shoulders; he himself was no bigger than Thumbelisa. He was the angel of the flower. In each of the flowers dwelt such a little man or woman, but this one was king over them all.

" Heavens! how beautiful he is! " whispered Thumbelisa to the swallow.

The little prince was very much frightened at the swallow; for it was quite a giant bird to him, who was so small and delicate. But when he saw Thumbelisa he was delighted; she was the prettiest maiden he had ever seen. Therefore he took his golden crown off his head and put it on hers, asked her name, and if she would be his wife, and then she should be queen of all the flowers. Yes, this was truly a different kind of man to the toad's son or the mole with the black velvet fur. So she said " Yes " to the charming Prince. And from every flower came a lady or a gentleman, so pretty to behold

that it was a delight; each one brought Thumbelisa a present. But the best of all was a pair of beautiful wings from a great white butter-fly; these were fastened to Thumbelisa's back, and then she too could fly from flower to flower. Then there was much rejoicing; and the swallow sat above them in his nest, and sang to them as well as he could; but in his heart he was sad, for he was so fond of Thumbelisa that he would have liked never to part from her.

174

"You shall not be called Thumbelisa," said the Flower Angel to her; "it is an ugly name, and you are so pretty. We will call you Maia!"

"Farewell, farewell!" said the swallow; and he flew away again from the warm countries, back to Denmark. There he had a little nest over the window where the man lives who can tell fairy tales. To him he sang, "Tweet-weet! tweet-weet!" and from him we have the whole story.

ELDER-TREE MOTHER

THERE was once a little boy who had caught cold: he had gone out and got wet feet. Nobody had the least idea how he had got them wet; the weather was quite dry. His mother undressed him, put him to bed, and ordered the teapot to be brought in that she might make him a good cup of tea from elder-tree blossoms, which is so warming. At the same time the amusing old man who lived by himself in the upper story of the house came in. He led a lonely life, for he had no wife and children; but he loved the children of others very much, and he could tell so many fairy tales and stories that it was a pleasure to hear him.

"Now, drink your tea," said the mother; "perhaps you will hear a story."

"Yes, if I only knew a fresh one," said the old man, and nodded smilingly. "But how did the little fellow get his wet feet?" he then asked.

"Yes, how indeed!" said the mother. "Nobody can understand."

"Will you tell me a story?" asked the boy.

"Yes, if you can tell me as nearly as possible how deep is the gutter in the little street where you go to school."

"Just half as high as my top-boots," replied the boy; "but then I must stand in the deepest holes."

"There, now we know where you got your wet feet," said the old man. "I ought by right to tell you a story now, but I do not know any more."

"You can make one up," said the little boy. "Mother says everything you look at you can turn into a fairy tale, and that you can tell a story about anything you touch."

"That is all very well, but such tales or stories are worth nothing! No, the right ones come by themselves and knock at my forehead, saying, ' Here I am.' "

"Will not one knock soon?" asked the boy; and the mother laughed while she put elder-tree blossoms into the teapot and poured boiling water over them. "A story! A story!"

"Yes, if stories came by themselves; but they are so proud they only come when they please. Wait," he said suddenly, "there is one. Look at the teapot; there is a story in it now."

And the little boy looked at the teapot; the lid rose up gradually, the elder-tree blossoms sprang forth one by one, fresh and white; long boughs came forth; even out of the spout they grew up in all directions, and formed a bush—nay, a large elder-tree, which stretched its branches up to the bed and pushed the curtains aside; and there were so many blossoms and such a sweet fragrance! In the midst of the tree sat a kindly looking old woman with a strange dress: it was as green as the leaves, and trimmed with large white elder-blossoms, so that it was difficult to say whether it was real cloth or the leaves and blossoms of the elder-tree.

"What is this woman's name?" asked the little boy.

"Well, the Romans and Greeks used to call her a dryad," said the old man; "but we do not understand that. Out in the sailors' quarter they give her a better name: there she is called Elder-tree Mother. It is to her you must pay attention now and look at the beautiful elder-tree.

"Just such a large tree, covered with flowers, stands out at Nyboder. It grew in the corner of a poor little yard; under this tree sat two old people one afternoon in the beautiful sunshine. He was an old, old sailor and she his old, old wife; they had already great-grandchildren, and were soon to celebrate their golden wedding, but they could not remember the date, and the elder-tree mother was sitting in the tree and looked pleased, just as she does here. 'I know very well when the golden wedding is,' she said; but they did not hear it—they were talking of bygone days.

"'Well, do you remember,' said the old sailor, 'when we were quite small and used to run about and play—it was in the very same yard where we now are—we used to put little branches into the ground and make a garden?'

"'Yes,' said the old woman, 'I remember it very well; we used to water the branches, and one of them, an elder-tree branch, took root, and grew and became the large tree under which we are now sitting as old people.'

"'Certainly, you are right,' he said; 'and over there in the corner stood a large water-tub. There I used to sail my boat, which I had cut out myself—how well it sailed. But soon I had to sail somewhere else.'

"'But first we went to school to learn something,' she said, 'and then we were confirmed. We both cried on that day, but in the afternoon we went hand in hand up the Round Tower and looked out upon the world over Copenhagen and the sea; then we walked to Fredericksberg, where the King and Queen were sailing about in their magnificent boat on the canals.'

"'But soon I had to sail about somewhere else, and for many years I was travelling about far away from home.'

"'And I often cried for you, for I was afraid you were dead and gone and lying rocked by the waves at the bottom of the sea. Many a time I got up in the night to look if the weathercock had turned; it turned often, but you did not return. I remember one day clearly: the rain was pouring down in torrents; the dustman had come to the house where I was in service; I went down with the dust-bin and stood for a moment in the doorway. What dreadful weather it was! As I stood there the postman came up and gave me a letter; it was from you. How it had travelled about! I tore it open and read it; I cried and laughed at the same time, I was so happy! There it was written that you were staying in the hot countries, where the coffee grows. They must be marvellous countries. You said a great deal about them, and I read it all while the rain was pouring down and I was standing there with the dust-bin. Then suddenly someone put his arm round my waist——'

"'Yes, and you gave him a hearty box on the ear, one that sounded!'

"'I did not know that it was you—you had come as quickly as your letter; and you looked so handsome, and so you do still. You

178

"WE WENT HAND IN HAND UP THE ROUND TOWER"

had a large yellow silk handkerchief in your pocket and a shining hat on. You were so fine! What weather it was, and what a state the street was in!'

"'Then we got married,' he said. 'Do you remember how we got our first boy, and then Mary and Niels and Peter and Hans Christian?'

"'Oh, yes; and now they have all grown up, and have become useful members of society, and everybody likes them.'

179

"'And their children have had little ones too,' said the old sailor. 'Yes, those great-grandchildren, they are of the right sort. If I am not mistaken, our wedding took place at this season of the year.'

"'Yes, to-day is your golden wedding-day,' said the little elder-tree mother, stretching her head down between the two old people, who thought that she was their neighbour who was nodding to them; they looked at each other and held each other's hands. Soon afterwards the children and grandchildren came, for they knew very well that it was the golden wedding-day. They had already wished them joy and happiness in the morning, but the old people had forgotten it, although they remembered things so well that had happened many years ago. The elder-tree smelt sweetly, and the setting sun shone on the faces of the two old people, so that they looked quite rosy. The youngest of the grandchildren danced round them, and cried merrily that there would be a feast in the evening, for they were to have hot potatoes. And the elder-tree mother nodded in the tree and cried 'Hooray' with the others."

"But that was not a fairy tale," said the little boy who had listened to it.

"Yes, if you understand it," said the old man who told the story. "But let us ask Elder-tree Mother about it."

"That was not a fairy tale," said the little elder-tree mother; "but now it comes! Out of real life come the most wonderful fairy tales; for otherwise my beautiful elder-bush could not have sprung from the teapot."

And then she took the little boy out of bed and held him to her bosom. The elder branches, full of blossoms, closed over them; it was as if they sat in a thick leafy bower, and away it flew with them through the air; it was beautiful beyond all description. Elder-tree Mother had suddenly become a charming young girl, but her dress was still of the same green material, covered with white blossoms as Elder-tree Mother had worn; she had a real elder-blossom on her bosom, and a wreath of elder-flowers on her curly yellow hair. Her eyes were so large and so blue that it was wonderful to look at them. She and the boy kissed each other, and then they became the same age and felt the same joys. They walked hand in hand out of the bower, and now stood in their beautiful flower-garden at home. Near the green lawn their father's walking-stick was tied to a post. There was life in this stick for the little ones, for as soon as they seated themselves upon it the polished knob turned into a neighing horse's head, a long black mane was fluttering in the wind, and four strong slender legs grew out. The animal was fiery and spirited; they galloped round the lawn. "Hooray! now we're going to ride many miles away!" said the boy; "we'll ride to the nobleman's estate where we were last year." And they rode round the lawn again, and the little girl, who, as we know, was no other than Elder-tree Mother, kept crying out, "Now we are in the country! Do you see the farmhouse there, with the large baking-stove which projects like a gigantic egg out of the wall into the road? The elder-tree spreads its branches over it, and the cock struts about and scratches for the hens. Look how proudly he struts! Now we are near the church; it stands on a high hill, under the spreading oak-trees; one of them is half dead! Now we are at the smithy, where the fire roars and the half-naked men beat with their hammers, so that the sparks fly far and wide. Let's be off to the beautiful farm!" And they passed by everything the little girl, who was sitting behind on the stick, described, and the boy saw it, and yet they only went round the lawn. Then they played in a side-walk, and marked out a little garden on the ground; she took elder-blossoms out of her hair and planted them, and they grew exactly like those the old people planted when they were children, as we have heard before. They walked about hand in hand, just as the old couple had done when they were little, but they did not go to the Round Tower nor to the Fredericksberg garden. No; the little girl seized the boy round the waist, and then they flew far into the country. It was spring, and it became summer; it was autumn, and it became winter; and thousands of pictures reflected themselves in the boy's eyes and heart, and the little girl always sang again, "You will never forget that!" And during their whole flight the elder-tree smelt so sweetly; he noticed the roses and the fresh beeches, but the elder-tree smelt much stronger, for its flowers hung near the little girl's heart, against which the boy often rested his head during the flight.

"It is beautiful here in spring," said the little girl, and they were again in the green beech-wood, where the thyme breathed forth sweet fragrance at their feet, and the pink anemones looked lovely in the green moss. "Oh! that it was always spring in the fragrant Danish beech-wood!"

"Here it is beautiful in summer!" she said, and they passed by old castles of the age of chivalry. The high walls and indented gables were reflected in the water of the canals, on which swans were swimming and looking into the old shady avenues. The corn waved in the fields like a yellow sea. Red and yellow flowers grew in the ditches, wild hops and convolvulus in full bloom in the hedges. In the evening the moon rose, large and round, and the hayricks in the meadows smelt sweet. "One can never forget it!"

"Here it is beautiful in autumn!" said the little girl, and the sky seemed twice as high and blue, while the wood shone with crimson, green, and gold. The hounds were running, flocks of wild fowl flew screaming over the Huns' Graves, while the bramble bushes twined round the old stones. The dark blue sea was covered with white-sailed ships, and in the barns sat old women, girls, and children picking hops into a large tub; the young ones sang songs, and the old people told fairy tales about goblins and trolls. It could not be more pleasant anywhere.

"Here it's beautiful in winter!" said the little girl, and all the trees were covered with hoar-frost, so that they looked like white coral. The snow creaked under one's feet, as if one had new boots on. One shooting star after another crossed the sky. In the room the Christmas-tree was lighted up, and there were presents and merriment. In the peasant's cottage the violin sounded, and games were played for slices of apples; even the poorest child said, "It is beautiful in winter!"

And indeed it was beautiful! And the little girl showed everything to the boy, and the elder-tree continued to breathe forth sweet perfume, while the red flag with the white cross was streaming in the wind; it was the flag under which the old sailor had served. The boy became a youth; he was to go out into the wide world, far away to the countries where the coffee grows. But at parting the little girl took an elder-blossom from her breast and gave it to him as a keepsake. He placed it in his prayer-book, and when he opened it in distant lands it was always at the place where the flower of remembrance was lying; and the more he looked at it the fresher it became, so that he could almost smell the fragrance of the woods at home. He distinctly saw the little girl, with her bright blue eyes, peeping out from behind the petals, and heard her whispering, " Here it is beautiful in spring, in summer, in autumn, and in winter," and hundreds of pictures passed through his mind.

Thus many years rolled by. He had now become an old man, and was sitting, with his old wife, under an elder-tree in full bloom. They held each other by the hand exactly as the great-grandfather and the great-grandmother had done, and, like them, they talked about bygone days and of their golden wedding. The little girl with the blue eyes and elder-blossoms in her hair was sitting high up in the tree, and nodded to them, saying, " To-day is the golden wedding! " And then she took two flowers out of her wreath and kissed them. They glittered at first like silver, then like gold, and when she placed them on the heads of the old people each flower became a golden crown. There they both sat like a king and queen under the sweet-smelling tree, which looked exactly like an elder-tree, and he told his wife the story of the elder-tree mother as it had been told him when he was a little boy. They were both of opinion that the story contained many points like their own, and these similarities they liked best.

" Yes, so it is," said the little girl in the tree. " Some call me Elder-tree Mother; others a dryad; but my real name is Remembrance. It is I who sit in the tree which grows and grows. I can remember things and tell stories! But let's see if you have still got your flower."

And the old man opened his prayer-book; the elder-blossom was still in it, and as fresh as if it had only just been put in. Remembrance nodded, and the two old people, with the golden crowns on their heads, sat in the glowing evening sun. They closed their eyes and—and——

Well, now the story is ended! The little boy in bed did not know whether he had dreamt it or heard it told. The teapot stood on the table, but no elder-tree was growing out of it, and the old man who had told the story was on the point of leaving the room, and he did go out.

" How beautiful it was! " said the little boy. " Mother, I have been to warm countries! "

" I believe you," said the mother; " if one takes two cups of hot elder-tea it is quite natural that one gets into warm countries! " And she covered him up well, so that he might not take cold. " You have slept soundly while I was arguing with the old man whether it was a story or a fairy tale! "

" And what has become of Elder-tree Mother? " asked the boy.

" She is in the teapot," said the mother; " and there she shall stay."

THE PRINCESS AND THE PEA

ONCE upon a time there was a prince and he wanted a princess; but she would have to be a *real* princess. He travelled all round the world to find one, but always there was something wrong. There were princesses enough, but he found it difficult to make out whether they were *real* ones. There was always something about them that was not quite right. So he came home again and was very sad, for he would have liked very much to have a real princess.

One evening a terrible storm came on; it thundered and lightened, and the rain poured down in torrents. It was really dreadful! Suddenly a knocking was heard at the city gate, and the old King himself went to open it.

It was a princess standing out there before the gate. But, good gracious! what a sight she was after all the rain and the dreadful weather! The water ran down from her hair and her clothes; it ran down into the toes of her shoes and out again at the heels. And yet she said that she was a real princess.

" Yes, we'll soon find that out," thought the old Queen. But she said nothing, went into the bedroom, took all the bedding off the bedstead, and laid a pea at the bottom; then she took twenty mattresses and laid them on the pea, and then twenty eiderdown beds on top of the mattresses.

On this the Princess was to lie all night. In the morning she was asked how she had slept.

" Oh, terribly badly! " said the Princess. " I have scarcely shut my eyes the whole night. Heaven only knows what was in the bed, but I was lying on something hard, so that I am black and blue all over my body. It is really terrible! "

Now they knew that she was a real princess, because she had felt the pea right through the twenty mattresses and the twenty eiderdown beds.

Nobody but a real princess could be as sensitive as that.

So the prince took her for his wife, for now he knew that he had a real princess; and the pea was put in the Art Museum, where it may still be seen, if no one has stolen it.

There, that is a real story!

WHAT THE OLD MAN DOES
IS ALWAYS RIGHT

I WILL tell you the story which I heard when I was a little boy. Every time I thought of the story it seemed to me to become more and more charming, for it is with stories as it is with many people—they become better and better the older they grow; and that is so delightful.

You have been in the country, of course! Well, then, you must have seen a very old farmhouse with a thatched roof, and mosses and weeds growing wild upon it. There is a stork's nest on the ridge of the roof, for we can't do without the stork. The walls of the house are aslant, and the windows low, and only one of the latter is made so that it will open. The baking-oven sticks out of the wall like a little fat body. The elder-tree hangs over the paling, and beneath its branches, at the foot of the paling, is a little pond with a duck and some ducklings under a knotted old willow-tree. There is a yard dog too, who barks at every passer-by.

Well, there was just such a farmhouse out in the country, and in it dwelt an old couple—a peasant and his wife. Small as was their property, there was one of their possessions that they could do without—a horse, which managed to live on the grass it found in the ditch by the side of the highroad. The old peasant rode it to town, and often his neighbours borrowed it, and rendered the old couple some service in return for the loan. But still they thought it would be best if they sold the horse or exchanged it for something that might be more useful to them. But what was it to be?

"You'll know that best, old man," said the wife. "It is fair-day to-day; so ride to town and get rid of the horse for money, or make a good exchange—whatever you do will be right to me. Ride off to the fair."

And she tied his neckerchief for him, for she could do that better than he could; and she tied it in a double bow and made him look quite smart. Then she brushed his hat round and round with the palm of her hand and gave him a kiss. So he rode away upon the horse that was to be sold or exchanged for something else. Yes, the old man knew what he was about.

The sun shone hot, and there was not a cloud in the sky. The road was very dusty, for many people who were all bound for the fair were driving, or riding, or walking upon it. There was no shade anywhere from the burning sun.

Among the rest a man was going along driving a cow to the fair. The cow was as pretty as a cow could be.

" She gives good milk, I'm sure," thought the peasant. " That would be a very good exchange—the cow for the horse.

" Hallo, you there with the cow! " he said. " Let's have a word together. I fancy a horse costs more than a cow, but I don't mind that; a cow would be more useful to me. If you like we'll exchange."

" To be sure I will," said the man with the cow. And so they exchanged.

So that was settled, and the peasant might just as well have turned back, for he had done the business he came to do, but as he had once made up his mind to go to the fair he thought he'd go all the same, if only to have a look at it; and so he went on to the town with his cow.

Leading the cow, he strode on briskly, and after a short time he overtook a man who was driving a sheep. It was a fine fat sheep, well covered with wool.

" I should like to have that," said our peasant to himself. " It would find plenty of grass by our fence, and in winter we could have it in the room with us. Perhaps it would be more practical to have a sheep instead of a cow. Shall we change? "

The man with the sheep was quite ready, and the exchange was made. So our peasant went on along the highroad with his sheep.

Soon he saw another man, who came into the road from a field, carrying a big goose under his arm.

" That's a heavy bird you have there. It has plenty of feathers and plenty of fat, and would look well tied by a string in our pond at home. That would be something for my old woman to save up her scraps for. How often she has said, 'If only we had a goose!' Now, perhaps, she can have one; and, if possible, it shall be hers. Shall we exchange? I'll give you my sheep for your goose, and say 'Thank you' into the bargain."

The other man had no objection; and so they exchanged, and our peasant got the goose.

By this time he was very near the town. The crowd on the high-road became greater and greater; there was quite a crush of men and cattle. They walked in the road and close by the palings, and at the toll-gate they even went into the toll-keeper's potato-field, where his only hen was strutting about with a string to her leg, lest she should take fright at the crowd, and run away and get lost. She had short feathers on her tail, and winked with one eye, and looked very cunning. "Cluck, cluck!" said the hen. What she meant by it I cannot tell you; but directly our good man saw her he thought, "That's the finest hen I've ever seen in my life! Why, she's finer than our parson's brood hen. Upon my word, I should like to have that hen. A fowl can always find a grain or two; she can almost keep herself. I think it would be a good exchange if I could get that for my goose.

"Shall we exchange?" he asked the toll-keeper.

"Exchange!" said the man. "Well, that wouldn't be a bad thing."

And so they exchanged, and the toll-keeper got the goose and the peasant got the hen.

Now he had done a good deal of business on his way to town, and he was hot and tired. He must have a drop of brandy and a bit to eat, and soon he was in front of the inn. He was just about to go in when the ostler came out, and they met in the doorway. The ostler was carrying a sackful of something on his back.

"What have you there?" said the peasant.

"Rotten apples," answered the ostler. "A whole sackful of them —enough to feed the pigs with."

"Why, that's terrible waste! I wish my old woman at home

could see that lot. Last year the old tree by the turf-stack only bore
a single apple, and we kept it in the cupboard till it was quite rotten
and spoiled. 'It's something, anyhow,' my old woman said; but here
she could see any quantity—a whole sackful. Yes, I should be glad to
show her that."

" What will you give me for the sackful? " asked the ostler.

" What'll I give? I'll give you my hen in exchange."

And so he gave him the hen and got the apples, which he carried
into the bar parlour. He stood the sack carefully by the stove, and
then went to the table. But the stove was hot; he had not thought of
that. There were many strangers in the room—horse-dealers, drovers,
and two Englishmen, and the two Englishmen were so rich that their
pockets were bursting with gold, and they were making bets too,
just as they are always supposed to.

Hiss-s-s! hiss-s-s! What was that by the stove? The apples were
beginning to roast!

" What's that? "

" Why, do you know——" said our peasant.

And he told the whole story of the horse that he had changed
for a cow, and all the rest of it, right down to the apples.

" Well, your old woman will give it you well when you get
home! " said the Englishmen. " There'll be a pretty row! "

" What? She'll give me what? " said the peasant. " She will
kiss me, and say, ' What the old man does is always right.' "

" Shall we have a bet? " said the Englishmen. We'll wager gold
by the ton—a hundred pounds to the hundredweight! "

" A bushel will be enough," said the peasant. " I can only set
the bushel of apples against it; and I'll throw in myself and my old
woman into the bargain—and that's piling up the measure, I should
say."

" Done! "

And so the bet was made. The innkeeper's cart was brought out,
and the Englishmen got in, and the peasant got in, and the rotten
apples, and away they went, and soon they reached the peasant's little
farm.

" Good evening, old woman! "

" Good evening, old man! "

" Well, I've made the exchange! "

" Yes, you know what you're about," said the woman, and she put her arms round him, paying no attention to the strangers, nor did she notice the sack.

" I got a cow in exchange for the horse," said he.

" Heaven be thanked! " said she. " What lovely milk we shall have now, and butter and cheese on the table! That was a most capital exchange! "

" Yes, but I changed the cow for a sheep."

" Why, that's better still! " said the old woman. " You always think of everything. We have just grass enough for a sheep. Ewe's milk and cheese, and woollen stockings, and even woollen jackets too! The cow cannot give those, and her hairs will only come off. How you think of everything! "

" But I gave away the sheep for a goose."

" Then this year we shall really have roast goose to eat, my dear old man. You are always thinking of something to give me pleasure. How lovely that is! We can let the goose walk about with a string to her leg, and she'll grow fatter still before Michaelmas."

" But I changed the goose for a hen," said the man.

" A hen? That *was* a good exchange! " replied the woman. " The hen will lay eggs and hatch them, and we shall have chickens; we shall have a whole poultry-yard! Oh, that's just what I was wishing for."

" Yes, but I exchanged the hen for a sack of rotten apples."

" Well! Now I must really kiss you for that," exclaimed the wife. " My dear, good husband! Now I'll tell you something. Do you know, you had hardly left me this morning before I began thinking how I could give you something very nice this evening. I thought it should be pancakes with savoury herbs. I had eggs, and bacon too; but I wanted herbs. So I went over to the schoolmaster's —they have herbs there, I know—but his wife is a mean woman, though she looks so sweet. I begged her to lend me a handful of

herbs. 'Lend!' she answered. 'Nothing at all grows in our garden, not even a rotten apple. I could not even lend you a rotten apple.' But now I can lend *her* ten—a whole sackful even. That I'm very glad of; that makes me laugh!" And with that she gave him a good smacking kiss.

"I like that!" said both the Englishmen together. "Always going downhill, and always happy; that's worth the money."

So they paid a bushel of gold to the peasant, who had not been cuffed, but kissed.

Yes, it always pays when the wife always sees and says that her husband is the wisest, and that whatever he does is right.

You see, that's my story. I heard it when I was a child, and now you've heard it too, and know that "What the old man does is always right."

THERE SHE WAS SITTING UNDER THE BEAUTIFUL CHRISTMAS TREE
''The Little Match Girl''

SHE CAME ACROSS A WHOLE FLOCK OF LITTLE CHILDREN
"The Little Mermaid"

THE LITTLE MATCH GIRL

IT was so terribly cold; it snowed, and it was almost dark; it was also the last evening of the year—New Year's Eve. In the cold and darkness a poor little girl, with bare head and naked feet, went along the streets. When she left home, it is true, she had had slippers on, but what was the use of that? They were very large slippers; her mother had worn them till then, so big were they. And the little girl lost them as she hurried across the street, to get out of the way of two carts driving furiously along. One slipper was not to be found again, and a boy had caught up the other and run away with it. He said he could use it for a cradle when he had children of his own. So the little girl had to go walking about in her little bare feet, which were red and blue with cold. She carried a lot of matches in an old apron and a box of them in her hand. No one had bought any from her the whole day; no one had given her a halfpenny.

Hungry and shivering, she went along, poor little thing, a picture of misery.

The snowflakes fell on her long yellow hair, that curled so prettily on her neck, but she did not think of that now. Lights were shining in all the windows, and there was a tempting smell of roast goose, for it was New Year's Eve. Yes, she was thinking of that.

In a corner formed by two houses, one of which projected a little beyond the other, she sat down and huddled herself together. She had tucked her little feet under her, but she felt colder and colder. She dared not go home, for she had not sold any matches nor earned a single halfpenny: her father would beat her, and it was cold at home, too; they had only the roof above them, through which the wind whistled, although the largest cracks had been stopped up with straw and rags.

Her little hands were almost dead with cold. Ah! One little match might do her good! If she dared take only one out of the

box, strike it on the wall, and warm her fingers! She took one out.
" Ritch! " How it sputtered and burned!

It was a warm, bright flame, like a little candle, when she held
her hands over it. It was a wonderful little light, and it really seemed
to the child as though she was sitting in front of a great iron stove
with polished brass feet and brass ornaments. How the fire burned
up, and how it warmed! But what was that? The little girl was
already stretching out her feet to warm these too, when—out went
the little flame, the stove vanished, and she had only the remains of
the burned match in her hand.

She struck a second one on the wall; it burned, and gave a light,
and where this fell upon the wall it became transparent, like a veil—
she could see right into the room. A white table-cloth was spread
upon the table, which was decked with shining china dishes, and
there was a lovely smell of roast goose stuffed with apples and
prunes. And what pleased the poor little girl more than all was that
the goose hopped down from the dish and, with a knife and fork
sticking in its breast, came waddling across the floor straight towards her. Just at that moment out went the match, and only the
thick, cold wall was to be seen. So she lighted another match. And
there she was sitting under the beautiful Christmas-tree; it was much
larger and more decorated than the one she had seen through the
glass doors at the rich merchant's. The green boughs were lit up
with thousands of candles, and gaily painted figures, like those in
the shop-windows, looked down upon her. The little girl stretched
her hands out towards them and—out went the match. The Christmas
candles rose higher and higher, till they were only the stars in the
sky; one of them fell, leaving a long fiery trail behind it.

" Now, someone is dying," said the little girl, for her old grandmother, the only person who had ever been good to her, and who
was now dead, had said that when a star falls a soul goes up to heaven.

She struck another match on the wall; it was alight at once, and
in its glow stood her old grandmother, so dazzling and bright, and
so kind and loving.

" Grandmother! " cried the little girl. " Oh, take me with you!

I know that you will go away when the match is burned out; you will vanish like the warm stove, like the beautiful roast goose and the big splendid Christmas-tree." And she quickly lighted the whole box of matches, for she did not wish to let her grandmother go. The matches burned with such a blaze that it was lighter than day, and the old grandmother had never appeared so beautiful or so tall before. Taking the little girl in her arms she flew up with her in brightness and joy, high, so high; and there was no cold, nor hunger, nor sorrow—for they were with God.

But in the corner by the houses, in the cold dawn, the little girl was still sitting, with red cheeks and a smile upon her lips—frozen to death on the last evening of the old year. The new year's sun shone on the little body. The child sat up stiffly, holding her matches, of which a box had been burned. " She must have tried to warm herself," someone said. No one knew what beautiful things she had seen, nor into what glory she had entered with her grandmother on the joyous new year.

EVERYTHING IN THE RIGHT PLACE

IT is over a hundred years ago! Behind the wood, near the great lake, stood an old mansion, and round it was a deep moat, in which reeds and bulrushes grew. Close by the bridge, at the entrance gate, stood an old willow-tree, which bent over the reeds.

From the narrow way came the sound of horns and the tramping of horses' feet; and therefore the little goose-girl hastened to drive her geese away from the bridge, before the hunting party came galloping up. They came, however, so fast that she had to jump up quickly on to one of the high corner-stones of the bridge in order to avoid being ridden over. She was still half a child and very delicately built; she had two lovely bright eyes and a gentle, sweet expression. But such things the baron did not notice; as he galloped past her he reversed the whip he had in his hand, and in rough play gave her such a push in the chest with the butt-end that she fell backward into the ditch.

"Everything in the right place!" he cried. "Into the ditch with you!" Then he burst out laughing, for that he called fun; the others

196

joined in; the whole party shouted and cried, and the hounds barked.

The poor goose-girl, happily for herself, caught hold of one of the branches of the willow-tree as she fell, by the help of which she held herself over the water, and, as soon as the baron with his company and the hounds had disappeared through the gate, the goose-girl tried to scramble up, but the branch broke off at the top, and she would have fallen backward among the rushes had not a strong hand from above seized her at the same moment. It was the hand of a pedlar, who had seen what had happened from a short distance, and had now hurried up to help her.

"Everything in the right place!" he said, imitating the noble baron, and he pulled her up to the dry ground. He wished to put the branch back in the place it had been broken off, but "everything in the right place cannot always be managed"; so he stuck the branch into the soft ground.

"Grow if you can, and provide a good flute for them up yonder at the mansion!" he said. It would have given him great pleasure to play the *Rogues' March* for the noble baron and his companions. Then he walked up and entered the mansion—but not the banqueting-hall, he was too humble for that. No, he went to the servants' hall, and the men-servants and the maids looked over his stock of goods and bargained with him; loud crying and screaming were heard from above, where the guests were at table; it was meant for singing—indeed, they could do no better. Laughter and the howls of dogs were heard through the open windows: there they were feasting and revelling; wine and old ale foamed in glasses and jugs; the favourite dogs ate with their masters; now and then they even kissed one of them, after having first wiped its muzzle with its long ears. They ordered the pedlar to come upstairs with his wares, but only to make fun of him. The wine had got into their heads, and the wit had gone out. They poured beer into a stocking for him to drink with them, but quickly! That's what they called fun, and it made them laugh. Then meadows, peasants, and farmyards were staked on a single card and lost.

"Everything in the right place!" the pedlar said when he had at last got well out of Sodom and Gomorrah, as he called it. "The open highroad—that is my right place. Up there I did not feel at ease." And the little goose-girl nodded to him from the wicket.

And days passed and weeks passed, and it could be seen that the broken willow branch which the pedlar had stuck into the ground near the ditch remained fresh and green—indeed it even had put forth fresh shoots. The little goose-girl saw that the branch had taken root, and she was very pleased; the tree, so she said, was her tree. Yes, the tree made good progress, but everything else at the mansion was going rapidly backward, through feasting and gambling, for these are two wheels upon which nobody runs safely. Less than six years afterwards the baron, with bag and stick, passed out of his castle gate a beggared man, while the estate had been bought by a rich tradesman. He was the very man they had made fun of and poured ale into a stocking for; but honesty and industry bring one to the front, and now the pedlar was the master of the baronial estate. From that time forward no card-playing was permitted there.

"That's a bad pastime!" he said. "When the devil saw the Bible for the first time he wanted to produce something in opposition to it, and so he invented card-playing."

The new master took a wife, and who was she? It was the little goose-girl, who had always remained good and faithful, and who looked as beautiful in her new clothes as if she had been of high birth. And how did all this come about? That would be too long a tale to tell in our busy time, but it really happened, and the most important part is yet to come.

It was pleasant and cheerful to live in the old mansion now; the mother looked after the household, and the father the affairs out-of-doors, and they were indeed very prosperous.

Where honesty leads the way prosperity is sure to follow. The old mansion was repaired and painted, the ditches were cleaned and fruit-trees planted; all was clean and pleasant, and the floors were scrubbed as white as a pastry-board. In the long winter evenings the mistress and her maids sat at the spinning-wheel in the large hall. Every Sunday the Justice of the Peace—for a justice the pedlar had become, although only in his old days—read aloud from the Bible. The children—for children came—all received the best education, but they were not all equally clever, as is the case in all families.

In the meantime the willow branch outside had grown into a fine tree, and stood there, free, and was never pollarded. "It is our genealogical tree," said the old people, and that tree must be held in honour and respect. So they told their children, even those who had not very good heads.

A hundred years had now gone by. It was in our own time; the lake had been transformed into marsh land, and the old mansion had almost disappeared. A narrow pool of water and some ruined walls by it, that was all that was left of the deep moat; and here still stood a magnificent old tree with overhanging branches—that was the genealogical tree. Here it stood, and showed how beautiful a willow can look if one does not interfere with it. The trunk, it is true, was cleft in the middle from the root to the crown; storms had twisted it a little, but it still stood, and out of every crevice and cleft, in which wind and weather had carried mould, blades of grass and flowers sprang forth. Especially near the top, where the great branches forked, there was quite a hanging garden, in which throve wild raspberries and ferns, and even a little mountain ash had taken root and grew gracefully in the old willow branches, which were reflected in the dark water beneath when the wind blew the chickweed into the corner of the pond. A footpath led across the fields close by the old tree.

High up, on the woody hillside, stood the new mansion. It had a splendid view, and was large and magnificent; its window-panes were so clear that one might have thought there were none there at all. The broad steps that led to the door looked like a bower covered with roses and big-leaved plants. The lawn was as green as if each blade of grass was cleaned separately morning and evening. In the hall valuable oil paintings were hanging on the walls. Here stood chairs and sofas covered with silk and velvet, which could be easily rolled about on castors; there were tables with polished marble tops, and books bound in morocco with gilt edges. Indeed, distinguished people lived here; it was the dwelling of the baron and his family.

Everything was in keeping with its surroundings. "Everything in the right place" was the motto still, and therefore all the paintings which had once been the honour and glory of the old mansion were now hung up in the passage which led to the servants' rooms. It was all old lumber, especially two portraits—one representing a man in a scarlet coat with a wig, and the other a lady with powdered and curled hair holding a rose in her hand, each of them being surrounded by a large wreath of willow branches. Both portraits had many holes in them, because the baron's sons used the two old people as targets for their cross-bows. They represented the councillor and his wife, from whom the whole family descended.

"But they did not properly belong to our family," said one of the boys; "he was a pedlar and she kept the geese. They were not like papa and mamma."

The portraits were old lumber, and "everything in its right place!" they said, and so the great-grandfather and great-grandmother had to go to the servants' passage.

The son of the clergyman was tutor in the great house. One day he was out with the young barons and their elder sister, who had lately been confirmed, and they walked by the footpath past the old willow-tree, and as they went along she picked a bunch of field-flowers. "Everything in the right place," and indeed the bunch looked very beautiful. At the same time she listened to all that was said, and she very much liked to hear the pastor's son speak about the works of Nature and about the great men and women in history. She had a healthy mind, noble in thought and deed, and with a heart full of love for everything that God had created.

They stopped at the old willow-tree, as the youngest of the baron's sons wished very much to have a flute from it, such as had been cut for him from other willow-trees, and the pastor's son broke a branch off.

"Oh, don't do that!" said the young baroness; but it was already done. "That is our famous old tree. I love it very much. They often laugh at me at home about it, but that does not matter. There is a story attached to this tree."

And now she told him all that we already know about the tree —the old mansion, the pedlar and the goose-girl, who had met there for the first time, and had become the ancestors of the noble family to which the young baroness belonged.

"They would not be ennobled, the good old people," she said. "Their motto was 'everything in the right place,' and it would not be right, they thought, to be given a title on account of their wealth. My grandfather, the first baron, was their son. They say he was a very learned man, a great favourite with the princes and princesses, and was invited to all Court festivities. The others at home love him best; but, I do not know why, there seemed to me to be something about the old couple that draws my heart to them! How homely, how patriarchal, it must have been in the old mansion, where the mistress sat at the spinning-wheel with her maids, while her husband read aloud out of the Bible!"

"They must have been excellent people, sensible people," said the pastor's son. And they went on to talk about noblemen and commoners, and from the manner in which the clergyman's son spoke about the meaning of nobility it seemed almost as if he were not himself a commoner.

"It is good fortune to be of a family that has distinguished itself, and to possess as it were in one's blood a spur to lead in all that is good. It is a splendid thing to have a noble name that is a card of admission into the highest circles. Nobility, besides nobleness, is a gold coin that bears the stamp of its own value. It is the fallacy of the time, and many poets express it, to say that all that is noble is bad and stupid, and that, on the contrary, the lower one goes among the poor, the more brilliant virtues one finds. I do not share this opinion, for it is a mistake—it is altogether wrong. In the upper classes one finds many kindly and beautiful traits; my own mother told me of such, and I could mention several. One day she was visiting a nobleman's house in town; my grandmother, I believe, had been the lady's nurse

when she was a child. My mother and the great nobleman were alone
in the room, when he noticed an old woman on crutches come limping
into the courtyard; she came every Sunday to get a penny.

" ' There is the poor old woman,' said the nobleman; ' it is such
difficulty to her to walk.'

" And before my mother understood, he was out of the door
and down the stairs, in order to save her the toilsome walk for the gift
she had come to fetch. Of course this is only a little incident, but,
like the widow's mite, it comes from the heart, from the depth of
human nature; and this is what the poet ought to show and point
out—more especially in our own time he ought to sing of this; it does
good, it soothes and reconciles. But when a man, simply because he
is of noble birth and has a pedigree, like an Arab horse, stands on his
hind legs and neighs in the streets, and says when a commoner has
been in a room, ' Some people from the street have been here,'
there nobility is decaying; it has become a mask of the kind that
Thespis created, and it is amusing when such a person is exposed in
satire."

Such was the speech of the parson's son; it was a little long, but
meanwhile the flute was being cut.

There was a great party at the mansion, many guests from the
neighbourhood and from the capital, ladies dressed with taste—and
without it. The big hall was quite crowded with people. The clergy-
men stood humbly together in a corner, and looked as if they were
preparing for a funeral, but it was a festival—only the amusement
had not yet begun.

A great concert was to take place, and that is why the baron's
young son had brought his willow flute with him; but he could not
make it sound, nor could his papa, and therefore it was good for
nothing.

There were music and songs of the kind which delight most those
that perform them; otherwise quite charming!

"You are a performer too?" said a cavalier—his father's son and
nothing else—to the tutor. "You play on the flute—you have made
it yourself; it is genius that rules—the place of honour is due to you.

For me, I only advance with the times, as one must. I hope you will delight us all with the little instrument—will you not? " Thus saying he handed him the little flute which had been cut from the willow-tree by the pool; and then announced in a loud voice that the tutor wished to perform a solo on the flute.

They wished to tease him—that was evident, and so the tutor declined to play, although he could do so very well, but they pressed and urged him so hard that at last he took up the flute and placed it to his lips.

That was a marvellous flute! Its sound was as shrill as the whistle of a steam engine—in fact, much stronger, for it was heard in the courtyard, in the garden, and in the wood, many miles round in the country; and with the note a storm arose and roared: " Everything in the right place! " And off flew papa, as if carried by the wind, out of the hall straight into the shepherd's cottage, and the shepherd flew—not into the hall, thither he could not come—but into the servants' hall, among the smart footmen strutting about in silk stockings; and these haughty servants looked horror-struck that such a person dared to sit at table with them.

But in the banqueting-hall the young baroness flew to the place of honour at the end of the table, where she was worthy to sit, and the parson's son had the seat next to her; the two sat there as if they were a bridal pair. An old count, belonging to one of the oldest families of the country, remained untouched in his place of honour; the flute was just, as it is one's duty to be. The sharp-tongued cavalier who had caused the flute to be played, and who was the child of his parents, flew headlong into the fowl-house, but not he alone.

The flute was heard a mile away, and strange events took place. A rich banker's family, who were driving in a coach and four, were blown out of it, and could not even find room on the footboard at the back. Two rich farmers, who had in our day grown too big for their own cornfields, were flung into the ditch; it was a dangerous flute! Luckily it burst at the first note, and that was a good thing, for then it was put back into its owner's pocket—" everything in the right place "!

The day after nobody spoke a word about what had taken place; and thence came the saying, " to pocket the flute! " Besides, every-thing was again in its usual order, except that the two old pictures of the pedlar and the goose-girl were hanging in the banqueting-hall, where they had been blown; and, as a real expert said that they were painted by a master's hand, they were allowed to remain there and were restored. " Everything in the right place," and to that it comes! Eternity is long, much longer than this story.

THE LITTLE MERMAID

FAR out in the ocean the water is as blue as the petals of the most beautiful corn-flower, and as clear as the purest glass. But it is very deep—much deeper, indeed, than any cable can sound. Many steeples would have to be piled one on top of the other to reach from the bottom to the surface of the water. Down there live the sea-folk.

Now you must not think that there is nothing but the bare white sand down at the bottom. No, there grow the strangest trees and plants, with such pliable stems and leaves that at the slightest movement of the water they stir as if they are alive. All the big and little fishes glide among their branches, as the birds do up above in the air. Where the ocean is deepest stands the sea-king's palace. Its walls are made of coral, and the high arched windows of the clearest amber. The roof is made of mussel-shells, which open and close in the current. It is very beautiful, for each of them is filled with gleaming pearls, a single one of which would make a fit jewel for a queen's crown.

The sea-king had been a widower for many years, but his old mother kept house for him. She was a clever woman, but very vain of her noble rank; so she wore twelve oysters on her tail, while other grand folk were only allowed to wear six. In other respects she deserved great praise, especially for her tender care of the little sea-princesses, her granddaughters. They were six lovely children, and the youngest was the most beautiful of all. Her skin was as clear and delicate as a rose-petal, and her eyes as blue as the deepest sea, but, like all the others, she had no legs—her body ended in a fish-tail. All day long they used to play in the great halls of the palace, where living flowers grew out of the walls. The large amber windows were thrown open, and the fishes came swimming in to them, as the swallows fly in to us when we open our windows; but the fishes swam right up to the little princesses, and ate out of their hands, and let themselves be stroked.

In front of the palace was a large garden, in which bright red and dark blue trees were growing. The fruit glittered like gold, and the flowers looked like flames of fire, with their ever-moving stems and leaves. The ground was covered with the finest sand, as blue as the flame of sulphur. A strange blue light shone over everything; one would imagine oneself to be high up in the air, with the blue sky above and below, rather than at the bottom of the sea. When the sea was calm one could see the sun; it looked like a huge purple flower, from whose centre the light streamed forth.

Each of the little princesses had her own little place in the garden, where she could dig and plant as she pleased. One gave her flower-bed the shape of a whale; another liked better to make hers like a little mermaid; but the youngest made hers as round as the sun, and only had flowers that shone red like it. She was a strange child, quiet and thoughtful. While her sisters made a great display of all sorts of curious objects which they found from wrecked ships, she only loved her rose-red flowers, like the sun above, and a beautiful marble statue of a handsome boy, carved out of clear white stone, which had sunk from some wreck to the bottom of the sea. She had planted by the statue a rose-coloured weeping-willow tree, which grew well, hanging over it with its fresh branches reaching down to the blue sand, and casting a violet shadow which moved to and fro like the branches, so that it seemed as if the top and the roots of the tree were playing at kissing each other.

Nothing gave her greater pleasure than to hear stories about the world of men above, and her old grandmother had to tell her all she knew about ships and towns, men and animals. It seemed strangely beautiful to her that on earth the flowers were fragrant, for at the bottom of the sea they have no scent, and that the woods were green, and that the fish which one saw there among the branches could sing so loudly and beautifully that it was a delight to hear them. The grandmother called the little birds fishes; otherwise her grand-daughter would not have understood her, as they had never seen a bird.

"When you are fifteen years old," said the grandmother, "you will be allowed to rise up to the surface of the sea and sit on the rocks in the moonlight, and see the big ships as they sail by. Then you will also see the forests and towns."

The following year one of the sisters would be fifteen; but the others—well, the sisters were each one year younger than the other; so the youngest had to wait fully five years before she could come up from the bottom of the sea and see what things were like on the earth above. But each promised to tell her sisters what she had seen and liked best on her first day; for their grandmother could not tell them enough—there were so many things about which they wanted to know. None of them, however, longed so much to go up as the youngest, who had the longest time to wait, and was so quiet and thoughtful. Many a night she stood at the open window and looked up through the dark blue water, where the fishes splashed with their fins and tails. She could see the moon and the stars, which only shone faintly, but looked much bigger through the water than we see them. When something like a dark cloud passed under them, and hid them for a while, she knew it was either a whale swimming overhead or a ship with many people, who had no idea that a lovely little mermaid was standing below stretching out her white hands towards the keel of their ship.

The eldest princess was now fifteen years old, and was allowed to rise to the surface of the sea. When she came back she had hundreds of things to tell: but what pleased her most, she said, was to lie in the moonlight on a sandbank, in the calm sea, and to see near the coast the big town where the lights twinkled like many hundreds of stars; to hear music and the noise and bustle of carriages and people, and to see the many church towers and spires and listen to the ringing of the bells. Oh, how the youngest sister listened to all this! And when, later on in the evening, she again stood at the open window, looking up through the dark blue water, she thought of the big town, with all its bustle and noise, and imagined she could hear the church bells ringing, even down where she was.

The year after the second sister was allowed to go up to the surface, and swim about as she pleased. She came up just as the sun was setting, and this sight she thought the most beautiful of all she saw. The whole sky was like gold, she said, and the clouds—well, she could not find words to describe their loveliness. Rose and violet, they sailed by over her head; but, even swifter than the clouds, a flock of wild swans, like a long white veil, flew across the water towards the sun. She followed them, but the sun sank, and the rosy gleam faded from the sea and clouds.

The year after the third sister went up. She was the boldest of them all, and swam up a broad river which flowed into the sea. She saw beautiful green hills covered with vines, and houses and castles peeped out from magnificent woods. She heard the birds sing, and the sun shone so warmly that she often had to dive under the water to cool her burning face. In a little creek she came across a whole flock of little children, who were quite naked and splashed about in the water; she wanted to play with them, but they ran away terrified. Then a little black animal—it was a dog, but she had never seen a dog before—came out and barked so ferociously at her that she was frightened, and hurried back as fast as she could to the open sea. But she could never forget the magnificent woods, the green hills, and the lovely children, who could swim even though they had no fish-tails.

The fourth sister was not so daring; she stayed far out in the open sea, and said that that was the loveliest place of all. There, she said, one could see for many miles round, and the sky above was like a great glass dome. She saw ships, but far away, and they looked to her like sea-gulls. The playful dolphins, she said, turned somer saults, and the big whales spouted out sea-water through their nostrils, as if a hundred fountains were playing all around her.

Now the fifth sister's turn came, and, as her birthday was in winter, she saw on her first visit things which the other sisters had not. The sea looked quite green; huge icebergs floated around her —they were like pearls, she said, and yet were much higher than the church steeples built by men. They were the strangest shapes and glittered like diamonds. She sat on one of the biggest, and all the passing sailors were terrified when they saw her sitting there, with the wind playing with her long hair. But towards evening the sky became overcast with black clouds; there was thunder and lightning, and the dark waves lifted up the big blocks of ice, which shone in each flash of lightning. On all the ships the sails were reefed, and there was anxiety and terror; but she sat quietly on her floating iceberg, and watched the blue lightning dart in zigzags into the foaming sea.

The first time each one of the sisters came to the surface all the new and beautiful things she saw charmed her; but now, when as grown-up girls they were allowed to come up whenever they liked, they became indifferent to them, longing for their home; and after a month they said that after all it was best down below, where one felt at home. On many an evening the five sisters would rise to the surface of the sea, arm-in-arm. They had beautiful voices, far finer than that of any human being; and when a storm was brewing, and they thought that some ships might be wrecked, they swam in front of them, singing so beautifully of how lovely it was at the bottom of the sea, and telling the people not to be afraid of coming down there. But the human beings could not understand the words, and thought it was only the noise of the storm; and they never saw the wonders below, for when the ship went down they were drowned, and were dead when they came to the sea-king's palace. When her sisters went up arm-in-arm to the top of the sea there stood the little sister, all alone, looking after them, and feeling as if she could cry; but mermaids have no tears, and so they suffer all the more.

"Oh, if I were only fifteen!" she said. "I know how much I shall love the world above, and the people who live in it."

At last she was fifteen years old.

"Well, now we have you off our hands," said her grandmother, the old dowager-queen. "Come now! Let me adorn you like your other sisters!" She put a wreath of white lilies on her head, but every petal of the flowers was half a pearl; and the old lady had eight big oysters fixed to the princess's tail, to show her high rank.

"But it hurts so!" said the little mermaid.

"Yes, one must suffer to be beautiful," said the old lady.

Oh, how gladly the little princess would have taken off all her ornaments and the heavy wreath! The red flowers in her garden would have suited her much better, but she dared not make any change now. "Good-bye!" she said, and rose as lightly as a bubble through the water.

The sun had just set when she lifted her head out of the water, but the clouds gleamed with red and gold, and the evening star shone in the rosy sky; the air was mild and fresh, and the sea as calm as glass. Near her lay a big ship with three masts; only one sail was set, as not a breath of wind was stirring, and the sailors were sitting about on deck and in the rigging. There was music and singing on board, and when it grew dark many hundreds of coloured lamps were lighted, and it looked as if the flags of all nations were floating in the air. The little mermaid swam up close to the cabin windows, and when the waves lifted her up she could see through the clear panes many richly dressed people. But the handsomest of them all was the young Prince, with large black eyes—he could not be older than sixteen; and it was his birthday that was the reason for all this celebration. The sailors were dancing on deck, and when the young Prince came out hundreds of rockets were sent off into the air, making the night as bright as day, so that the little mermaid was frightened, and dived under water. But soon she lifted up her head again, and then it seemed to her as if all the stars of heaven were falling down upon her. Never had she seen such fireworks! Great suns whirled round, gorgeous fiery fish flew through the blue air, and everything was reflected in the calm and glassy sea. The ship was so brilliantly lighted up that one could see everything distinctly, even to the smallest rope, and the people still better. Oh, how beautiful was the young Prince! He shook hands with the people and smiled graciously, while the music sounded dreamily through the starry night.

It grew very late, but the little mermaid could not turn her eyes away from the ship and the handsome Prince. The coloured lamps were put out, no more rockets were sent off nor cannons fired. But deep down in the sea was a strange moaning and murmuring, and the little mermaid sitting on the waves was rocked up and down, so that she could look into the cabin. Soon the ship began to make greater headway, as one sail after another was unfurled; then the waves rose higher and higher; dark clouds gathered, and flashes of lightning were seen in the distance. Oh, what a terrible storm was brewing! Then the sailors reefed all the sails, and the big ship rushed at flying speed through the wild sea; the waves rose as high as great black mountains, as if they would dash over the masts, but the ship dived like a swan between them, and then was carried up again to their towering crests. The little mermaid thought this was great fun; but not so the sailors. The ship creaked and groaned, her strong timbers bending under the weight of the huge waves; the sea broke over her; the mainmast snapped in two, like a reed; and the ship lay over on her side while the water rushed into her hold. The little mermaid then realized that the crew was in danger; she herself had to be careful of the beams and planks floating about in the water. For one moment it was so dark that not a thing could be seen, but flashes of lightning made everything visible, and she could see all on board. The little mermaid looked out for the young Prince, and as the ship broke up she saw him sinking into the deep sea. At first she was very pleased, for now he would come down to her; but then she remembered that men cannot live in the water, and only if he were dead could he come to her father's palace. No, he must not die! Heedless of the beams and planks floating on the water, which might have crushed her, she dived down into the water and came up again in the waves, in search of the Prince. At last she found him. His strength was failing him, and he could hardly swim any longer in the stormy sea; his arms and legs began to grow numb, and his beautiful eyes closed; he would certainly have died if the little mermaid had not come to his assistance. She held his head above the water and let the waves carry them where they would.

Next morning the storm was over, but not a plank of the ship was to be seen anywhere. The sun rose red and brilliant out of the water, and seemed to bring new life to the Prince's cheeks; but his eyes remained closed. The little mermaid kissed his beautiful high forehead, and smoothed back his wet hair; she thought he looked very much like the white marble statue in her little garden. She kissed him again and again, and prayed that he might live.

Then she saw before her eyes the mainland, where lay high, blue mountains, on whose summits snow was glistening, so that they looked like swans. Down by the shore were beautiful green woods, and in front of them stood a church or convent—she did not know which, but it was some sort of building. Lemon-trees and orange-trees grew in the garden, and before the gate stood lofty palm-trees. The sea formed a little bay here, and was quite calm, though very deep; she swam straight to the cliffs, where the fine white sand had been washed ashore, and laid the handsome Prince on the sand, taking special care that his head lay raised up in the warm sunshine. Then all the bells began to ring in the big white building, and many young girls came out into the garden. The little mermaid swam farther out and hid behind some rocks, covering her hair and breast with sea-foam, lest anybody should see her little face; and from there she watched to see who would come to the poor Prince.

It was not long before a young girl came to the spot where he lay. At first she seemed very frightened, but only for a moment, and then she called some of the others. The little mermaid saw that the Prince came back to life, and smiled at all who stood round him; but at her he did not smile—he little knew who had saved him. She was very sad; and when they had taken him into the big building she dived sorrowfully down into the water, and so went back to her father's palace.

She had always been silent and thoughtful, and now she became still more so. Her sisters asked her what she had seen when she went up for the first time, but she told them nothing. Many a morning and many an evening she went back to the place where she had left the Prince. She saw how the fruit in the garden ripened and was gathered, and how the snow melted on the high mountains, but she never saw the Prince; and each time she returned home she was more sorrowful than before.

Her only comfort was to sit in her little garden and put her arms round the marble figure which was so like the Prince; but she no longer looked after her flowers. Her garden became a wilderness; the plants straggled over the paths, and twined their long stalks and leaves round the branches of the trees, so that it became quite dark there.

At last she could bear it no longer, and confided her troubles to one of her sisters, who, of course, told the others. These and a few other mermaids, who also told their intimate friends, were the only people who were in the secret. One of them knew who the Prince was, and could tell them where his kingdom lay. She also had watched the festivities on board the ship.

"Come, little sister!" said the other princesses, and arm-in-arm, in a long row, they rose to the surface of the sea, in front of where the Prince's palace stood. It was built of bright yellow stone, and had broad marble staircases, one of which reached right down to the sea. Magnificent gilt cupolas surmounted the roof, and in the colonnades, which ran all round the building, stood lifelike marble statues. Through the clear panes of the high windows could be seen splendid halls, hung with costly silk curtains and beautiful tapestries, and on all the walls were paintings which were a joy to look at. In the centre of the largest hall a big fountain was playing. Its jets rose as high as the glass dome in the ceiling, through which the sun shone on the water and on the beautiful plants which grew in the great basin.

Now she knew where he lived, and came there many an evening

and many a night across the water. She swam much closer to the shore than any of the others would have ventured, and she even went up the narrow channel under the magnificent marble terrace which cast a long shadow over the water. Here she would sit and gaze at the young Prince, who thought that he was all alone in the bright moonlight.

Many an evening she saw him sailing in his stately boat, with music on board and flags waving. She watched from behind the green rushes, and when the wind caught her long silvery-white veil, and people saw it, they thought it was a swan spreading its wings. Many a night when the fishermen were out at sea fishing by torch-light she heard them say many good things about the Prince, and she was glad that she had saved his life when he was drifting half dead upon the waves. She remembered how heavily his head had lain upon her breast, and how passionately she had kissed him, but he knew nothing about it, and did not even see her in his dreams.

More and more she grew to love the human beings, and more and more she longed to be able to live among them, for their world seemed to her so much bigger than hers. They could sail over the sea in great ships and climb mountains high above the clouds, and the lands which they owned stretched, in woods and fields, farther than her eyes could see. There were still so many things she wanted to know about, and her sisters could not answer all her questions; so she asked her grandmother, who knew the upper world very well, and rightly called it " the countries above the sea."

" If human beings are not drowned," asked the little mermaid, " can they live for ever? Don't they die as we do down here in the sea ? "

" Yes," said the old lady, " they also die, and their life is even shorter than ours. We can live to be three hundred years old, but when we cease to exist we are turned into foam on the water, and have not even a grave down here among our dear ones. We have not got immortal souls, and can never live again. We are like the green rushes, which, when once cut down, can never grow again. Human beings, however, have a soul which lives for ever, lives even after

215

the body has become dust; it rises through the clear air up to the shining stars. As we rise out of the water and see all the countries of the earth, so they rise to unknown, beautiful regions which we shall never see."

"Why don't we also have an immortal soul?" said the little mermaid sorrowfully. "I would gladly give all the hundreds of years I have yet to live if I could only be a human being for one day, and afterwards have a share in the heavenly kingdom."

"You must not think about that," said the old lady. "We are much happier and better off than the human beings up there."

"So I must die, and float as foam on the sea, and never hear the music of the waves or see the beautiful flowers and the red sun! Is there nothing I can do to win an immortal soul?"

"No," said the grandmother. "Only if a man loved you so much that you were dearer to him than father or mother, and if he clung to you with all his heart and all his love, and let the priest place his right hand in yours, with the promise to be faithful to you here and to eternity—then would his soul flow into your body, and you would receive a share in the happiness of mankind. He would give you a soul and yet still keep his own. But that can never happen! What is thought most beautiful here below, your fish-tail, they would consider ugly on earth—they do not know any better. Up there one must have two clumsy supports, which they call legs, in order to be beautiful."

The little mermaid sighed and looked sadly at her fish-tail.

"Let us be happy!" said the old lady. "Let us hop and skip through the three hundred years of our life! That is surely long enough! And afterwards we can rest all the better in our graves. This evening there is to be a Court ball."

Such a splendid sight has never been seen on earth. The walls and ceiling of the big ballroom were of thick but transparent glass. Several hundred colossal mussel-shells, red and grass-green, stood in rows down the sides, holding blue flames, which illuminated the whole room and shone through the walls, so that the sea outside was brightly lit up. One could see innumerable fish, both big and small, swimming outside the glass walls; some with gleaming purple scales and others glittering like silver and gold. Through the middle of the ballroom flowed a broad stream, in which the mermen and mermaids danced to their own beautiful singing. No human beings have such lovely voices. The little mermaid sang most sweetly of all, and they all applauded her. For a moment she felt joyful at heart at the thought that she had the most beautiful voice on land or in the sea; but soon her mind returned to the world above, for she could not forget the handsome Prince and her sorrow at not possessing an immortal soul like his. So she stole out of her father's palace, while all within was joy and merriment, and sat sorrowfully in her little garden.

Suddenly she heard the sound of a horn through the water, and thought: " Now he is sailing above, he whom I love more than father or mother, and into whose hands I would entrust my life's happiness. I will dare anything to win him and an immortal soul. While my sisters are dancing in my father's palace I will go to the sea-witch, whom I have always feared so much. Perhaps she may be able to give me advice and help."

Then the little mermaid left her garden, and went out towards the roaring whirlpools where the witch lived. She had never been that way before; no flowers, no seaweed even, were growing there— only bare, grey sand stretching to the whirlpools, where the water swirled round like rushing mill-wheels, dragging everything it got hold of down into the depths. She had to pass right through these dreadful whirlpools to reach the witch's territory. For a long way the only path led over bubbling mud, that the witch called the peat-bog. Behind this her house stood, in a strange forest, for all the trees and bushes were polyps—half animals and half plants—which looked like hundred-headed snakes growing out of the ground. All the branches were slimy arms with fingers like wriggling worms, and they moved joint by joint from the root to the topmost branch. Everything that they could lay hold of in the sea they clutched and held fast, and never let it go again. The little mermaid stopped timidly in front of them. Her heart was beating with fear, and she nearly turned back; but then she thought of the Prince and man's immortal soul, and took courage. She twisted her long flowing hair round her head, in case the polyps should seize her by it, and, crossing her hands on her breast, darted through the water as fast as a fish, right past the hideous polyps, who stretched out their writhing arms and fingers after her. She saw that each one of them had seized something, and held it tightly with hundreds of little arms like bands of iron. The bleached bones of men who had perished at sea and sunk into the depths were tightly grasped in the arms of some, while others clutched ships' rudders and sea-chests, skeletons of land animals, and a little mermaid whom they had caught and strangled, which was the most terrifying sight of all to her.

She now came to a big marshy place in the forest, where big, fat water-snakes were writhing about, showing their ugly yellow bellies. In the middle of this place stood a house built of the white bones of shipwrecked men, and there sat the sea-witch, letting a toad eat out of her mouth, as we should feed a little canary with sugar. The ugly, fat water-snakes she called her little chickens, and allowed them to crawl all over her hideous bosom.

"I know quite well what you want!" said the sea-witch. "It is silly of you! But you shall have your way, for it is sure to bring you misfortune, my pretty princess! You want to get rid of your fish-tail and have instead two stumps which human beings use for walking, so that the young Prince may fall in love with you, and you may win him and an immortal soul!" As she said this the old witch laughed so loudly and horribly that the toad and the snakes fell to the ground, where they crawled about. "You have only just come in time," said the witch, "for if you had come after sunrise to-morrow I should not have been able to help you till another year had passed. I will make you a drink, and before sunrise you must swim ashore and sit on the beach and drink it. Then your tail will split in two and shrink into what human beings call legs; but it will hurt you, as if a sharp sword were running through you. Every one who sees you will say that you are the most beautiful child of man they have ever seen. You will keep your gracefulness, and no dancer will be able to move as lightly as you; but at each step you take you will feel as if you were treading on a sharp knife, and as if your blood must flow. Are you willing to suffer all this, and shall I help you?"

"Yes," said the little mermaid in a trembling voice, and thought of the Prince and of winning an immortal soul.

"But remember!" said the witch. "When once you have taken the human form you can never become a mermaid again. You will never again be able to dive down through the water to your sisters and your father's palace. And if you fail to win the Prince's love, so that for your sake he will forget father and mother, and cling to you with body and soul, and make the priest join your hands as man and wife, you will not be given an immortal soul. On the first morning after he has married another your heart will break, and you will turn into foam on the water."

"I will do it," said the little mermaid, as pale as death.

"But you will have to pay me," said the witch, "and it is not a trifle that I ask. You have the most beautiful voice of all who live at the bottom of the sea, with which you probably think you can enchant the Prince: but this voice you must give to me. I must have the best thing you possess in return for my precious drink, for I have to give you my own blood in it, so that the drink may be as sharp as a two-edged sword."

"But if you take away my voice," said the little mermaid, "what have I got left?"

"Your lovely figure," said the witch, "your grace of movement, and your speaking eyes! With these surely you can capture a human heart. Well, have you lost your courage? Put out your little tongue, so that I may cut it off in payment, and you shall have the powerful drink."

"Do it," said the little mermaid, and the witch put her cauldron on the fire to prepare the magic drink. "Cleanliness is a good thing," she said, and scoured the cauldron with snakes which she had tied into a bundle. Then she pricked her breast and let her black blood drip into it, and the steam rose up in the weirdest shapes, so that one could not help being frightened and horrified. Every moment the witch threw some new thing into the cauldron, and when it boiled the sound was like crocodiles weeping. At last the drink was ready, and it looked like the clearest water.

"Here it is!" said the witch, and cut off the little mermaid's tongue, so that now she was dumb and could neither sing nor speak. "If the polyps should catch hold of you when you go back through my wood," said the witch, "you need only throw one drop of this liquid over them, and their arms and fingers will fly into a thousand pieces!" But the little mermaid had no need to do this, for the polyps shrank back from her in terror at the sight of the sparkling drink, which gleamed in her hand like a glittering star. So she came quickly through the forest and the bog and the roaring whirlpools.

She could see her father's palace: in the ballroom the lamps were all darkened, and every one was asleep, but she dared not go in to them, now that she was dumb and about to leave them for ever. She felt as if her heart would break with sorrow. She stole into the garden, took a flower from each of her sisters' flower-beds, kissed her hand a thousand times to the palace, and swam up through the dark blue sea.

The sun had not yet risen when she came in sight of the Prince's palace and reached the magnificent marble steps. The moon was shining bright and clear. The little mermaid drank the sharp, burning draught, and it felt as if a two-edged sword went through her tender body; she fainted, and lay as if dead.

When the sun shone over the sea she awoke, and felt a stabbing pain; but there before her stood the beautiful young Prince. He fixed his black eyes on her, so that she cast hers down, and saw that her fish-tail had disappeared, and that she had the prettiest little white legs that any girl could possess; but she was quite naked; so she wrapped herself in her long, thick hair. The Prince asked her who she was and how she came there, and she looked at him tenderly and yet sadly with her deep blue eyes, for she could not speak. Then he took her by the hand and led her into the palace. Every step she took was, as the witch had warned her, as if she trod on pointed needles and sharp knives, but she bore it gladly, and walked as lightly as a soap-bubble by the side of the Prince, who, with all the others, admired her grace of movement.

She was given wonderful dresses of silk and muslin to put on,

THE POLYPS SHRANK BACK FROM HER IN TERROR

and she was the greatest beauty in the palace; but she was dumb, and unable either to sing or speak. Beautiful slaves, dressed in silk and gold, came to sing before the Prince and his royal parents. One of them sang better than all the rest, and the Prince clapped his hands and smiled at her. Then the little mermaid grew sad, for she knew that she had been able to sing far more beautifully; and she thought: "Oh, if he only knew that to be with him I have given away my voice for ever!"

Now the slaves began to dance light, graceful dances to the loveliest music; and then the little mermaid lifted her beautiful white arms, rose on her toes, and glided across the floor, dancing as none of the others had danced. At every movement her beauty seemed to grow, and her eyes spoke more deeply to the heart than the songs of the slave girls. Every one was charmed by her, especially the Prince, who called her his little foundling, and she danced again and again, although every time her feet touched the ground she felt as if she were treading on sharp knives. The Prince said that she should always be near him, and let her sleep on a velvet cushion before his door.

He had a man's dress made for her, so that she might ride with him. They rode through fragrant woods, where the green branches brushed her shoulders and the little birds sang among the fresh leaves. She climbed with the Prince up the high mountains, and, though her tender feet bled so that even others could see it, she smiled and followed him, till they saw the clouds sailing beneath their feet, like a flock of birds flying to foreign lands.

At home, in the Prince's palace, when all the others were asleep at night, she would go out on to the broad marble steps. It cooled her burning feet to stand in the cold sea-water, and then she thought of those she had left down below in the deep.

One night her sisters came up arm-in-arm, singing sorrowfully as they swam through the water, and she beckoned to them, and they recognized her and told her how sad she had made them all. After that they came to see her every night, and one night she saw far out her old grandmother, who had not been up to the surface for many, many years, and the sea-king, with his crown on his head. They stretched out their hands towards her, but did not venture so close to land as her sisters.

Day by day the Prince grew fonder of her; he loved her as one would love a good, sweet child, but he never had the slightest idea of making her his queen; and yet his wife she must be, or she could not win an immortal soul, but on his wedding morning would turn into foam on the sea.

"Don't you love me more than them all?" the little mermaid's eyes seemed to say when the Prince took her in his arms and kissed her beautiful forehead.

"Yes, you are the dearest to me," he said, "for you have the best heart of them all. You are the most devoted to me, and you are like a young girl whom I once saw, but whom I fear I shall never meet again. I was on board a ship which was wrecked, and the waves washed me ashore near a holy temple where several young maidens were serving in attendance. The youngest of them found me on the beach, and saved my life. I only saw her twice. She is the only girl in the world I could love, but you are like her, and you almost drive her image from my heart. She belongs to the holy temple, and so by good fortune you have been sent to me, and we shall never be parted."

"Alas! He doesn't know that it was I who saved his life!" thought the little mermaid. "I carried him across the sea to the wood where the temple stands; and I was hidden in the foam, watching to see if anyone would come to him. I saw the beautiful girl whom he loves better than me." She sighed deeply, for she could not weep. "The girl belongs to the holy temple, he said. She will never come out into the world, and they will never meet again; but I am with him, and see him every day. I will care for him, love him, and give up my life for him."

But soon the rumour spread that the Prince was to marry the beautiful daughter of a neighbouring king, and that that was why they were fitting up such a magnificent ship. The Prince is going to visit the neighbouring king's country, they said, but really he is going to see his daughter, and a large suite is to accompany him. The little mermaid shook her head and smiled, for she knew the Prince's thoughts much better than the others. "I must go," he said to her. "I must see the beautiful princess, for my parents wish it; but they will not force me to bring her home as my bride. I cannot love her: she will not be like the beautiful girl in the temple whom you are like. If one day I were to choose a bride I would rather have you, my dumb foundling with the eloquent eyes." And he kissed her red lips, and played with her long hair, and laid his head on her heart, so that she began to dream of human happiness and an immortal soul.

"You are not afraid of the sea, my dumb child?" he said to her, when they were standing on board the stately ship which was to carry him to the neighbouring king's country. He told her of the storm and of the calm, of the strange fish in the deep, and of the marvellous things which divers had seen down there, and she smiled at his words, for she knew more about the things at the bottom of the sea than anyone else.

At night, in the moonlight, when all were asleep except the man at the helm, she sat by the ship's rail, gazing down into the clear water, and thought she could see her father's palace, and her grandmother, with her silver crown on her head, looking up through the swirling currents at the ship's keel. Then her sisters came up out of the water, looking sorrowfully at her and wringing their white hands. She beckoned to them, and smiled, and wanted to tell them that she was well and happy, but a cabin-boy came up to her, and her sisters dived under, so that he thought the white things he had seen were just foam on the sea.

The next morning the ship reached the harbour of the neighbouring king's magnificent city. All the church-bells were ringing, and from the high towers trumpets sounded, while soldiers paraded with flying colours and glittering bayonets. Every day there were festivities; balls and receptions followed one another; but the princess had not yet arrived. She was being brought up in a holy convent far away, they said, where she was learning every royal virtue. At last she came. The little mermaid was anxious to see her beauty, and she had to admit that she had never seen a lovelier being: her skin was clear and delicate, and behind her long dark lashes smiled a pair of deep blue, loyal eyes.

"You are she!" said the Prince. "She who saved me when I

**SHE PUT HER ARMS ROUND THE MARBLE FIGURE WHICH WAS SO
LIKE THE PRINCE**
"The Little Mermaid"

"BUT HE HAS NOTHING ON AT ALL," SAID A LITTLE CHILD

"The Emperor's New Clothes"

lay almost dead on the shore!" And he clasped his blushing bride in his arms.

"Oh, I am too happy!" he said to the little mermaid. "My greatest wish, which I have never dared to hope for, has come true. You will rejoice at my happiness, for you love me more than them all." The little mermaid kissed his hand, and felt as if her heart was already breaking: his wedding morning, she knew, would bring death to her, and she would turn into foam on the sea.

The church-bells pealed, and heralds rode through the streets announcing the betrothal. On all the altars sweet-smelling oil was burning in costly silver lamps. The priests swung their censers, and the bride and bridegroom joined hands and received the bishop's blessing. The little mermaid, dressed in silk and gold, stood holding the bride's train, but her ears did not hear the joyous music, and her eyes saw nothing of the sacred ceremony—she was thinking of the night of her death, and of all that she had lost in this world.

That same evening the bride and bridegroom came on board the ship; cannons roared, flags were waving, and in the middle of the ship was erected a royal tent of purple and gold, with the most magnificent couch, where the bridal pair were to rest through the still, cool night.

The sails swelled in the wind, and the ship glided smoothly and almost without motion over the clear sea. When it grew dark coloured lamps were lighted, and the sailors danced merrily on deck. The little mermaid could not help thinking of the first time she had risen to the surface and had seen the same splendour and revelry. She threw herself among the dancers, darting and turning as a swallow turns when it is pursued, and they all applauded her, for she had never danced so wonderfully before. It was like sharp knives cutting her tender feet, but she did not feel it, for the pain in her heart was much greater. She knew that it was the last evening that she would be with him—him for whom she had left her family and her home, sacrificed her lovely voice, and daily suffered endless pain, of which he had not the slightest idea. It was the last night that she would breathe the same air as he, and see the deep sea and the starry sky. An

unending night, without thoughts or dreams, was waiting for her
who had no soul and could not win one. On board the ship the
rejoicing and revelry lasted till long past midnight, and she laughed
and danced with the thought of death in her heart. The Prince kissed
his beautiful bride, and she played with his dark hair, and arm-in-arm
they retired to rest in the magnificent tent.

Then everything grew quiet on board; only the steersman stood
at the helm, and the little mermaid laid her white arms on the rail,
and looked towards the east for the rosy glimmer of dawn, for she
knew that the first sunbeam would kill her.

Then she saw her sisters rising out of the waves; they were as
pale as she was, and their beautiful hair no longer floated in the wind,
for it had been cut off. "We have given it to the witch, to get her
help, so that you need not die to-night. She has given us a knife: here
it is. See how sharp it is! Before the sun rises you must thrust it
into the Prince's heart, and when the warm blood sprinkles your feet
they will grow together again into a fish-tail. Then you will be a
mermaid again, and you can come down with us into the sea, and
live your three hundred years before you turn into dead, salt sea-
foam. Hurry! For he or you must die before sunrise. Our old
grandmother is so full of grief for you that her white hair has all
fallen off, as ours fell under the witch's scissors. Kill the Prince and
come back to us! Hurry! Do you see that red streak in the sky?
In a few moments the sun will rise, and then you must die!" They
gave a deep sigh, and disappeared beneath the waves.

The little mermaid drew back the purple curtain of the tent, and
saw the lovely bride lying asleep with her head on the Prince's
breast, and she bent down and kissed him on his beautiful forehead.
She looked up at the sky, where the rosy glow was growing brighter
and brighter, and then at the sharp knife, and again at the Prince, who
murmured his bride's name in his dreams. Yes, she alone was in his
thoughts, and for a moment the knife trembled in the little mermaid's
hand. But suddenly she flung it far out into the waves, that shone
red where it fell, so that it looked as if drops of blood were splashing
up out of the water. Once more she looked with dimmed eyes at

THE LITTLE MERMAID WAS SLOWLY RISING UP OUT OF THE FOAM

the Prince, then threw herself from the ship into the sea, and felt her body dissolving into foam.

Now the sun rose out of the sea, and its rays fell with gentleness and warmth on the deathly cold sea-foam, and the little mermaid felt no pain of death. She saw the bright sun and, floating above her, hundreds of beautiful transparent beings, through whom she could see the white sails of the ship and the red clouds in the sky. Their voices were melodious, but so ethereal that no human ear could hear them, just as no earthly eye could see them, and without wings they floated through the air. The little mermaid saw that she had a body like theirs and was slowly rising up out of the foam.

"Where am I going to?" she asked, and her voice sounded like that of the other spirits—so ethereal that no earthly music was like it.

"To the daughters of the air," answered the others. "Mermaids have no immortal soul, and can never have one unless they win the love of a human being. Their eternal life must depend on the power of another. The daughters of the air have no immortal soul either, but by their own good deeds they can win one for themselves. We fly to the hot countries where the pestilent winds kill the human beings, and we bring them cool breezes. We spread the fragrance of the flowers through the air, and bring life and healing. When for three hundred years we have striven to do all the good we can we are given an immortal soul, and share the eternal happiness of mankind. You, poor little mermaid, have struggled with all your heart for the same goal, and have suffered and endured. Now you have risen to the spiritual world, and after three hundred years of good deeds you will win an immortal soul for yourself."

And the little mermaid lifted her eyes to the sun, and for the first time she felt tears in them.

On the ship there was life and noise once more. She saw the Prince and his beautiful bride looking for her, and gazing sadly at the gleaming foam, as if they knew that she had thrown herself into the waves. Unseen, she kissed the bride's forehead and smiled at the Prince. Then she rose with the other children of the air up to the rosy clouds which sailed across the sky.

" In three hundred years we shall float like this into the kingdom of God!"

" But we may get there sooner!" whispered one of them. " Unseen, we fly into houses where there are children, and for every day on which we find a good child that gives its parents joy and deserves their love God shortens our time of probation. The child does not know when we fly through the room, and if we smile for joy one of the three hundred years is taken off; but if we see a naughty and wicked child we must shed tears of sorrow, and every tear adds a day to our time of probation."

THE TRAVELLING COMPANION

Poor John was in a great trouble, for his father was very ill, and could not be cured. There was no one but these two in the little room; the lamp on the table had nearly burnt out, and it was quite late in the evening.

"You have been a good son, John," said the sick father. "The Lord will help you on in the world." And he looked at him with his mild, earnest eyes, drew a deep breath, and died; it was just as if he had fallen asleep. But John wept; now he had no one in the whole world, neither father nor mother, sister nor brother. Poor John! He knelt down by the bed, kissed his dead father's hand, and shed very many salt tears; but at last his eyes closed, and he went to sleep, lying with his head against the hard bedpost.

Then he dreamt a strange dream: he saw the sun and moon bowing before him, and he saw his father again alive and well, and heard him laugh as he had always laughed when he was very happy. A beautiful girl, with a golden crown upon her long shining hair, gave John her hand, and his father said, "Do you see what a bride you have won? She is the most beautiful in the whole world!" Then he awoke, and all the splendour was gone. His father was lying dead and cold in the bed, and there was no one at all with them. Poor John!

The week after the dead man was buried. John walked close behind the coffin. He could now no longer see the good father who had loved him so much. He heard how they threw the earth down upon the coffin, and watched till only the last corner could be seen; but the next shovelful of earth hid even that; then he felt as if his heart must burst into pieces, so sorrowful was he. Around him they were singing a psalm; it sounded so beautiful that the tears came into John's eyes; he wept, and that did him good in his sorrow. The sun shone brightly on the green trees, as if it would say, "You must no

longer be sorrowful, John! Do you see how beautiful the sky is?
Your father is up there, and prays to the Father of all that it may
always be well with you."

"I will always do right, too," said John; "then I shall go to
heaven to my father, and what joy it will be when we see each other
again! How much I shall then have to tell him! And he will show
me so many things, and explain to me the glories of heaven, just as
he taught me here on earth. Oh, what joy that will be!"

John saw it all so plainly that he smiled, while the tears were still
running down his cheeks. The little birds sat up in the chestnut-trees,
and twittered, "Tweet-weet! tweet-weet!" They were joyful and
merry, though they too had been at the burying. But they seemed to
know that the dead man was up in heaven, and that he had wings, far
larger and more beautiful than theirs, and that he was now happy,
because he had been a good man upon earth, and they rejoiced at it.
John saw how they flew from the green tree out into the world, and
he felt a longing to fly with them. But first he carved a great cross of
wood to put on his father's grave, and when he brought it there in
the evening the grave was already strewn with sand and flowers.
Strangers had done this, for all loved the good father who was now
dead.

Early next morning John packed his little bundle, and put in his
belt his whole inheritance, which consisted of fifty dollars and a few
silver shillings; and with this he intended to wander out into the
world. But first he went to the churchyard to his father's grave,
repeated the Lord's Prayer, and said, "Farewell, my dear father! I
will always try to be a good man, and so do thou beg the good God
that all may go well with me."

In the fields through which he passed all the flowers were fresh
and blooming in the warm sunshine; and they nodded in the wind,
as if they wished to say, "Welcome to the green wood! Is it not
lovely here?" But John turned round once more to look at the old
church, where he had been christened when he was a little child, and
where he had been to service every Sunday with his father, and had
sung his psalm. High up in one of the openings of the tower he saw

the little church-goblin standing with his little pointed red cap, shading his face with his bent arm to keep the sun from shining in his eyes. John nodded a farewell to him, and the little goblin waved his red cap, laid his hand on his heart, and kissed his hand to John a great many times, to show him that he wished him well and hoped he would have a prosperous journey.

John thought what a number of fine things he would see in the great splendid world, and he went on farther and farther—farther than he had ever been before. He did not know the places he came through nor the people he met. Now he was far away in a strange country.

The first night he had to lie down on a haystack in a field to sleep, for he had no other bed. But it was very nice, he thought; the king could have no better. There was the whole field, with the brook, the haystack, and the blue sky above; it was certainly a lovely bedroom. The green grass with the little red and white flowers was the carpet, the elder-bushes and the wild-rose hedges were bouquets of flowers, and for a wash-hand basin he had the whole brook with the clear fresh water, and the rushes bowing before him and wishing him " Good night " and " Good morning." The moon was really a fine night-light, high up under the blue ceiling, and one that would never set fire to the curtains. John could sleep quite safely, and he did so too, and never woke until the sun rose and all the little birds round about were singing, " Good morning ! good morning ! Are you not up yet ? "

The bells were ringing for church; it was Sunday. The people went to hear the priest, and John followed them, and sang a psalm and heard God's word, just as if he was in his own church, where he had been christened and had sung psalms with his father.

Out in the churchyard were many graves, and on some of them the grass grew high. Then he thought of his father's grave, which would one day look like these, as he could not weed or trim it. So he sat down and pulled up the long grass, set up the wooden crosses which had fallen down, and put back in their places the wreaths which the wind had blown away from the graves. For he thought,

"Perhaps someone will do the same to my father's grave, as I cannot do it."

Outside the churchyard gate stood an old beggar, leaning upon his crutch. John gave him the silver shillings which he had, and then went on his way, happy and cheerful, into the wide world. Towards evening a dreadful storm came on. He made haste to get under shelter, but very soon the dark night set in. At last he came to a little church, which stood quite by itself on the top of a hill.

"I'll sit down in here in a corner," said he. "I am quite tired and sorely in need of a little rest." So he sat down, folded his hands, and said his evening prayer; and before he was aware of it he was asleep and dreaming, while it thundered and lightened outside.

When he awoke it was midnight; but the bad weather had passed away, and the moon shone in upon him through the windows. In the middle of the aisle stood an open coffin with a dead man in it, for he had not yet been buried. John was not at all afraid, for he had a good conscience, and he knew very well that the dead do not harm anyone. It is the living evil-doers who are the danger. Two such bad men were standing close to the dead man, who had been placed here in the church till he should be buried. They were evilly disposed towards him, and would not let him lie at rest in his coffin, but were going to throw him outside the church door—poor dead man!

"Why do you do that?" asked John. "It is bad and wicked. Let him rest, in Christ's name!"

"Nonsense!" said the two bad men. "He has cheated us. He owed us money and could not pay it, and now he's dead, and we shall never get a penny! So we mean to have our revenge; he shall lie like a dog outside the church door!"

"I have no more than fifty dollars," said John; "that is my whole inheritance; but I will gladly give it you if you will promise me on your honour to leave the poor dead man in peace. I shall be able to get on without the money; I have sound, strong limbs, and God will always help me."

"Yes," said the horrible men. "If you will pay his debt we will do nothing to him, you may depend upon that!" And then they

233

took the money he gave them, laughed aloud at his good nature, and went their way. But he laid the dead body out again in the coffin, folded its hands, took leave of it, and went away contentedly through the great forest.

All around, wherever the moon could shine between the trees, he saw the graceful little elves playing about merrily. They did not let him disturb them—they knew that he was a good, innocent man, and it is only the bad people who are never allowed to see the elves. Some of them were not bigger than a finger-breadth, and had fastened up their long yellow hair with golden combs. They were rocking themselves, two and two, on the big dewdrops that lay on the leaves and the long grass. Sometimes the dewdrops rolled off, and then they fell down between the long grass-stalks, and that caused much laughter and noise among the other tiny creatures. It was great fun! They sang, and John recognized quite plainly the pretty songs which he had learnt as a little boy. Great gay-coloured spiders, with silver crowns on their heads, had to spin long hanging bridges and palaces from one hedge to another, and as the tiny dewdrops fell on these they looked like gleaming glass in the moonlight. This went on until the sun rose. Then the little elves crept into the flower-buds, and the wind caught their bridges and palaces, which flew through the air like great cobwebs.

John had just come out of the wood, when a man's strong voice called out behind him, " Hullo, comrade! Whither are you journeying? "

" Out into the wide world! " said John. " I have neither father nor mother, and am but a poor lad; but God will help me."

" I am going out into the wide world too," said the strange man. " Shall we two keep company? "

" Yes, certainly," said John, and so they went on together. Soon they became very fond of each other, for they were both good men. But John saw that the stranger was much wiser than he was. He had travelled almost all over the world, and could tell him about almost everything that existed.

The sun already stood high in the heavens when they seated themselves under a great tree to eat their breakfast; and just then an old woman came up. She was very old, and walked quite bent, leaning upon a crutch, and carrying on her back a bundle of firewood which she had gathered in the forest. Her apron was fastened up, and John saw three big rods of fern and some willow twigs sticking out of it. Just when she was quite close to them her foot slipped; she fell and gave a loud scream, for she had broken her leg, the poor old woman!

John proposed at once that they should carry her home to where she lived, but the stranger opened his knapsack, took out a little jar, and said that he had a salve in it which would immediately make her leg whole and strong, so that she could walk home herself, just as if she had never broken her leg at all. But for that he wanted her to give him the three rods that she had in her apron.

"That would be paying well!" said the old woman, and she nodded her head in a strange way. She did not like to give away the rods, but then it was not pleasant to lie there with a broken leg! So she gave him the rods, and as soon as he had rubbed the salve on her leg the old mother got up and walked much better than before—such was the power of this ointment. But then it was not to be bought at the chemist's.

"What do you want with the rods?" John asked his travelling companion.

"They are three capital fern brooms," said he. "Just the sort I like, for I am a whimsical fellow."

And they went on a good way.

"See how the sky is becoming overcast," said John, pointing straight before them. "Those are awfully thick clouds."

"No," said his travelling companion, "they are not clouds, they are mountains—lovely great mountains, where you can get high up above the clouds into the pure air. It is delightful, I can tell you! To-morrow we shall be far on our way out into the world."

But they were not so near as they looked; they had to walk for a whole day before they came to the mountains, where the black woods grew straight up towards heaven, and there were rocks almost as big as a whole town. It certainly might be hard work to get right across them, and so John and his comrade went into an inn to rest themselves well and gather strength for the morrow's journey.

Down in the big common room in the inn a great many people were assembled, for there was a man there with a puppet-show. He had just put up his little theatre, and the people were sitting round to see the play. Right in front a fat butcher had taken his seat in the very best place. His great bulldog—ugh! how fierce he looked—sat by his side and stared with all his might, as all the rest were doing.

Then the play began; and it was a nice play, with a king and a queen in it; they sat upon a beautiful throne, and had gold crowns on their heads and long trains to their clothes, for they were very rich. The prettiest of wooden dolls, with glass eyes and great moustaches, stood at all the doors, and opened and shut them so that fresh air might come into the room. It was a very pleasant play, and not at all mournful. But—goodness knows what the big bulldog can have been thinking about!—just as the queen stood up and was walking across the boards, as the fat butcher did not hold him, he made a spring on to the stage and seized the queen by her slender waist so that one heard it go ' crick-crack.' It was terrible!

The poor man who managed the whole show was very frightened and in great distress about his queen, for she was the most beautiful doll he had, and now the ugly bulldog had bitten her head off. But afterwards, when the people had gone away, the stranger who had come with John said that he would put her to rights again, and he brought out his little jar once more and rubbed the doll with the ointment with which he had cured the old woman when she broke her leg. As soon as the doll had been rubbed she was whole again. Yes, she could even move all her limbs by herself—it was no longer necessary to pull the strings. The doll was just like a living person, except that she could not speak. The man who owned the little puppet-show was very glad, for now he had not to hold this doll by the strings any more, for she could dance by herself. None of the others could do that.

When night came on, and all the people in the inn had gone to bed, there was some one sighing so fearfully, and it went on so long,

that everybody got up to see what it could be. The man who had
shown the play went to his little theatre, for it was there that the
sighing came from. All the wooden dolls lay mixed together, the
king and all his followers; and it was they who were sighing so
pitifully and staring with their glass eyes; for they wished to be
rubbed a little as the queen had been, so that they might be able to
move by themselves. The queen at once went down on her knees,
and held out her beautiful crown, and begged, " Take this from me,
but rub my husband and my courtiers! " Then the poor man, the
owner of the little theatre and the dolls, could not help crying, for
he really was so sorry for them. He promised the travelling companion at once that he would give him all the money he received
the next evening for the show if he would only anoint four or five
of his dolls. But the travelling companion said he would not ask anything at all but the big sword the man wore by his side; and when
he got it he anointed six of the dolls, who immediately began to
dance so gracefully that all the girls, the living human girls who
were watching, fell a-dancing too. The coachman and the cook
danced, the waiter and the chambermaid, and all the strangers, and
even the fire-shovel and tongs, but these last fell down flat at the
very first jump they made. Yes, it was indeed a merry night!

Next morning John with his travelling companion went away
from them all, up the high mountains and through the great pine-
woods. They got so high up that the church steeples below looked
at last like little red berries among all the green; and they could see
very far, many, many miles away, where they had never been. So
much beauty in this lovely world John had never seen before. And
the sun shone warm in the fresh blue air, and among the mountains
he could hear the huntsmen blowing their horns so gaily and sweetly
that tears of joy came into his eyes, and he could not help calling out,
" How kind has Heaven been to us to give us all the loveliness that
there is in the world! "

The travelling companion also stood there with folded hands,
and looked out over the forest and the towns in the warm sunshine.
At the same time they heard the most wonderful music over their

heads: they looked up, and there was a large white swan soaring in the air, and singing as they had never heard a bird sing before. But the song became weaker and weaker; he bowed his head and sank slowly down at their feet, where he lay dead, the beautiful bird!

"Two such splendid wings," said the travelling companion, "so white and large as those which this bird has are worth money; I will take them with me. Do you see that it was good I took the sabre?"

And so, with one blow, he cut off both the wings of the dead swan, which he wanted to have.

They now travelled for many, many miles over the mountains till at last they saw a great town before them with hundreds of towers, which shone like silver in the sun. In the middle of the town was a splendid marble palace, roofed with pure red gold, and there lived the King.

John and the travelling companion would not go into the town at once, but stopped at the inn outside the town, that they might make themselves tidy; for they wished to look neat as they went about the streets. The landlord told them that the King was a very good man, who never did harm to anyone one way or another; but as for his daughter—Heaven preserve us! she was a bad princess. Beauty enough she had indeed—no one could be so pretty and so charming as she was—but what good was that? She was a wicked witch, through whose fault many gallant princes had lost their lives. She had given out that all men might seek her hand. Anyone might come, be he prince or beggar: it was all the same to her. He had only to guess three things she had just thought of, and about which she questioned him. If he could do that she would marry him, and he was to be king over the whole country when her father died, but if he could not guess the three things she ordered him to be hanged or to have his head cut off! Indeed she was wicked, was this beautiful princess! Her father, the old King, was very sad about it; but he could not forbid her to be so wicked, because he had once said that he would have nothing to do with her lovers; she might do as she liked. Every time a prince came, and tried to guess in order to gain the Princess, he failed, and was hanged or lost his head. They had all been warned in time, you see, and need never have gone a-wooing. The old King was so sorry for all this misery and woe that he used to spend a whole day in every year on his knees with all his soldiers, praying that the Princess might become good; but that she would not, by any means. The old women who drank brandy used to colour it black before they drank it, they were in such deep mourning —and more than that they certainly could not do.

"The hateful Princess!" said John. "She ought really to have the rod; that would do her good. If I were only the old King she should be flogged till the blood ran!"

As he spoke they heard the people outside shouting "Hurrah!" The Princess came by; and she was really so beautiful that all the people forgot how wicked she was, and they shouted "Hurrah!" Twelve beautiful maidens, all in white silk gowns, and each with a golden tulip in her hand, rode on coal-black horses by her side. The Princess herself had a snow-white horse, decked with diamonds and rubies. Her riding-habit was all of cloth of gold, and the whip she held in her hand looked like a sunbeam; the golden crown on her head shone just like stars from the sky, and her mantle was sewn together out of more than a thousand beautiful butterflies' wings. In spite of this, she herself was much more lovely than all her clothing.

When John saw her his face became as red as a drop of blood, and he could hardly utter a word. The Princess looked just like the beautiful maiden with the golden crown of whom he had dreamt on the night his father died. He found her so enchanting that he could not help loving her greatly. It could not be true that she was a wicked witch, who caused people to be hanged or beheaded if they could not guess the riddles she put to them.

"Every one is free to woo her, even the poorest beggar. I will really go to the castle, I cannot help it!"

They all told him not to attempt it, for he was certain to fare as all the rest had done. His travelling companion too tried to dissuade him; but John thought it would end well. He brushed his shoes and his coat, washed his face and hands, combed his nice beautiful

239

yellow hair, and then went all by himself into the town and up to
the palace.

"Come in!" said the old King, when John knocked at the door.

John opened it, and the old King came to meet him in his dressing-
gown and embroidered slippers. He had the crown on his head, and
the sceptre in one hand and the golden apple in the other. "Wait a
little!" said he, and put the apple under his arm, so that he could hold
out his hand to John. But as soon as he learnt that his visitor was
a suitor he began to cry so violently that both the sceptre and the
apple fell to the ground, and he was obliged to wipe his eyes with his
dressing-gown. Poor old King!

"Give it up!" said he. "You will fare as badly as all the others
have done. Now come and see!"

Then he led him out into the Princess's pleasure garden. There
was a terrible sight! On every tree there hung three or four kings'
sons who had wooed the Princess, but had not been able to guess the

240

riddles she put to them. Each time that the breeze blew all the skeletons rattled, so that the little birds were frightened, and never dared to come into the garden. All the flowers were tied up to human bones, and in the flower-pots were grinning skulls. It was a strange garden indeed for a princess.

"Now you see," said the old King. "It will fare with you just as it has fared with all these whom you see here; therefore you had better give it up. You will really make me unhappy, for I take these things very much to heart."

John kissed the good old King's hand, and said all would be well, for he was quite enchanted by the beautiful Princess.

At that moment the Princess herself came riding into the courtyard with all her ladies, so they went to meet her and wished her good day. She was beautiful to look at, and she gave John her hand, and then he could not help loving her more than before; she could never be the cruel, wicked witch people said she was. Then they went into the hall, and the little pages offered them preserves and ginger-nuts. But the old King was so distressed that he could not eat anything at all. Besides, ginger-nuts were too hard for him.

It was settled that John should come up to the palace again the next morning; the judges and the whole council would then be assembled, and would hear how he succeeded with his answers. If it went well with him that time he would have to come twice more; but no one yet had come who had succeeded in guessing right even the first time, and so they had lost their lives.

John was not at all anxious as to how he would fare. On the contrary, he was quite merry, thought only of the beautiful Princess, and felt quite sure that God would help him, but how he did not know, nor did he want to think of it. He danced along on the highroad on his way back to the inn, where his travelling companion was waiting for him.

John could not stop telling him how gracious the Princess had been to him and how beautiful she was. He declared he already longed for the next day, when he was to go to the palace and try his luck at guessing.

But the travelling companion shook his head and was greatly downcast. "I am so fond of you!" said he. "We might have been together a long time yet, and now I am to lose you already! You poor dear John! I should like to cry, but I will not disturb your happiness on the last evening perhaps we shall ever spend together. We will be merry, right merry! To-morrow, when you are gone, I can weep undisturbed."

All the people in the town had soon heard that a new suitor for the Princess had arrived, and there was great sorrow on that account. The theatre was closed; all the cake-women tied bits of crape round their sugar men, and the King and the priests were on their knees in the churches. There was great lamentation, for they all thought that John would fare no better than the other suitors.

Towards evening the travelling companion mixed a big bowl of punch, and said to John, "Now we will be very merry, and drink the health of the Princess." But when John had drunk two glasses he became so sleepy that he found it impossible to keep his eyes open, and sank into a deep sleep. The travelling companion lifted him very gently from his chair and laid him in the bed, and when it was quite dark he took the two great wings which he had cut off the swan and bound them fast to his own shoulders, and he put in his pocket the longest of the rods he had got from the old woman who had fallen and broken her leg, opened the window and flew away over the town, straight to the palace, where he sat himself in a corner under the window which looked into the bedroom of the Princess.

Everything was quiet in the whole town. As the clock struck a quarter to twelve the window opened, and the Princess, in a long white cloak, and with long black wings on her shoulders, flew out and away over the town to a great mountain. But the travelling companion made himself invisible, so that she could not see him at all, and flew behind her, and whipped the Princess with his rod, so that the blood came at every stroke. Ugh! what a journey that was through the air! The wind caught her cloak, so that it spread out on all sides like a great sail, and the moon shone through it.

"How it hails! how it hails!" said the Princess at every blow she got from the rod, and it served her right. At last she arrived at the mountain, and knocked. There was a rolling like thunder, the mountain opened, and the Princess went in. The travelling companion followed her, for no one could see him, as he was invisible. They went through a great, long passage, where the walls glistened in a strange manner; there were more than a thousand gleaming spiders running up and down the walls and shining like fire. Then they came to a great hall built of silver and gold; flowers as big as sunflowers, red and blue, shone on the walls; but no one could pluck these flowers, for the stems were ugly poisonous snakes, and the flowers were flames of fire pouring out of their mouths. The whole of the ceiling was covered with shining glow-worms and sky-blue bats, flapping their thin wings. It looked terrific! In the middle of the floor was a throne, borne by four skeleton horses, with harness made by fiery red spiders; the throne itself was of milk-white glass, and the cushions were little black mice, biting each other's tails. Above it was a canopy of rose-red spiders' web, beset with the prettiest little green flies, which shone like precious stones. On the throne sat an old troll, with a crown on his ugly head and a sceptre in his hand. He kissed the Princess on the forehead, made her sit beside him on the costly throne, and then the music began. Great black grasshoppers played on jews'-harps, and the owl beat her wings upon her body, because she hadn't a drum. It was a ridiculous concert. Little black goblins with a jack-o'-lantern on their caps danced about the hall. But no one could see the travelling companion; he had placed himself just behind the throne, and heard and saw everything. The courtiers who now came in were very grand and noble; but anyone with common sense could see what they really were. They were nothing more than broomsticks with cabbage-heads on them, which the troll had brought to life by magic and given embroidered clothes. But that did not matter, for they were only used for show.

After there had been some dancing the Princess told the troll that she had a new suitor, and therefore she asked him what she should think of for him to guess when he should come next morning to the palace.

"Listen!" said the troll. "I will tell you something. You must choose something very easy, for then he won't guess it. Think of one of your shoes. That he will not guess. Let him have his head cut off, but don't forget, when you come to me to-morrow night, to bring me his eyes, for I'll eat them."

The Princess curtsied very low, and said she would not forget the eyes. The troll opened the mountain, and she flew home again, but the travelling companion followed her, and beat her again so hard with the rod that she groaned aloud at the heavy hailstorm, and hurried as much as she could to get back into the bedroom through the window. The travelling companion flew back to the inn, where John was still asleep, took off his wings, and lay down upon the bed, for he might well be tired.

It was very early in the morning when John awoke. The travelling companion got up too, and told him he had had a wonderful dream in the night about the Princess and one of her shoes, and he therefore begged John to ask if the Princess had not thought of her shoe. For that was what he had heard from the troll in the mountain.

"I may just as well ask that as anything else," said John. "Perhaps it is quite right what you have dreamt, for I always believe that the Lord God will help me. But I will bid you farewell, for if I guess wrong I shall never see you more."

Then they kissed each other, and John went into the town and to the palace. The whole hall was filled with people: the judges sat in their armchairs and had eider-down pillows behind their heads, for they had a great deal to think about. The old King stood up, and wiped his eyes with a white pocket-handkerchief. Then the Princess came in. She was much more beautiful than yesterday, and bowed to them all in a very gracious manner, but to John she gave her hand, and said, "Good morning to you."

Then John had to guess what she had thought of. Oh, how kindly she looked at him! But as soon as she heard him utter the word 'shoe' she turned deathly pale and trembled all over. But that could not help her, for he had guessed right!

Goodness! How glad the old King was! He turned a somersault

it was a joy to see, and all the people clapped their hands for him and for John, who had guessed right the first time!

The travelling companion was very glad too when he heard how well things had gone. But John folded his hands and thanked God, Who, he was sure, would help him the second and the third time, as He had helped him the first. The next day he was to guess again.

The evening passed just like that of the day before. While John was asleep the travelling companion flew behind the Princess to the mountain, and beat her even harder than the time before, for now he had taken two rods. No one saw him, and he heard everything. The Princess was to think of her glove, and this again he told to John as if it had been a dream. In this way John was able to guess right, which caused great rejoicing in the palace. The whole Court turned somersaults, just as they had seen the King do the first time; but the Princess lay on the sofa, and would not say a single word. Now the question was whether John could guess aright the third time. If he succeeded he was to have the beautiful Princess and inherit the whole kingdom after the old King's death. If he failed he was to lose his life, and the troll would eat his beautiful blue eyes.

That evening before the third trial John went early to bed, said his prayers, and went to sleep quite peacefully. But the travelling companion bound his wings to his back and the sword to his side, and took all three rods with him, and flew away to the palace.

It was a very dark night. The wind blew so hard that the tiles flew off the houses, and the trees in the garden on which the skeletons were hanging bent like reeds before the storm. The lightning flashed every minute, and the thunder rolled just as if it were one peal lasting the whole night. The window was thrown open, and the Princess flew out. She was as pale as death; but she laughed at the bad weather, and declared it was not bad enough yet. And her white cloak whirled round in the wind like the great sail of a ship; but the travelling companion beat her with the three rods till the blood ran down upon the ground and she could scarcely fly any farther. At last, however, she reached the mountain.

245

"It hails and it storms!" she said. "I have never been out in such weather."

"One can have too much of a good thing," said the troll.

Then she told him that John had guessed right the second time too, and if he did the same the next morning he would have won and she would never be able to come to the mountain again, and never be able to practise her magic arts any more; and so she was in great distress.

"He shall not guess it this time," said the troll. "I shall think of something of which he has never thought, or he must be a greater troll than I am. But now we will be merry." And he took the Princess by both hands, and they danced about with all the little goblins and jack-o'-lanterns in the room. The red spiders jumped just as merrily up and down the walls: it looked as if fiery flowers were throwing out sparks. The owl beat the drum, the crickets piped, and the black grasshoppers played on the jews'-harps. It was a merry ball.

When they had danced long enough the Princess had to go home, or else she might have been missed at the palace. The troll said he would go with her—then they would have each other's company on the way.

Then they flew away through the storm, and the travelling companion broke his three rods across their backs. Never had the troll been out in such a hailstorm. Outside the palace he said good-bye to the Princess, and whispered to her at the same time, "Think of my head." But the travelling companion heard it; and the moment the

HE TOOK THE PRINCESS BY BOTH HANDS, AND THEY DANCED ABOUT WITH ALL
THE LITTLE GOBLINS

Princess slipped through the window into her bedroom, and the troll was about to turn back, he seized him by his long beard, and with his sword cut off the ugly troll's head at the shoulders, so that the troll did not even see him. The body he threw out into the sea to the fishes; but the head he only dipped into the water, and then tied it in his silk handkerchief, took it with him to the inn, and then lay down to sleep.

Next morning he gave John the handkerchief, and told him not to untie it until the Princess asked him what she had thought of.

There were so many people in the great hall of the palace that they stood as close together as radishes in a bunch. The council sat in the chairs with their soft cushions, and the old King had new clothes on; his golden crown and sceptre had been polished, and he looked quite stately. But the Princess was very pale, and had a coal-black dress on, as though she was going to a funeral.

"What have I thought of?" said she to John. And he immediately untied the handkerchief, and was himself quite frightened when he saw the horrible troll's head. All the people shuddered, for it was dreadful to look at; but the Princess sat just like a stone statue, and could not utter a single word. At last she stood up and gave John her hand, for he had guessed right. She did not look at anyone, but only sighed deeply and said, "Now you are my lord!—this evening we will hold our wedding."

"That's what I like!" said the old King. "And so we'll have it!"

All the people shouted "Hurrah!" The soldiers' band played music in the streets, the bells rang, and the cake-women took the black crape off their sugar dolls, for now there was joy; three oxen roasted whole, and stuffed with ducks and fowls, were placed in the middle of the market-place, that every one might cut himself a slice; the fountains ran with the finest wine; and whoever bought a penny cake at a baker's got six buns as a present, and the buns had currants in them.

In the evening the whole town was illuminated; the soldiers fired off the cannon, and the boys crackers; and there was eating and drinking, clinking of glasses, and dancing in the palace. All the noble gentlemen and pretty ladies danced with each other, and one could hear a long way off how they sang:

> Here are many pretty girls,
> Longing to be swung around!
> Calling for the drummer's march!
> Pretty maiden, whirl around!
> Dance and stamp the whole night through
> Till the sole falls from your shoe.

But the Princess was still a witch and did not at all like John. The travelling companion had thought of that; and so he gave John three feathers from the swan's wings and a little bottle with a few drops in it, and told him that he must have a large tub of water put near the bridal bed; and when the Princess was about to get into bed he must give her a little push, so that she should fall into the tub; and then he must duck her three times, after he had cast the feathers in and the drops; and she would then be free from her enchantment and love him very much.

John did everything the travelling companion had advised him. The Princess screamed loudly while he ducked her under the water and struggled in his hands in the form of a great coal-black swan with fiery eyes. When she came the second time out of the water the swan was white, with the exception of a black ring round her neck. John prayed devoutly to Our Lord and let the water close for the third time over the bird, and the same moment she was changed again to the beautiful Princess. She was more beautiful even than before, and thanked him with tears in her lovely eyes for having freed her from the magic spell.

The next morning the old King came with his whole Court, and there were congratulations till late in the day. Last of all came the travelling companion; he had his staff in his hand and his knapsack on his back. John kissed him many times, and said he must not go: he must stay with the friend of whose happiness he was the cause. But the travelling companion shook his head, and said mildly and kindly: "No, my time is up. I have only paid my debt. Do you remember the dead man whom the wicked men wanted to ill-treat? You gave all you possessed in order that he might rest in his grave. I am that man."

And the next moment he had vanished.

The wedding festivities lasted a whole month. John and the Princess loved each other truly, and the old King lived to see many happy days, and to let their little tiny children ride on his knee and play with his sceptre. And John became king over the whole country.

THE EMPEROR'S NEW CLOTHES

MANY years ago there lived an emperor who thought so much of new clothes that he spent all his money in order that he might be very fine. He did not care for his soldiers, nor for going to the play; or driving in the park except to show his new clothes. He had a coat for every hour of the day, and just as they say of a king, "He is in the council-room," so they always said of him, "The Emperor is in his dressing-room."

The great city where he lived was very gay; and every day many strangers came there. One day there came two swindlers; they gave out that they were weavers, and said they could weave the finest cloth to be imagined. Their colours and patterns, they said, were not only exceptionally beautiful, but the clothes made of their material possessed the wonderful quality of being invisible to any man who was unfit for his office or hopelessly stupid.

"Those must be wonderful clothes," said the Emperor. "If I wore such clothes I should be able to find out which men in my empire were unfit for their places, and I could tell the clever from the stupid. Yes, I must have this cloth woven for me without delay." And he gave a lot of money to the two swindlers in advance, so that they should set to work at once. They set up two looms, and pretended to be very hard at work, but they had nothing whatever on the looms. They asked for the finest silk and the most precious gold; this they put in their own bags, and worked at the empty looms till late into the night.

"I should very much like to know how they are getting on with the cloth," thought the Emperor. But he felt rather uneasy when he remembered that he who was not fit for his office could not see it. He believed, of course, that he had nothing to fear for himself, yet he thought he would send somebody else first to see how matters stood. Everybody in the town knew what a wonderful property the

251

stuff possessed, and all were anxious to see how bad or stupid their neighbours were.

"I will send my honest old Minister to the weavers," thought the Emperor. "He can judge best how the stuff looks, for he is intelligent, and nobody understands his office better than he."

So the good old Minister went into the room where the two swindlers sat working at the empty looms. "Heaven preserve us!" he thought, and opened his eyes wide. "I cannot see anything at all," but he did not say so. Both swindlers bade him be so good as to come near, and asked him if he did not admire the exquisite pattern and the beautiful colours. They pointed to the empty looms, and the poor old Minister opened his eyes wider, but he could see nothing, for there was nothing to be seen. "Good Lord!" he thought, "can I be so stupid? I should never have thought so, and nobody must know it! Is it possible that I am not fit for my office? No, no, I cannot say that I was unable to see the cloth."

"Well, have you got nothing to say?" said one, as he wove.

"Oh, it is very pretty—quite enchanting!" said the old Minister, peering through his spectacles. "What a pattern, and what colours! I shall tell the Emperor that I am very much pleased with it."

"Well, we are glad of that," said both the weavers, and they named the colours to him and explained the curious pattern. The old Minister listened attentively, that he might relate to the Emperor what they said; and he did so.

Now the swindlers asked for more money, more silk and gold, which they required for weaving. They kept it all for themselves, and not a thread came near the loom, but they continued, as hitherto, to work at the empty looms.

Soon afterwards the Emperor sent another honest courtier to the weavers to see how they were getting on, and if the cloth was nearly finished. Like the old Minister, he looked and looked, but could see nothing, as there was nothing to be seen.

"Is it not a beautiful piece of cloth?" said the two swindlers, showing and explaining the magnificent pattern, which, however, was not there at all.

"I am not stupid," thought the man; "is it therefore my good appointment for which I am not fit? It is ludicrous, but I must not let anyone know it"; and he praised the cloth, which he did not see, and expressed his pleasure at the beautiful colours and the fine pattern. "Yes, it is quite enchanting," said he to the Emperor.

Everybody in the whole town was talking about the splendid cloth. At last the Emperor wished to see it himself while it was still on the loom. With a whole company of chosen men, including the two honest councillors who had already been there, he went to the two clever swindlers, who were now weaving as hard as they could, but without using any thread.

"Is it not *magnifique*?" said both the honest statesmen. "Will your Majesty see what a pattern and what colours?" And they pointed to the empty looms, for they imagined the others could see the cloth.

"What is this?" thought the Emperor. "I do not see anything at all. This is terrible! Am I stupid? Am I unfit to be emperor? That would indeed be the most dreadful thing that could happen to me."

"Yes, it is very fine," said the Emperor. "It has our highest approval"; and, nodding contentedly, he gazed at the empty loom, for he did not like to say that he could see nothing. All his attendants who were with him looked and looked, and, although they could not see anything more than the others, they said, like the Emperor, "It is very fine." And all advised him to wear the new magnificent clothes at a great procession which was soon to take place. "It is *magnifique*! beautiful, excellent!" went from mouth to mouth, and everybody seemed to be delighted. The Emperor gave each of the swindlers the cross of the order of knighthood and the title of Imperial Court Weavers.

All through the night before the procession was due to take place the swindlers were up, and had more than sixteen candles burning. People could see that they were busy getting the Emperor's new clothes ready. They pretended to take the cloth from the loom, they snipped the air with big scissors, they sewed with needles without thread, and said at last: "Now the Emperor's new clothes are ready!"

The Emperor with all his noblest courtiers then came in; and both the swindlers held up one arm as if they held something, and said: "See, here are the trousers! Here is the coat! Here is the cloak!" and so on. "They are all as light as a cobweb! They make one feel as if one had nothing on at all, but that is just the beauty of it."

"Yes!" said all the courtiers; but they could not see anything, for there was nothing to be seen.

"Will it please your Majesty graciously to take off your clothes?" said the swindlers. "Then we may help your Majesty into the new clothes before the large looking-glass!"

The Emperor took off all his clothes, and the swindlers pretended to put the new clothes upon him, one piece after another; and the Emperor looked at himself in the glass from every side.

"Oh, how well they look! How well they fit!" said all. "What a pattern! What colours! That is a splendid dress!"

"They are waiting outside with the canopy which is to be borne over your Majesty in the procession," said the chief master of the ceremonies.

"Yes, I am quite ready," said the Emperor. "Does not my suit fit me marvellously?" And he turned once more to the looking-glass, that people should think he admired his garments.

The chamberlains, who were to carry the train, fumbled with their hands on the ground as if they were lifting up a train. Then they pretended to hold something up in their hands; they dare not let people know that they could not see anything.

And so the Emperor marched in the procession under the beautiful canopy, and all who saw him in the street and out of the windows exclaimed: "How marvellous the Emperor's new suit is! What a long train he has! How well it fits him!" Nobody would let others know that he saw nothing, for then he would have been unfit for his office or too stupid. None of the Emperor's clothes had ever been such a success.

"But he has nothing on at all," said a little child. "Good heavens! hear what the little innocent says!" said the father, and then each whispered to the other what the child said. " He has nothing on—a little child says he has nothing on at all! " " He has nothing on at all," cried all the people at last. And the Emperor too was feeling very worried, for it seemed to him that they were right, but he thought to himself, " All the same, I must keep the procession going now." And he held himself stiffer than ever, and the chamberlains walked on and held up the train which was not there at all.

THE SNOW MAN

"IT is so delightfully cold that my whole body creaks," said the snow man. "The wind is wonderfully invigorating. How that glowing thing up there is staring at me!" He meant the sun, which was just setting. "He shall not make me wink; I will hold the pieces tightly." For you must know that he had two large three-cornered pieces of red tile in the place of eyes in his head; an old rake represented his mouth, and so he had also teeth. He was born amid the cheering of the boys, and greeted by the tinkling of sledge-bells and the cracking of whips.

The sun set, the full moon rose large, round, and clear in the blue sky. "There he is again on the other side!" said the snow man. Of course he fancied the sun was showing himself again. "I thought I had cured him of staring. Now let him hang there, and give me a light, so that I may see myself. I wish I knew how to move: I should so much like to walk about. If I could, I should like to go down and slide on yonder ice, as I have seen the boys do. But I don't know how—I can't even walk."

"Go! Go!" barked the old dog in the yard; he was somewhat hoarse, and could no longer well pronounce the proper "Wow, wow." He had become hoarse since he used to live indoors and lie all day long under the warm stove. "The sun will soon teach you how to run; I saw him teach your predecessor last year, and his predecessors before him. Go! Go! They are all gone."

"I do not understand you, friend," said the snow man. "Do you mean to say that he up there is to teach me to walk?" He meant the moon. "I certainly saw him walk a little while ago when I looked him straight in the face, but now he comes creeping from the other side."

"You are dreadfully ignorant," replied the dog; "but that is no wonder, for you have only just been put up. She whom you see up there is the moon; he whom you have seen going off a little while ago was the sun; he is returning to-morrow, and is sure to teach you how to run down into the ditch. We shall soon have a change in the weather; I feel it by the pain I have in my left hind-leg; the weather is going to change."

"I do not understand him," said the snow man; "but it strikes me that he speaks of something disagreeable. He who was so staring at me and afterwards went off—the sun, as he calls him—is not my friend; so much I know for certain."

"Go! Go!" barked the dog, turned three times round, and crept back into his kennel to sleep.

The weather really changed. On the next morning the whole country was enveloped in a dense fog. Later on an icy wind began to blow, it was bitter cold; but when the sun rose, what a splendour! Trees and bushes were covered with hoar-frost—they looked like a wood of white coral; all the branches seemed to be covered with shiny white blossoms. The many delicate boughs and twigs, which are in the summer completely hidden by the rich foliage, were all visible now. It looked very much like a snowy white cobweb; every twig seemed to send forth rays of white light. The birch-tree moved its branches in the wind, as the trees do in the summer; it was marvellously beautiful to look at.

And when the sun rose all glittered and sparkled as if small diamonds had been strewed over everything, with large diamonds on the snowy carpet below. Or as if innumerable lights were shining even more white than the snow itself.

"How lovely!" said a young girl who stepped out into the garden with a young man. They stopped near the snow man, and looked admiringly at the glittering trees. "There is no more beautiful scene in the summer," she said, and her eyes were beaming. "And we can't possibly have such a fellow there in the summer," replied the young man, pointing at the snow man.

The girl laughed, nodded to the snow man, and then both walked over the snow, so that it creaked under their feet like starch.

" Who were those two? " asked the snow man of the dog. " You have been longer in the yard than I; do you know them? "

" Certainly I do," replied the dog. " She has stroked me, and he has given me a meat-bone. I shall never bite those two."

" But what are they? " asked the snow man again.

" Lovers," said the dog. " They are going to live together in one kennel, and gnaw on the same bone. Go! Go! "

" Are they beings like ourselves? " asked the snow man.

" They are members of the master's family," said the dog. " Of course, one knows very little if one has only been born yesterday. I can see that from you! I have the age and the knowledge too. I know all in the house. I also knew a time when I was not obliged to be chained up here in the cold. Go! Go! "

" The cold is splendid," said the snow man. " Go on, tell me more. But you must not rattle so with the chain, for you make me shudder if you do."

" Go! Go! " barked the dog. " They say I was once a dear little puppy. Then I used to lie on a chair covered with velvet, up in the mansion, or sit on the mistress's lap. They kissed me on the nose and wiped my paws with an embroidered handkerchief. They called me Ami, dear, sweet Ami. But later on I became too big for them, and they gave me to the housekeeper; and so I came down into the basement. You can look in at the window from where you are standing. You can look down into the room where I was one day master, for master I was at the housekeeper's. The rooms were not so grand as upstairs in the mansion, but they were more homely. I was not continually mauled and pulled about by the children, and the food was just as good, if not better. I had my own cushion, and there was a stove in the room, which is at this time of the year the best thing in the world. I used to creep under the stove; there was enough room for me. I am still dreaming of this stove. Go! Go! "

" Does a stove look nice? " asked the snow man. " Does it re-semble me? "

" The very contrary of you! It is as black as a raven, and has a long neck with a broad brass band round it. It eats so much fuel

that the fire comes out of its mouth. One must keep at its side, close by or underneath it; there one is very comfortable. Perhaps you can see it from your place."

The snow man looked and saw something, brightly polished, with a broad brass band round it; in its lower parts the fire was visible. A strange feeling overcame the snow man. He had no idea what it was, nor could he explain the cause of it; but all people know it, even those who are not snow men.

"Why did you leave her?" asked the snow man, for he had a notion that the stove was a woman. "How could you leave such a place?"

"I had to," said the dog. "They turned me out of the house and fastened me up here with the chain. I had bitten the youngest son of the squire in the leg, because he kicked away the bone which I was gnawing with his foot. Bone for bone, I think. But this they took very ill, and from that time forward I was chained up. And I have lost my voice too—do you not hear how hoarse I am? Go! Go! I can no longer bark like other dogs. Go! Go! That's how it ended."

The snow man was no longer listening to him; he looked down unswervingly into the basement, into the housekeeper's room, where the stove was standing on its four legs, as tall as the snow man.

"What a strange noise I hear within me," he said. "Shall I never get in there? It is such an innocent wish of mine, and they say innocent wishes are sure to be fulfilled. I must go in there, and lean against her, even if I must break the window."

"You will never get in there," said the dog; "and if you went close to the stove you'd be gone. Go! Go!"

"I am already as good as gone now," replied the snow man. "I believe I am fainting."

The snow man was all day long looking in at the window. In the twilight the room appeared still more inviting; a gentle light shone out of the stove, not like that of the moon or the sun, but such light as only a stove can give after being filled with fuel. When the door of the room was opened the flame burst out at the mouth of the stove—that was its custom. And the flame was reflected on the white face and chest of the snow man, and made him appear quite ruddy.

"I can no longer stand it," he said. "How well it suits her to put out her tongue!"

The night was long, but it did not appear so to the snow man, for he was standing there deeply lost in his pleasant thoughts, which were so freezing that he creaked.

In the morning the window-panes of the basement were covered with ice: the most beautiful ice-flowers that one could wish for were upon them; but they concealed the stove.

The ice on the window-panes would not thaw; the snow man could not see the stove which he imagined to be such a lovely woman. It groaned and creaked within him; it was the very weather to please a snow man; but he did not rejoice—how could he have been happy with this great longing for the stove?

"That is a dreadful disease for a snow man," said the dog. "I suffered myself from it one day, but I have got over it. Go! Go! We shall soon have a change in the weather."

The weather changed; it was beginning to thaw. The warmer it became, the more the snow man melted away. He said nothing, he did not complain, and that is the surest sign.

One morning he broke down; and lo! in the place where he had stood something like a broomstick was sticking in the ground, round which the boys had built him up.

"Well, now I understand why he had such a great longing," said the dog. "I see there is an iron scraper attached to the stick, which people use to clean stoves with. The snow man had a stove-scraper in his body, that was what moved him so. Now all is over. Go! Go!"

And soon the winter was over too. "Go! Go!" barked the hoarse dog, but the girls in the house were singing:

> Thyme, green thyme, come out, we sing,
> Soon will come the gentle spring.
> Willow-trees, your catkins don;
> The sun shines bright and the days roll on.
> Cuckoo and lark sing merrily too;
> We also will sing cuckoo! cuckoo!

And nobody thought of the snow man.

THE GOLOSHES OF FORTUNE

I. A Beginning

IT was in Copenhagen at a house in East Street, not far from the King's New Market, that a very large party was being given, for you must give a party now and then, and get it over, and then you can expect to be invited in return. Half of the company already sat at the card-tables, while the other half seemed to be waiting for the answer to their hostess's question, "What shall we do now?" They had progressed so far, and conversation was going on as best it could. Among other subjects the conversation turned on the Middle Ages. Some held the opinion that the Middle Ages were much more interesting than our own time; Councillor Knap, indeed, upheld this opinion so warmly that the lady of the house sided with him at once, and both eagerly declaimed against Oersted's treatise in the Almanac on ancient and modern times, in which the preference is given to our own age. The Councillor held that the times of King Hans were the best and most prosperous.

While this is the subject of the conversation, which was only interrupted for a moment by the arrival of a newspaper containing nothing worth reading, let us look into the anteroom, where the overcoats, sticks, umbrellas, and goloshes had been left. Here sat two maids, one young, the other old. One might have thought they were servants who had come to fetch their mistresses, some old maiden lady or widow, but, on looking more closely, one soon saw that they were not common servant-girls—their appearance was too dignified, their hands too delicate, and their dresses too uncommon. They were two fairies; the younger was not Fortune herself, it is true, but lady's maid to one of her ladies of the bedchamber who brings round the smaller gifts of Fortune. The elder one looked somewhat more severe; she was Care, who goes about her business

262

herself in her own exalted person, for only then does she know that
it is well done.

They were telling each other where they had been during the
day. The lady of the bedchamber's maid, who was also Fortune's
messenger, had only carried out some unimportant commissions:
for instance, she had saved a new hat from a shower of rain, procured
an honest man a bow from a titled nobody, and so forth; but she
had now something of greater consequence to do. " I must also tell
you," she said, " that to-day is my birthday, and in honour of it a
pair of goloshes have been entrusted to me, which I am to give to
mankind. These goloshes have the property that whoever puts
them on is instantly transported to the place and the time where he
most desires to be; every wish regarding time or place is at once
realized, and so for once a man can be happy here below."

" Believe me," said Care, " he will be most unhappy, and bless
the moment when he is once more rid of the goloshes! "

" That is your opinion! " replied the other. " Now I shall put
them down near the door; someone will take them, and become
the fortunate man! "

You see, that's what they were talking about.

II. WHAT HAPPENED TO THE COUNCILLOR

It was late; Councillor Knap, deeply in thought over the times
of King Hans, wished to go home; but fate so arranged that, instead
of his own goloshes, he put on those of Fortune, and walked out
into East Street; but the magic power of the goloshes instantly
carried him back to the times of King Hans, and his feet sank deeply
into the mud and mire of the street, which was not paved in those
days.

" This is dreadful! How dirty it is here," said the Councillor.
" Why, the pavement's all gone, and all the lamps are out! "

The moon had not yet risen high enough, and it was rather foggy,
so that all around was buried in the darkness. When he came to the
next corner he found a lamp before a picture of the Madonna, but

the light it gave was so small that he only noticed it when he was passing beneath it, and his eyes fell upon the painted figures of the Mother and Child.

"That is evidently an art dealer's," he thought, "and they have forgotten to take in their sign."

Several people in the costume of a former age passed by him.

"How oddly they are dressed up! They must be coming from a masquerade!"

Suddenly there was a sound of drums and fifes. The Councillor saw the flaring light of torches, and stopped, and an extraordinary procession passed by him. First marched a band of drummers, beating their instruments with great skill. They were followed by attendants with bows and cross-bows. The principal person in the procession was a clergyman. The astonished Councillor asked what all this meant, and who the clergyman was.

"The Bishop of Zealand," was the answer.

"Good Lord!" sighed the Councillor. "What on earth has come over the Bishop?" Then he shook his head; he could not believe it possible that the man was the Bishop.

Still puzzling over this, he passed through East Street and over High Bridge Place. The bridge which he used to cross in order to reach Castle Square was nowhere to be found. He at last reached the bank of a shallow river, where he saw two men with a boat.

"Would the gentleman like to cross over to the Holm?" they asked him.

"To the Holm?" said the Councillor, who was quite unconscious that he lived in a different age. "I wish to go to Christian's Haven, to Little Turf Street."

The two men stared at him.

"Only tell me where the bridge is!" he said. "It is scandalous that they have not lighted the lamps here, and it is as muddy as if it was a marsh!"

The more he talked to the boatmen, the less intelligible their language became to him.

"I do not understand your Bornholmish," he said at last in an angry voice, and turned his back on them. He could not find the bridge, nor was there any fence. " It is a scandal how things are here," he said. He had never thought his own times more miserable than this evening. " I think it will be best for me to take a droshky," he thought. But where were the droshkies? None were to be seen. " I shall have to return to the King's New Market to find one, or I shall never reach Christian's Haven." Then he went back to East Street, and had nearly come to the end of it when the moon broke through the clouds.

" Good Lord! What strange building have they put up here! " he said, when he saw the East Gate, which in those days stood at the end of East Street. One of the wickets was still open, however, and he passed through it, in the hope of reaching what is now the King's New Market; but there he found there were wide meadows before him, with a few bushes here and there, and a broad canal or river streaming through them. A few wretched wooden huts, belonging to Dutch sailors, stood on the opposite bank. " Either what I see is a *fata Morgana*, or I am tipsy," lamented the Councillor. " If I only knew what all this means! " He returned again, firmly believing that he was ill. Walking back through the same streets, he looked more closely at the houses, and noticed that most of them were only built of lath and plaster, and that many had only thatched roofs.

" No, I do not feel at all well," he sighed, " and yet I only drank one glass of punch. But punch does not agree with me, and it is altogether wrong to serve punch with hot salmon. I shall say so to our hostess—the agent's lady. I wonder whether to go back now, and let them know how I feel. No, no, it would look too ridiculous; and then, after all, the question is whether they are still up." He looked about for the house, but was unable to find it.

" This is dreadful! I cannot even recognize East Street again. I do not see a single shop; there are only wretched old houses, as if I were in Roeskilde or Ringstedt. There is no doubt about it; I am ill, and it is useless to stand on ceremony. But where in all the world is the agent's house? It is no longer the same; but in the house over there I see some people are up still. Alas! I am very ill! " He soon reached a half-open door, and saw the light inside. It was an inn of that period, a sort of public-house. The room looked very much like a Dutch bar: a number of people—sailors, citizens of Copenhagen, and a few scholars—sat there in lively conversation, with their mugs before them, and paid little attention to the Councillor coming in.

"I beg your pardon," said the Councillor to the landlady. "I have been suddenly taken ill. Would you kindly send for a cab to drive me to Christian's Haven?"

The woman looked at him and shook her head. Then she addressed him in German. The Councillor, supposing that she could not speak Danish, repeated his request in German. This, in addition to his dress, made the woman feel sure that he was a foreigner; but she understood that he was unwell, and brought him a jug of water. It tasted very much of sea-water, although it had been fetched from the well outside.

The Councillor rested his head upon his hand, drew a deep breath, and thought over all the strange things around him.

"Is that this evening's number of the *Day*?" he asked mechanically when he saw the woman putting aside a big sheet of paper.

She did not know what he meant, but she gave him the paper. It was a woodcut representing a strange appearance in the air that had been seen in the city of Cologne.

"That is very old," said the Councillor, and became quite cheerful at the sight of this old curiosity. "How did you get this rare cut? It is highly interesting, although the whole is but a fable. These phenomena are now explained as polar lights; they probably are caused by electricity."

Those who sat next to him, and heard what he said, looked at him with great surprise, and one of them rose, politely raised his hat, and said in a serious tone, "You are certainly a very learned man, monsieur."

"Not at all," replied the Councillor. "I can only talk about things that everybody is supposed to understand."

"*Modestia* is a fine virtue," said the man. "Moreover, I have to add to your explanation *mihi secus videtur*; yet in the present case I willingly suspend my *judicium*."

" May I ask with whom I have the honour to speak? " replied the Councillor.

" I am a Bachelor of Divinity," said the man.

This answer was enough for the Councillor; title and dress were in accordance with each other. " Surely," he thought, " this man is an old village schoolmaster, such a specimen as one still meets with sometimes in the upper parts of Jutland."

" Although here we are not in a *locus docendi*," began the man again, " I beg you to take the trouble to give us a speech. You are surely well read in the ancients."

" Oh, yes," replied the Councillor, " I am very fond of reading old and useful books, but I am also interested in new ones—with the exception of everyday stories, of which we have enough in real life."

" Everyday stories? " asked the Bachelor of Divinity.

" Why, yes—I mean the modern novels."

" Oh! " said the man, smiling, " they certainly contain a great deal of wit, and are read at Court. The King especially likes the romance of Sir Iffven and Sir Gaudian, which treats of King Arthur and his valiant knights of the Round Table. He has made jokes about it to his courtiers."

" This one certainly I have not read yet," said the Councillor. " It must be quite a new one, published by Heiberg."

" No," replied the man, " Heiberg is not the publisher, but Gotfred von Gehmen."

" Is he the author? " asked the Councillor. " That is a very old name. Was it not the name of the first Danish printer? "

" Yes, he is our first printer," said the scholar.

So far everything went fairly well; but now one of the citizens began to speak of the dreadful plague which had raged a few years ago, meaning that of the year 1484. The Councillor thought he spoke of the cholera, and so they could discuss it, unaware of the fact that each spoke of something else. The war against the freebooters had happened so lately that it was unavoidably mentioned; the English pirates, they said, had seized some ships that were in the harbour. The Councillor, in the belief that they meant the events of 1801, was strongly against the English. The latter part of the conversation, however, did not go off so smoothly; they could not help contradicting each other every moment; the good Bachelor of Divinity was dreadfully ignorant, so that the simplest remarks of the Councillor seemed to him too daring or too fantastic. They often looked at each other in astonishment, and when matters became too complicated the scholar began to talk Latin, hoping to be better understood, but it was of no use.

"How do you feel now?" asked the landlady, pulling the Councillor's sleeve. Only then his memory returned; in the course of the conversation he had forgotten all that had happened.

"Good heavens! Where am I?" he said, and he felt quite dizzy when he thought of it.

"Let us have some claret, or mead, or Bremen beer!" cried one of the guests. "And you shall drink with us!"

Two girls came in; one had on a cap of two colours. They poured the wine out, and made curtsies. The Councillor felt a cold shiver run down his back. "What does all this mean?" he said. But he had to drink with them, they asked him so politely. He was quite in despair, and when one of them said that he was intoxicated he did not doubt it for a moment, and only requested them to get him a droshky. Then they thought he spoke the Muscovite language. Never in his life had he been in such rough and vulgar company. "One would think that the country had gone back to paganism!" he thought. "This is the most terrible moment in all my life."

Just then the idea struck him that he would stoop under the table and creep towards the door. He carried this out, but when he was near the door the others discovered his intention; they took hold of his feet, and, to his great good fortune, pulled off the goloshes, and at once the whole spell was broken.

The Councillor distinctly saw a street lamp burning, and behind it a big house; it all seemed familiar to him. He was in East

Street, as we know it now, and was lying on the pavement with his legs towards the door, and opposite to him sat the watchman, asleep.

"Goodness gracious! Have I really been lying here in the street dreaming?" he said. "Yes, this is East Street. How beautifully light and pleasant! That glass of punch must have had a dreadful effect upon me."

Two minutes later he sat in a cab, and drove to Christian's Haven. He thought of all the anguish he had suffered, and praised the present, his own age, with all his heart, as being, in spite of its shortcomings, much better than the age in which he had found himself a little while ago. And that, you know, was very sensible of the Councillor.

III. THE WATCHMAN'S ADVENTURES

"Why, there's a pair of goloshes!" said the watchman. "They must belong to the lieutenant who lives up there. They are close to his door." The honest man would gladly have rung the bell and returned them to their owner, for there was still a light upstairs, but he did not wish to wake up the other people in the house; so he left them there. "I am sure a pair of such things must keep one's feet very warm," he said. "How nice and soft the leather is!" They fitted his feet exactly. "How strange things are in this world! This man, now, might go into his warm bed, and yet he does not do so, but walks up and down in his room. He is a fortunate man. He has neither wife nor child; he is out every evening. I wish I were in his place, I should certainly be happy."

No sooner had he uttered this wish than the goloshes he had put on brought it about; the watchman became the lieutenant in body and mind.

There he was, standing upstairs in his room, holding a sheet of pink note-paper between his fingers, on which was written a poem —a poem from the lieutenant's own pen. Who has not had, once in his life, a poetical moment? Then, if one writes down one's thoughts, they are poetry.

OH, WERE I RICH!

" Oh, were I rich! " Such was my wish, yea, such,
When hardly three feet high; I longed for much.
Oh, were I rich! An officer were I,
With sword and uniform and plume so high!
And the time came—an officer was I!
But yet I grew not rich. Alas! poor me!
Have pity, Thou Who all man's wants dost see!

I sat one evening sunk in dreams of bliss—
A maid of seven years old gave me a kiss.
I at that time was rich in poesy
And tales of old, though poor as poor could be;
But all she asked for was this poesy.
Then was I rich, but not in gold, poor me!
As Thou dost know Who all men's hearts canst see.

Oh, were I rich! Oft asked I for this boon.
The child grew up to womanhood full soon.
She is so pretty, clever, and so kind;
Oh, did she know what's hidden in my mind—
A tale of old. Would she to me were kind!
But I'm condemned to silence. Oh, poor me!
As Thou dost know Who all men's hearts canst see.

Oh, were I rich in calm and peace of mind,
My grief you then would not here written find!
Oh, Thou to Whom I do my heart devote,
Oh, read this page of glad days now remote,
A dark, dark tale, which I to night devote!
Dark is the future now. Alas! poor me!
Have pity Thou Who all men's pains dost see!

Such poems people only write down when they are in love, but
a prudent man never has them printed. To be a lieutenant, poor and
in love—that's a triangle; or one might better describe it as half the
broken die of fortune. That is just what the lieutenant thought at
this moment, and so he leaned his head against the window-frame and
sighed. " The poor watchman down in the street is much happier

than I. He does not know what I call want. He has a home, a wife and children, who share his joys and sorrows. I should be much happier if I could change places with him, and live with only his hopes and expectations. I am sure he is much happier than I."

Instantly the watchman became a watchman again, for, through the goloshes of Fortune, he had become, body and soul, the lieutenant; but as such he felt less contented than before, and preferred to be what he had despised a short time ago. And so the watchman was a watchman again.

" That was a hideous dream," he said, " but very curious. I felt as if I were the lieutenant up there, and it was by no means a pleasure. I missed my wife and children, who are always ready to smother me with their kisses."

He sat down again and nodded; he could not quite get over the dream; the goloshes were still on his feet. A shooting star passed over the sky.

" There it goes," he said, " and yet there are plenty left. I should like to look a little more closely at these things, especially at the moon, for she would not slip so easily out of one's hands. The student my wife does washing for says that when we are dead we shall fly from one planet to another. That's a story, although it would not be at all bad. I wish I could take a little leap up there. I should not mind leaving my body here on the steps."

There are some things in this world that must be spoken of with caution, and one ought to be still more careful when one has the goloshes of Fortune upon one's feet. Now, let us see what happened to the watchman.

Everybody knows how quickly one can move from one place to another by steam: we have done it either on a railway or a steamboat. But this speed is not more than the crawl of the sloth or creeping of a snail in comparison to the swiftness with which light travels. It flies nineteen million times faster than the quickest railway engine. Death is an electric shock to our hearts: the liberated soul flies away on the wings of electricity. Sunlight requires about eight minutes and a few seconds to perform a journey of more than ninety-five millions of miles; the soul travels as quickly on the wings of electricity. The distance between the various celestial bodies is not greater to it than we should find the distance between the houses of friends living in the same town quite close together. The electric shock to our hearts costs us our bodies, unless we have by chance the goloshes of Fortune on our feet, like the watchman.

In a few seconds the watchman had traversed the distance of two hundred and sixty thousand miles to the moon, which consists, as everybody knows, of much lighter material than our earth—something like new-fallen snow, as we should say. He had arrived on one of the numerous circular mountains which one sees on Dr Maedler's large map of the moon. The inside was a basin of about half a mile in depth. Down below was a town; to get an idea of its appearance the best thing would be to pour the white of an egg into a glass of water. The substance here was just as soft, and formed similar transparent towers, domes, and terraces, floating in the thin air like sails. Our globe hung above his head, like a dark red ball.

He soon noticed a great many beings, surely intended to be what we call 'men,' but they were very different from us. They also had a language, but how could the soul of a watchman be expected to understand it? Nevertheless, it did understand the language of the inhabitants of the moon very well. They were discussing our earth, and had doubts as to its being inhabited; they asserted the air there must be too thick for any moon-being to live in. They were of opinion that the moon only was inhabited; that it was *the* celestial body where the ancient inhabitants of the world lived.

But let us leave them, and return to East Street, and see what happens to the watchman's body. He was still sitting motionless on the steps; his spiked staff had fallen out of his hand, while his eyes looked fixedly towards the moon, where his honest soul was rambling about.

"What o'clock, watchman?" asked one of the passers-by. But the watchman gave no answer. Then the man gently filliped his nose, which caused him to lose his balance and fall, full length, on the ground, like a dead man. His comrades were frightened; the watchman was dead, and dead he remained. It was reported and taken note of, and later on in the morning the body was taken to the hospital.

It would have been a good joke if the soul had come back and looked for its body in East Street, without being able to find it. Probably it would first go to the police station, from thence to the lost property office, to make inquiries, and finally to the hospital. But we need not trouble our minds about that, for souls are cleverest when they act on their own responsibility; only the bodies make them stupid.

As I have stated, the watchman's body was carried to the hospital. There it was taken to the room where the bodies were washed, and, naturally, the first thing they did was to take off the goloshes. Whereupon the soul was obliged to return to the body. It at once started straight for the body, and in a few moments the man was alive again. He declared that he had never in all his life passed such a dreadful night, and not if you paid him ten marks would he go through such an experience again; but he got over it all right.

He was able to leave the hospital the same day, but the goloshes remained there.

IV. A Critical Moment: A Most Extraordinary Journey

Every one who comes from Copenhagen knows the entrance to Frederick's Hospital in Copenhagen, but, as probably some people who do not come from Copenhagen will read this story, it will be well to give a short description of it.

Towards the street the hospital is surrounded by an iron railing of considerable height, the thick bars of which stand so far apart that sometimes, so the story goes, some of the thinnest young medical students have squeezed themselves through and paid little visits to town. The part of the body most difficult to get through was the head, and so in this case, as often happens in this world, the smallest heads were the luckiest. This will do for an introduction.

One of the students, of whom one could say that he had a big head in one sense only, was on duty one evening; the rain was pouring down; but in spite of these two obstacles he wished to go out.

Just for a quarter of an hour, he thought; he need not trouble the porter, especially if he could slip through the bars. He noticed the goloshes which the watchman had forgotten; it never occurred to him in the least that they were those of Fortune. They would do him good service in the bad weather, he thought, and so he put them on. The point now was, could he squeeze himself through the bars?—he had never tried before. There he stood.

" I wish to goodness I had my head outside," he said, and instantly, although it was very thick and big, it slipped smoothly and easily through the bars; the goloshes seemed to know how to do that very well. Then he tried to get his body through too, but this was impossible.

" I am too fat," he said. " I thought my head was the worst; but it is my body that I can't get through."

Now he tried to pull his head back again, but he couldn't; he could move his neck about comfortably, and this was all. At first he felt very angry, but soon became discouraged. The goloshes of Fortune had placed him in this awkward position, and unluckily it never came into his mind to wish himself free again. Instead of wishing, he could only struggle, but all his attempts were in vain. The rain was pouring down; not a soul was to be seen in the street; he could not reach the bell at the porter's lodge. How could he get out? He felt certain he would have to stop there until the next morning. Then they would be obliged to send for a blacksmith to file through the iron bars. But all this would take time; all the charity children would be going to their school opposite, all the inhabitants of the adjoining sailors' quarter would flock together to see him in the stocks—there would be a large crowd, no doubt! "Ugh!" he cried, " the blood is rushing to my head! I shall go mad! Yes, I am going mad! Oh, I wish I was free! Then perhaps I might feel better." He ought to have said this sooner, for the thought was

scarcely expressed when his head was free, and he rushed up to his room, quite upset by the fright the goloshes had caused him.

Now we must not think it was all over for him. No—the worst was still to come.

The night and the following day passed; nobody claimed the goloshes. In the evening an entertainment was to take place in the little theatre in Kannike Street. The house was filled in every part; the student from the hospital was among the audience, and seemed to have entirely forgotten what had happened to him the night before. He had put on the goloshes, as no one had claimed them, and they were very useful to him, for the streets were very dirty. A new poem, entitled *Granny's Spectacles*, was being recited, in which the spectacles were described as enabling the person who wore them to read people like cards, and to foretell from them all that would happen in the coming year.

The idea pleased him; he would have very much liked to have such a pair. He thought, one might perhaps be able to look straight into people's hearts if one made good use of them, and that surely would be much more interesting than to see what would happen in the coming year; the latter one would be sure to see, but not the former.

"I think if I could look into the hearts of the ladies and gentlemen in the first row they would seem to me to form a sort of large shop. Oh, how my eyes would wander about in it! In the heart of that lady, sitting there, I am sure I should find a milliner's shop; in the next one the shop is empty, but a cleaning out would do it no harm. Would there not also be some shops where real solid articles are to be found? Yes, yes," he sighed. "I know one in which everything is genuine, but there is already a shopman in it, and that, in fact, is the only thing I have to find fault with. One might be invited to come into various others and inspect them. I wish I could pass like a little thought through these hearts!"

That was the word of command for the goloshes; the student shrunk to nothing, and at once began a most extraordinary journey through the hearts of the spectators in the first row. The first heart through which he passed belonged to a lady. It seemed to him that he was in one of the rooms of an orthopædic museum, where the plaster casts of deformed limbs are arranged on the walls, the only difference being that, while in the museum the casts are formed when the people enter, they were formed and kept in this heart after they had left. There were casts of the bodily and mental deformities of her lady friends carefully preserved.

Quickly he slipped into another lady's heart. It appeared to him to be like a big holy church; the white dove of innocence fluttered over the high altar. He would have gladly knelt down, but he had no time—he had to go on into the next heart. The sound of the organ was still ringing in his ears, and he felt he had become a new and better man, so that he did not feel unworthy to enter the next sanctuary, where he saw a sick mother in a miserable garret. But God's bright sun was shining through the window, splendid roses

276

were growing in the little flower-box on the roof, and two heavenly blue birds were singing of the joys of childhood, while the sick mother prayed to God to bless her daughter.

Then he crept on all fours through an overcrowded butcher's shop; wherever he turned there was nothing but meat. It was the heart of a rich and respectable man, whose name you will certainly find in the directory.

Thence he came into the heart of this gentleman's wife; it was nothing but an old dilapidated pigeon-house. The husband's portrait served as a weathercock, and was connected with the doors, so that they opened and shut whenever he turned his head.

In the next heart he found a cabinet of mirrors, like those one sees in the castle of Rosenburg. But the mirrors magnified in an incredible degree. The insignificant *I* of the proprietor sat in the centre of the floor, like the Dalai Lama, admiringly contemplating his own greatness.

Next he thought he had entered a narrow needle-case, full of sharp needles, and said, " No doubt, this is the heart of an old maid." But such was not the case; it belonged to a young officer with several orders, whom people considered a man of intellect and heart. The poor student was quite dizzy when he came out of the last heart in the row; he could not collect his thoughts, and fancied his too strong imaginative powers had run away with him.

" Good heavens! " he sighed. " I have a strong tendency to go mad, without doubt, and in here it is intolerably hot; the blood is rushing to my head." Just then he remembered his critical situation the evening before, when he had stuck fast between the bars of the hospital railing.

" Surely that was when I caught it! " he thought. " I must do something for it in time. Perhaps a Russian bath would do me good. I wish I was already on the top-shelves."

And there he lay on the top-shelf of the vapour bath, fully dressed, with boots and goloshes still on, and the water dropped down from the ceiling on his face.

" Ugh! " he cried, and jumped down to take a plunge bath.

277

The attendant cried out loudly in his surprise at seeing a man with all his clothes on.

The student fortunately had enough presence of mind to whisper in his ear, " It is for a bet! "

Upon arriving home he at once placed a large mustard plaster on his neck and another on his back, to draw out the madness.

The next morning he had a very sore back, and that was all he gained through the goloshes of Fortune.

V. The Clerk's Transformation

The watchman, whom we surely have not yet forgotten in the meantime, remembered the goloshes which he had found and carried with him to the hospital.

He went to fetch them, and when neither the lieutenant nor anybody else in the same street recognized them as their property he took them to the police office.

" They look exactly like my own goloshes," said one of the clerks, looking at the goloshes, and placing them by the side of his own. " It requires more than a shoemaker's eye to distinguish the difference——"

" Mr Clerk," said an attendant, who entered the room with some papers. The clerk turned round and spoke to him. Afterwards, when he looked at the goloshes again, he was uncertain whether the pair on the left or on the right were his. " The wet ones must be mine," he thought; but in this he was wrong—they were the goloshes of Fortune; and after all it is not so wonderful, for a police clerk can make mistakes, like anybody else.

He put the goloshes on, thrust some papers into his pocket, took some others under his arm (the latter he was to read at home, and make abstracts of their contents), and went out. By chance it was Sunday morning, and splendid weather. " A trip to Fredericksberg would do me good," he thought, and thither he bent his steps.

No one could be more quiet and steady than this young clerk. We will not grudge him the little walk: after so much sitting it will no doubt be beneficial to him. At first he walked on mechanically, without thinking of anything at all, and therefore gave the goloshes no opportunity of proving their magic powers. In the avenue he met an acquaintance, a young Danish poet, who told him that he intended to start the next day for a summer tour.

"Are you really off again?" asked the clerk. "You are indeed a luckier and freer man than one of us. You can go wherever you like, but we always have a chain to our feet."

"But it is fastened to the bread-tree," replied the poet. "You need not have a care for the morrow, and when you grow old you will receive a pension."

"But you are better off, after all," said the clerk. "It must be a pleasure to sit down and write poetry. Everybody has something pleasant to say to you, and you are your own master. Come and try what it is like to be obliged to sit in court and listen to all sorts of frivolous cases."

The poet shook his head; the clerk did the same, and so they parted, each retaining his own opinion.

"They are peculiar people, these poets," thought the clerk. "I should very much like to try and enter into such a nature, and become a poet myself, for I am certain I should not write such lamentations as the others. To-day is a splendid spring day for a poet! The air is exceptionally clear, the clouds look beautiful, and the green grass has such a fragrance! For many years I have not felt as I do now!"

From these remarks we see that he had already turned a poet. To express such feelings would in most cases be considered ridiculous. It is foolish to think a poet is a different being from other men. There may be some among the latter who have far more poetical minds than professional poets. But a poet has a better memory— he can retain ideas and thoughts until they are clearly fixed and expressed in words; and that others cannot do. But the transition of an ordinary nature to a poetical one must needs be noticeable, and so it was with the clerk.

"What a delicious fragrance!" he said. "How much it reminds

279

me of the violets at Aunt Laura's! That was when I was a small boy. Dear me! I have not thought of that for a long time. Good old lady! She used to live near the canal. She always kept a green branch or a few green shoots in water, however hard the winter was. The violets smelt sweet when I was putting hot pennies against the frozen window-panes to make peep-holes. And I had a fine view through them. There lay the ships out in the canal, frozen in and deserted by their crews; a lonely crow was the only living thing on board. But when spring came all became alive; with cries and shouting the ice was broken, the ships were tarred and rigged, and then they started for distant lands. I have always remained here, and shall always be obliged to do so, and sit in a police office, while other people take passports for abroad. That's my fate." And he sighed deeply. Suddenly he stopped. " Good heavens! What can be the matter with me? I have never thought and felt like this. The spring air must be the cause of it. It alarms me, and yet it is not disagreeable!" He felt in his pockets for his papers. " They will soon make me think of something else," he said, and his eyes glided over the first page:

" *Mrs Sigbirth: Original Tragedy, in Five Acts,*" he read. " What's this? It's my own handwriting! Have I written this tragedy? *The Intrigue on the Promenade; or, Fast Day: a Vaudeville.* But wherever have I got these things? Somebody must have put them into my pocket! And here is a letter!"

It was from a theatrical manager; the plays were refused, and the letter was written in not over-polite language.

" Hm! Hm!" said the clerk, and seated himself on a bench. His thoughts were very elevated, and his nerves highly strung. Involuntarily he plucked a flower growing near him; it was a common daisy. What botanists tell us in many a lecture this flower tells us in a minute. It told the story of its birth, of the power of the sunlight, which, spreading out the fine petals, compels them to breathe forth sweet fragrance. Then he thought of the struggle of life, which in the same way awakens feelings in our breast. Air and light are the flower's lovers, but light is the favoured one. It turns towards the light, and when light vanishes it folds its petals and sleeps in the arms of the air.

"Light adorns me," said the flower.

"But the air enables thee to breathe," whispered the poet.

A little way off a boy was splashing with a stick in the water of a marshy ditch, so that the drops of water flew up to the green branches. The clerk thought of the millions of animalculæ which were thrown up in each drop of water, which, considering their size, must produce in them the same feeling as if we were thrown up high into the clouds. When the clerk thought of the great change that had taken place in him he smiled.

"I am asleep and dreaming! It is strange how naturally one can dream, and all the time one knows that one is only dreaming! I hope I may be able to remember this dream to-morrow when I am awake. I feel unusually excited. What a clear perception I have of everything, and how free I feel! But I am sure, should I remember anything of it to-morrow, it will seem stuff and nonsense; something the same has happened to me before. All the clever and beautiful things one hears of and speaks about in dreams are like the elves' buried gold: when one receives it it looks rich and beautiful, and in the daylight it is only stones and dead leaves. Ah!" he sighed, and looked at the singing birds hopping merrily from branch to branch. "They are much better off than I! Flying is a fine art. Happy is he who has been born with wings. If I could transform myself into a bird I should choose to be a lark."

Immediately his coat-tails and sleeves became wings, his clothes feathers, and the goloshes claws. He noticed it, and smiled to himself. "Well, now! I see that I am dreaming, but I never had such a foolish dream!"

He flew up into the green branches and sang, but there was no poetry in his song; the poetical mind was gone. The goloshes, like anybody else who wishes to do a thing well, could only do one thing at a time. He wished to be a poet: he became one. Then he desired to be a little bird, and by becoming one his former character disappeared.

"This is charming indeed!" he said. "In the daytime I sit at the police office among the most uninteresting official papers; at night I can dream, and fly about as a lark in the park of Fredericksberg! One might really write a popular comedy about all this!"

Then he flew down into the grass, turned his head from side to side, and pecked the flexible blades of grass with his beak, which, in proportion to his present size, appeared to him as large as palm-leaves in North Africa. The next moment all became as dark as night around him. Something, as it seemed to him, of enormous size was thrown over him—it was a sailor boy's cap. A hand then came underneath the cap, and seized the clerk by the back and wings so tightly that he cried out. In his fright he instinctively shouted out, "You rascal, I am a clerk in the police office." But this only sounded to the sailor boy like "Tweet! tweet!" He tapped the bird on its beak and walked off.

In the avenue he met two schoolboys of the upper class—that is, from the social point of view; for as far as their abilities were concerned they belonged to the lowest class in the school. They bought the bird for a small sum, and so the clerk was brought back to Copenhagen.

"It is a good thing that I am dreaming!" said the clerk. "Otherwise I should certainly feel very angry! First I was a poet, now I am a lark! Surely the poetical nature has transformed me into this little bird! It is a very poor story, especially if one falls into boys' hands. I should very much like to know how it will end."

The boys took the bird into a very elegantly furnished room; a stout, amiable-looking lady received them. She was not at all pleased to see that they had brought home such a common field bird, as she called the lark. She would only allow them to keep it for the day, and they had to put the bird into an empty cage near the window.

"Perhaps it will please Polly," she added, and nodded to a large green parrot which was proudly rocking itself in its ring in a beautiful brass cage. "To-day is Polly's birthday," she said foolishly. "The little field bird wants to congratulate it."

Polly did not reply a single word, and continued to rock itself, but a pretty canary, which had been brought away from its warm native country only the last summer, began to warble sweetly.

"Squaller!" cried the lady, and threw a white cloth over the cage.

"Tweet! tweet!" it sighed. "This is a terrible snowstorm." And then became silent.

The clerk, or, as the lady called him, the field bird, was put into a small cage close by the canary and not far from the parrot. All that Polly could say (and it sounded sometimes most comical) was, "No, let us be men!" What it said besides was no more intelligible than the warbling of the canary; but the clerk, being now a bird himself, understood his comrades very well.

"I flew about beneath green palms and flowering almond-trees," sang the canary. "I used to fly with my brothers and sisters over the beautiful flowers and smooth, clear lakes, at the bottom of which one could see the plants waving their leaves. I also saw many fine-looking parrots, who could tell the most amusing tales."

"They were wild birds," replied the parrot; "they were not educated. No, let us be men! Why don't you laugh? When the lady and all the other people laugh you ought to do so also. It is a great shortcoming not to be able to appreciate fun. No, let us be men!"

"Do you remember the handsome girls who used to dance in the tents near the flowering trees?" asked the canary. "Have you forgotten the sweet fruit, and the cooling juice of the wild herbs?"

"Oh, yes, I remember it all," replied the parrot; "but I am much more comfortable here. I have good food, and am well treated; I know I am clever, and I do not ask for more. Let us be men! You are a poet, as men call it; I possess sound knowledge and wit; you are a genius, but you lack discretion. You rise up to those high notes of yours, and then they cover you over. They dare not treat me like that. I was more expensive. My beak gains me consideration, and I can be witty. No, let us be men!"

"Oh, my warm native country!" sang the canary. "I will sing of your dark green trees, your calm bays, where the branches kiss the smooth, clear water. I will sing of all my shining comrades' joy, where the plants grow by the desert springs."

" Leave off those mournful strains!" said the parrot. " Sing something that makes one laugh. By laughing you show that you possess the highest mental accomplishments. Have you ever seen a horse or a dog laugh? No, they can cry out; but laugh—only man has the gift of laughing." Then it laughed " Ha! ha! ha!" and added, " Let us be men!"

" You poor little grey bird of the North," said the canary, " you are a prisoner here, like us. Although it is cold in your woods, you have freedom there. Fly away!—they have forgotten to close the door of your cage, and the top window is open. Fly away!"

The clerk instinctively obeyed, and hopped out of the cage. At the same moment the half-open door leading into the next room creaked, and stealthily, with green, shining eyes, the cat came in and chased him. The canary fluttered in the cage, the parrot opened its wings and cried, " Let us be men!" The clerk felt a mortal fright and flew out through the window, over houses and streets, until he was obliged to rest himself a little.

The house opposite his resting-place seemed familiar to him; the windows stood open; he flew in—it was his own room.

He perched himself on the table and said, " Let us be men!" involuntarily imitating the parrot. Instantly he became the clerk again, but he was sitting on the table.

" Oh, dear!" he said; " I wonder how I came up here and fell asleep! That was a disagreeable dream. After all, it was nothing but stuff and nonsense."

VI. THE BEST THING THE GOLOSHES DID

The next day, early in the morning, when the clerk was still in bed, somebody knocked at his door. His neighbour, a young student of theology, who lived on the same floor, walked in.

" Lend me your goloshes," he said; " it is damp in the garden, but the sun shines so brightly that I should like to smoke a pipe out there." He put on the goloshes and was soon in the garden below, in which a plum-tree and a pear-tree were growing. Even such a small garden is considered a wonderful treasure in the centre of big cities.

The student walked about in the garden; it was only six o'clock, and from the street he heard the sound of a post-horn.

" Travelling! travelling!" he exclaimed. " That is the most desirable thing in the world; that is the aim of all my wishes. The restlessness which I often feel would be cured by travelling. But I ought to be able to go far away. I should like to see beautiful Switzerland, to travel through Italy, and——"

It was well that the goloshes acted instantly; otherwise he might have gone too far, not only for himself, but for us too.

He was travelling in the heart of Switzerland, closely packed with eight others in a diligence. He had a headache; his neck was stiff with fatigue; the blood had ceased to circulate in his feet; they were swollen; and his boots pinched. He was half asleep and half awake. In his right-hand pocket he carried his letters of credit; in his left the passport; and some gold coins sewn in a little bag he wore on his chest. Whenever he dozed off he woke up imagining he had lost one or other of his valuables, and started up suddenly; then his hand would move in a triangle from the right over the breast to the left, to feel if they were still in their places. Umbrellas, sticks, and hats were swinging in a net in front of him, and almost entirely deprived him of the view, which was very imposing. He looked at it, but his heart sang what, at least, one poet we know of has sung in Switzerland, although he had not yet printed it:

> I dreamt of beauty, and I now behold it:
> Mont Blanc doth rise before me, steep and grey!
> Were my purse full I should esteem it
> The greatest joy in Switzerland to stay.

Grand, serious, and dark was all Nature around him. The pine-woods looked as small as heather on the high rocks, the summits of which towered into the misty clouds; it began to snow; an icy wind was blowing.

"Ugh!" he shivered. "I wish we were on the other side of the Alps! There it would be summer, and I should have raised money on my credit notes. I am so anxious about my money that I do not enjoy Switzerland. Oh! I wish I had already come to the other side!"

And there he was on the other side, in Central Italy, between Florence and Rome. The lake Thrasymene lay before his eyes, and looked in the evening light like fiery gold between the dark blue mountains. Here, where Hannibal defeated Flaminius, vines were peacefully growing; by the wayside lovely, half-naked children watched over a herd of swine under the flowering laurel-trees. If we could describe this picture correctly all would exclaim, "Beautiful Italy!"

But neither the student nor any of his travelling companions in the carriage of the *vetturino* said anything of the sort. Poisonous flies and gnats flew into the carriage by thousands; they tried to drive them away with myrtle branches, but in vain; the flies stung them nevertheless. There was not one among them whose face was not swollen from their painful stings. The poor horses looked dreadful; the flies covered them in swarms, and it was only a momentary relief when the coachman dismounted and swept the flies off.

Then the sun set, and a sudden icy cold pervaded all Nature—much like the cold air in a tomb when we enter it on a hot summer day; the mountains round about appeared wrapped in that peculiar green which we see in some old oil paintings, and which, if we have not witnessed it in the South, we believe to be unnatural. It was a superb spectacle, but the travellers' stomachs were empty and their bodies exhausted with fatigue; all they were longing for were good night quarters, but what could they find? They looked more longingly for this than they did at the magnificent scenery before them.

The road led through an olive grove, much like a road between pollard willow-trees at home. Here was at last a lonely inn. A dozen crippled beggars were lying down before it; the liveliest of them looked, to use one of Marryat's phrases, "like the eldest son of Hunger having just come of age." The others were either blind or had paralysed feet, and crept about on their hands, or they had crippled arms and fingerless hands. That was misery in rags, indeed!

"*Excellenza, miserabili!*" they sighed, and stretched out their crippled limbs. The landlady herself, barefooted and with disorderly hair and a soiled blouse, received the guests.

The doors were fastened with strings; the floors of the rooms consisted of bricks, and were broken in many places; bats flew about under the ceilings, and there was a vile odour within.

"Lay the table down in the stable," said one of the travellers. "There, at least, we know what we breathe."

The windows were opened to allow the fresh air to enter; but the crippled arms and continual lamenting, "*Miserabili, excellenza,*" came in quicker than the air. Many inscriptions covered the walls; half of them were not in favour of *Bella Italia*!

Supper, when served, consisted of watery soup, with pepper and rancid oil. The latter was the chief ingredient in the salad. Musty eggs and fried cockscombs were the best dishes; even the wine had a peculiar taste; it was a nauseous mixture.

At night the travellers' boxes were placed against the door, and one of them had to watch while the others slept. It was the student's turn to watch. Oh, how unbearably close the room was! The heat was oppressive; the gnats buzzed and stung; the *miserabili* outside groaned in their dreams.

"Travelling," said the student, "would be a pleasure if one had no body. If the body could rest and the mind fly about. Wherever I go I feel a want that oppresses me. I wish for something better than the moment can give me; something better—nay, the best! But where and what is it?"

No sooner had he uttered this wish than he was at home again. The long white curtains were hanging before the window, and in the middle of the room stood a black coffin; in it he slept the sleep of death. His wish was fulfilled: his body rested, his spirit was free to travel.

"Consider no man happy until he rests in the grave," were the words of Solon. In this case their truth was confirmed. Every dead body is a sphinx of immortality. The sphinx in the black coffin answered the questions which the student two days before had written down:

> O Death, thou stern dark angel, do we find
> Nought but the tombs that thou dost leave behind!
> Will not the soul on Jacob's ladder upward pass,
> Or only rise as sickly churchyard grass?
>
> The world doth seldom see the greatest woes—
> Ye lonely suffering ones! Ye now repose!
> Your hearts were often more oppressed by care
> Than by the earth your coffin-lid doth bear.

Two beings were moving about in the room; we know them already. One was the fairy Care, the other was the messenger of Fortune. They bent over the dead.

"Now you see," said Care, "what happiness your goloshes have brought to mankind!"

"They, at least, brought a lasting gift to him who slumbers here," answered Fortune's messenger.

"Oh, no," said Care. "He passed away at his own wish; he was not summoned. His mental power was not strong enough to discern the treasures Fate had destined him to discover. I will render him a good service now."

And she pulled the goloshes from his feet; the sleep of death was at once ended; the awakened man raised himself. Care disappeared, and with her the goloshes. Probably she considered them her property.